PRAISE FOR

Love from the Cosmos

"Mowa Badmos is a cosmic force on the horizon of romance."
—J. L. SEEGARS, author of *Restore Me*

"Mowa Badmos brings a new level of brilliance to the art of storytelling in this stunningly witty and deliciously spicy debut."
—NATASHA BISHOP, author of *Only for the Week*

"*Love From the Cosmos* is a joyful, witty, heartwarming story that will leave you starry-eyed. From the friends you'll instantly wish you were in a group chat with to the romance that will leave you smiling from ear to ear, Badmos's refreshingly original novel deftly explores what it means to fight for the life and love of your dream."
—RUFARO FAITH MAZARURA, author of *Let the Games Begin*

"What a gift to read a rom-com that's both celestial and grounded—full of laughter, longing, and the kind of sisterhood that catches you when the stars fall out of alignment. Mowa Badmos writes for the soft girls, the star-crossed, and the ones still learning how to choose themselves."
—CHARISH REID, author of *Jewel Me Twice*

"From the electric chemistry and visionary world-building to the effort-less weaving of Nigerian culture, *Love From the Cosmos* is the reminder we all need to keep our hearts open to love. Mowa Badmos writes with a voice both tender and expansive, and this debut proves just how much we need originality in romance, especially from African writers."
—JESSICA CARMICHAEL, author of *The Full Picture*

"*Love From the Cosmos* by Mowa Badmos is a joyful, starlight filled ro-mance decked out with flirty dialogue, charming characters, and an absolutely unique and engaging world. Readers eager for a delightful and heavenly story that will have you believing in fate, soulmates, and the perfect movie night should make this book their next read. Badmos, through her humorous and lovely writing, shows that the best love story can feel handwritten in the stars."

—**CELESTINE MARTIN**, author of *Deja Brew*

"Mowa Badmos has written a charming slow burn exploring the intersection of technology and astrology in meeting your soulmate. Equal parts sweet and spicy, you'll root for Moyo and Niyi as they discover the truest algorithm—following one's heart. One thing's for sure—you're destined to love this book!"

—**JEN MICHALSKI**, author of *All This Can Be True*

Keylight Books
an imprint of Turner Publishing Company
Nashville, Tennessee
www.turnerpublishing.com

Love from the Cosmos

Cover and book design by Ashlyn Inman
Cover illustration by Alex Copeman

Library of Congress Cataloging-in-Publication Data
Names: Badmos, Mowa author
Title: Love from the cosmos / by Mowa Badmos.
Description: Nashville, Tennessee : Keylight Books, 2026.
Identifiers: LCCN 2025019868 (print) | LCCN 2025019869 (ebook) | ISBN 9798887981307 hardcover | ISBN 9798887981314 paperback | ISBN 9798887981321 epub
Subjects: LCGFT: Novels
Classification: LCC PR9387.9.B256 L68 2026 (print) | LCC PR9387.9.B256 (ebook)
LC record available at https://lccn.loc.gov/2025019868
LC ebook record available at https://lccn.loc.gov/2025019869

Printed in the United States of America

*To Ozor, my beautiful angel in heaven,
thank you for always inspiring me to chase
my dreams.
The story lives on.*

*To anyone wondering if they should take a
leap of faith, here's your sign. Do it.*

Pronunciation Guide

Moyosore (Moyo) — Moe-your-sor-eh (Moe-your)
Anjola (Anjie) — Anne-jaw-lah (Anne-jee)
Sewa — Sh-eh-wah
Niyi — Nee-yee

Prologue

Cupid's Bow

The App for Love Destined By the Stars!

Welcome to *Cupid's Bow*, where your soulmate is guaranteed.

At *Cupid's Bow*, we take the guesswork out of love by using your astrological makeup to find the best person to support, challenge, and complement *you*. Our system isn't based on superficial looks but on your essence, your personality—your astrology.

Everyone has a unique astrological makeup—no two people are alike (even twins, please stop asking). The moment you are born is an exact snapshot of the planets, perfectly assigning the correct zodiac signs which correlate to a unique human—you.

You might receive multiple matches through our app. That's because you're a dynamic and fluid individual. You are constantly changing as you move with the stars, and, unlike other apps, we honor and encourage your fluidity. Your needs, based on the astrological weather, will change from time to time; therefore, so will your matches.

So, trust us, trust our process, and, most importantly, trust yourself.

We know user error is possible: some people have the wrong birth time or location, or they just go ahead and guess. Please, try to be as accurate as possible when using our system. Additionally, some people think they are ready for a soulmate but really aren't—so please refrain from our app if you're unsure. At *Cupid's Bow*, our science is exact.

And now, to serve you better, the *Cupid's Bow* Complaints Department is here to directly handle your concerns, staffed by our competent core team.

We are happy to serve! We hope you enjoy using *Cupid's Bow*.

Yours sincerely,

Vinny "Mercury" Carr

Moyo

CHOCOLATES AREN'T MY THING, AND I'M NOT THE BIGGEST fan of roses, so shoving them in the supply closet as I prepare for my next patient is a no-brainer. But before I do, I bring the red bouquet to my nose and inhale the floral scent, hoping this time I'll like it.

I don't.

A second glance at the heart-shaped chocolate box also does nothing for me. Luckily, their existence is temporary—the roses will fade, and Anjie and Sewa will eat the chocolates—but it's the thought that counts.

"Dr. Adegbite," Sally, the older receptionist, calls, returning to my office for the third time before 8:30 AM.

"Are they here already?" I jump up from my seat, and my heart pounds at the prospect of finally meeting the family I've fought to work with for weeks.

Sally shakes her head, and I deflate a little. "Your boyfriend sure must love you," she says. I collect a white envelope from her hand and place it beside my *Beetlejuice* mug.

"He really does," I say, thinking of Cole. It's been almost a year, and his thoughtfulness, although sometimes misguided, still warms my heart. Once Sally leaves, I snap a quick photo of the beautiful envelope and add it to the growing thread in the group chat with my girls.

Three gifts from Cole on a Thursday morning, all before my first client.

> Anjie: Another thing?? Woah, he's going all out. I'm OBSESSED!

> Sewa: I'm actually impressed. Maybe that man ain't half bad.

Anjie sends a series of laughing emojis, and I shake my head. Where Anjie is true love's cheerleader, mascot, and marching band all-in-one, Sewa is the skeptic, looking for a proper reason before hopping on board. For some reason, she's never bought into Cole. But my happiness is enough to keep her sly comments to a minimum.

> Me: Are we still on for tonight?

> Sewa: You telling us the big secret?

My eyes roll before I respond.

> Me: Yes

I can keep a secret, unlike those two. They couldn't even keep my thirtieth birthday party a surprise. I mean, who leaves their phone face-up when there's a notification for a "popcorn machine delivery" and then "randomly" asks for horror movie recs, a genre neither of them watches? It wasn't rocket science. But no, I plan to reveal my good news in my own time.

> Sewa: Well, then. Getting you hot and ready for tomorrow's surprise? Aye, aye, Captain!

> Anjie: By the time we're done, Little Caesar's Pizza might send us a cease and desist.

I'm laughing when my pager beeps, and all thoughts of Cole and his gifts dissipate, replaced by a bubbling giddiness that only means one thing—my new patient is here. Putting my phone away, I gather the signed documentation stating I can work with the sweetest little girl, Danaya, and her family at no financial cost to the hospital. The only cost is my soul, which is now owned by the administration. You'd think the hospital would be happy to flaunt my work at the Foundation Gala at the end of the year, but evidently not.

There's a high chance fighting to work pro bono will bite me in the ass, but as a developmental-behavioral pediatrician, my clients are my joy, especially my Black, low-income families, like this one. They're the reason I applied to medical school and spent many nights crying on the phone to my dad. They're why I fight, regardless of how much it pisses off a lot of senior staff members.

With my brightest smile of the morning, I readjust my pink scrubs, pat down my slicked-back hair, and make my way to reception.

· ✧ ✳ ♄ ✳ ✧ ·

Even more exciting than Cole's gifts is whatever Sewa and Anjie have planned for our girls' night. The one secret they've managed to keep. Tomorrow is a special day, but spending the night before with my girls is the icing on the cake.

My jaw drops when I open the door to my transformed living room.

"Surprise!" they yell, popping out from behind the kitchen island.

Hanging up my trench coat, I laugh. "I knew y'all were here."

Sewa collects the chocolates and partially crumpled flowers from me. "Sorry for trying to be festive."

"Welcome to your glam squad!" Anjie says, pulling me into a quick hug.

"We're doing hair and nails ahead of tomorrow. Plus we got dinner," Sewa says.

The setup of the wine glasses and food looks so good, it's hard to believe the food is from our regular place a few miles away. The appetizers—spring rolls, crab Rangoon, and chicken wings—sit on paper plates on my coffee table, while the delicious, salty, umami-filled fried rice and Kung Pao chicken are in the glass serving bowls my mother made me purchase when I moved in. Sewa, the cosmetic guru among us, has three different press-on nail sets for me to choose from. Tears spring to my eyes, and I pull both of them into a hug.

"Thank you," I whisper, and they rub circles into my back.

Pulling back, Sewa grabs the nail options.

"We have classic French tip, almond nude, or green-and-clear ombre."

I point to the green ones—the obvious choice.

Anjie connects to my speakers, and Styl-Plus' R&B hit "Olufunmi" pours into the room. The familiar tune slips past our lips, the English verses coming easily to all of us, while Sewa preps my nails. As the song's Yoruba chorus starts, her previously dutiful hand grabs my forearm. Anjie palms my shoulder. It only takes a second's glance for our minds to sync. Like a rehearsed band, we belt the refrain in unison.

We're not singers, but Anjie takes the lower harmony. Sewa does her best impression of a soprano with the nail file as a microphone, and I sing the melody, as we've done many times before. We spend the next ten minutes doing impromptu karaoke, Anjie grabbing the remote while I use my phone as a mic, easily flowing between English and Yoruba as each new song demands. We give in to the music, waists whining, bodies shaking, and asses twerking with no regard. When 112's "Dance With Me" directs us to clap—because we are sexy, and we know it—we do.

"You clap like someone's grandma at church," I tell Anjie.

"Those women clap with conviction. I have conviction," she says, continuing her thunderous applause.

"You're not a serious person," Sewa snickers.

When the song ends, Anjie pauses the playlist.

"Let's pause for now 'cause we really need to get things moving. If not, we'll dance all through the night," she says, grabbing a spring roll. I attempt to pick up a crab Rangoon, but Sewa swats my hand.

"Don't get your fingers dirty," she says. "Anjie, feed her." My oldest friend rolls her eyes, and I open my mouth and close my eyes.

"See how this babe opened her mouth?" Anjie hisses at Sewa. "Where does she think she is? Ancient Rome?"

I open my eyes. "In this house, I'm Zeus—wait, that's wrong. Roman myth is the planets. In this house, I'm Jupiter."

The girls look at me like I've grown another head.

"*Cupid's Bow* got you mythological?" Sewa asks, referencing the astrology dating app that matched Cole and me using our birth charts.

"It was fun to learn. Did y'all know that in astrology, the houses rule over different parts of your life?" I ask excitedly as Sewa preps my left hand.

"Houses?" Anjie bites into a buffalo wing.

"Yep! For example, romantic and professional relationships are ruled by the seventh house. My seventh house is in Capricorn, which is ruled by Saturn." I pause. Are they still engaged? Anjie and I make eye contact, and she nods along.

"Still listening, keep going," Sewa says, the sound of the nail buffer filling the space.

"Saturn rules over longevity, time, aging, rigidity—"

"That really is you." Sewa's head pops up, and she shoots me a cheeky grin.

"Don't be rude." I kick her playfully. "But it makes sense. It has taken me a long time to find someone. And Cole is a year older, so it all tracks with Saturn." I shrug.

"That was so insight—" Anjie begins, but I cut her off.

"There's one more thing. It's called a Saturn return, where Saturn wrecks your life, breaks you down, and makes you reassess all your habits and responsibilities. You're literally forced to reconsider everything and become a new person."

"So, it's a coming-of-age period?" Sewa asks.

"But for adults."

Anjie's eyebrows scrunch. "Does this happen to be around thirty? Cause that was a bitch. It was when I was trying to secure the restaurant a new building."

"I was contemplating leaving my job and returning to school," Sewa says.

"And I got back into dating," I say, following their leads. "That's the Saturn return for you. New changes that influence the rest of adulthood."

After college, I wasn't thinking about love. However, once I turned thirty, even though I had a steady job in the U.S. and best friends a girl would kill for, it felt like something was missing. Call it a Saturn return or simply aging, but I owed it to myself to stop letting a failed college relationship hold me back.

"That was deep." Anjie holds a spring roll to my mouth. Sewa nudges her, and she cuts off a piece and plops it into her mouth too.

"What about the signs?" Sewa asks. "Virgo, Aries, those things."

"Okay, so aside from the houses, the signs play a role, but the houses influence them," I try to explain, pinching at the air with my free hand. "Think of it this way. There's a house, and it has amenities. The astrological signs live in this house, but depending on the conditions, it could go sideways. In my case, Saturn controls my relationships. But I'm a Cancer Venus, which also deals with my dating life. Cancer is protective, soft. And Saturn is—"

"Rigid," Anjie says, resting her cheek on her palm.

"So, when a soft babe is in a hard house?"

"She has to develop tough skin," Sewa responds, pressing a nail into the glue on my left index finger.

"But..." I trail off, pointing at Anjie like a conductor directing her symphony.

"She's still a soft babe on the inside despite the outer shell. Like a crab. That's Cancer. Right?"

"Precisely!" I exclaim.

"Wow. I recommended the app to you, but your knowledge has surpassed mine," Anjie says.

"No vex." I blow her a kiss for putting the app on my radar.

Initially, I was skeptical because a dating app with a 99 percent success rate sounds like a scam, but after I read reviews and watched videos about people's positive experiences, I was sold.

"So, how does your man Cole fit into all of this? Is he a Capricorn...?" Anjie snaps her fingers. "Oh, you know what I mean."

Her frustration makes me giggle. "He's not a Capricorn Venus, but it doesn't have to be one-to-one like that. He's business-oriented, stable, direct, and a huge gift giver. Very Capricorn. So, we're good," I explain.

"Oh, it's giving me a headache. I'll be back." Anjie rubs her temples. She gets up from the couch and heads to the kitchen.

"I wonder how the *Cupid's Bow* people do it since they claim not to use an algorithm." Sewa's accusatory tone doesn't escape me. I've also wondered, but since I found love with Cole so quickly, I don't care what they do. It's magic. And who am I to question magic?

I'm about to say as much when she brushes off my left hand, and I stare in awe. The clear, nude base fades into a gorgeous forest green that matches most of my belongings.

"Thanks, babe, I love them," I gush.

"No worries. Glad to be part of this important post-Saturn return milestone," she says, and her left eye squints. "Did I say that right?"

"Exactlyyy," I say, drawing out the final syllable as I stretch my back.

Anjie returns with three plates perfectly balanced in her arms. One in each hand and one on her forearm. My stomach growls, ready to devour the fried rice and chicken.

Several spoonfuls later, I'm revitalized. "Do y'all wanna hear the secret?"

Groans fill the air.

"I thought we were gonna have to force it out of you," Sewa says.

Ignoring them, I run to my room and retrieve the cold steel key Cole gave me almost a week ago. The white silk rope I tied around it makes the plain item match the beauty of his gesture.

I dangle the metal in their faces.

Anjie is the first to scream. "Ah! He gave you a key!"

"Holy shit," Sewa says.

"Holy shit is right," I say, happy it's off my chest. He gave me a key. Cole, the man I've fallen in love with over the past year, is *finally* ready to take our relationship to the next level.

"How did it happen?" Anjie sets her food down and gives me her undivided attention.

"Okay, we're watching this Nolan flick, and he keeps touching me during the movie, and getting distracted on his phone, something about his new TA with many questions." I stop myself and wave my hands. "Long story short, you know I don't like that—"

"Yeah, you film purist. But go on," Sewa interrupts, and I shoot her a mild glare.

"Anyways, I tell him to stop, kinda blowing up—"

This time, it's Anjie's turn to interrupt. "Like you usually do."

I ignore her. "As I was saying, I ramble a bit about how our anniversary is soon, and we don't have any plans, and then..." I pause for dramatic effect. "He pulls out the key!"

"When you say 'pulls out,' like in a box or...?" Sewa peters off with her signature brow raise.

"Well...I technically ruined the surprise—"

"Like you usually do," Anjie says, referencing my failed surprise birthday party, and they both laugh. I roll my eyes, fighting the urge to laugh as well. Regardless of my mood, upset or annoyed, if my girls are laughing, I simply can't help it.

Sewa brings us back to the initial topic. "How are you feeling?"

I rub the soft white fabric attached to the precious key and my heart swells. "Like all my research and hard work paid off. Like it's everything I wanted from *Cupid's Bow*."

"Soulmate material?" Sewa asks.

"A whole ten yards of it." I laugh, and she smiles.

"We're so happy for you, babes. You deserve this and a lot more," Anjie cuts in. "Do you know what you're getting him?" She asks politely, but, knowing her, it's eating her up inside. Sewa looks up from the haircare products and flexi rods she is laying out.

A wicked smile grows on my face.

"Follow me," I say, and they scramble after me to the bedroom.

I reach under my bed and grab the white bow-tied box housing the main character of my carefully thought-out plan. After unexpectedly receiving the key, I pivoted from my simple plan of his favorite out-of-production perfume to something more worthy of an anniversary.

Their jaws drop when I untie the bow and open the box.

"Moyo," Sewa breathes.

"You're gonna kill this man." Anjie stares at the intricate, black lace lingerie set I bought from my favorite plus-size store.

Of all the things I've done in this relationship—planned movie dates, at-home paint and sips, bowling nights—this is my magnum opus. And I can't wait for his five-star review.

Nuyi

A LOT OF PEOPLE WOULDN'T SAY THIS, BUT NEPOTISM ruins lives.

I foolishly thought I was immune because never in this lifetime did I dream my dad would retire from the role of Saturn after one term. He was supposed to do at least two and then name an actual successor. Not the child he's barely spoken to in years.

Clearly, my disdain for the man and his job was my blind spot. I should've known that after his first twenty-nine-year term—the time it takes Saturn to orbit the sun—he would find a way to drag me back into the world I'd turned my back on.

My dad has always been big on legacy, even though he didn't do anything to foster our relationship once my mother died. After she passed, his parenting turned colder and absences lengthened, his only focus the family business, like those before him. Ever since the Saturn mantle was transferred to us after a mishap with the Jakande family, the Bankoles have worked tirelessly to ensure the next generation is primed and ready to serve. Until me.

I wasn't ready on that early spring day at the start of Aries season. Mars was throwing her annual Spring Equinox party before returning to her latest coaching gig. During Mars's first term, the event was small, but this being her sixth term—thanks to Mars's short two-year orbit, the commitment to serve was frequently renewed—she invited everyone. For once, I'd agreed to attend after an onslaught of pleading from my beloved cousins, Vee and Merc, who had already received their godhood. Venus, or Victoria, my favorite cousin, and Mercury, or Vinny, the most audacious member of the family.

The three of us stood near the bar, barely drinking, mostly talking. Alcohol doesn't do much for my godly cousins as they are conduits of fast-moving planets, which gives them fast metabolisms. But I, with my 100 percent human self, was enjoying the plum notes of the fabulous red wine.

Indulging in the drink and lost in the chatter as our trio expanded with Moon and Mars joining the fray, I didn't notice my dad walking up. Years ago, I would've recognized him by his footsteps. But after living away from him for so long, I'd forgotten what it was like to be alert.

He came up to me, gray hairs peeking out of his full beard. That should've been my first red flag: Saturns age more slowly to allow us to complete one or two full terms. But here he was, looking every bit a man in his late fifties.

"What are you—" Before I could finish my question, he shoved the fading leather Saturn notebook he always kept on his person into my hands.

His voice boomed out the most unexpected words: "I am retiring."

Then, as if I had already inherited his powers, time slowed. The words rang like cymbals.

"You're the next Saturn."

The younger me, before Mom passed and everything went to shit, would've loved to hear those words and get my father's approval. But now? The role is a death sentence. Unfortunately for me, a death sentence with no chance at clemency.

Soon after the party, we had the transfer ceremony. I became Saturn—day one of the next twenty-nine years of my life—and Dad booked the next one-way flight to Lagos.

I had to quit my cozy, San Francisco tech job and move to the arctic tundra commonly known as Boston, where I assumed my new duties as one-third of the core matchmaking staff at *Cupid's Bow*, despite knowing practically nothing about astrology.

Everyone, including Dad, had said the job would get easier once the Saturn powers transferred to me. At the transfer ceremony, he encouraged me to study his ratty old book, claiming every crucial moment of the Bankole-Saturn dynasty had been transcribed there. But it's been eighteen months since the powers transferred, and all I can do is useless shit like aging wine. Okay, not entirely useless since it's allowed me to upgrade my wine collection. But still.

I'm missing the one thing necessary to make me an equal partner, both in *Cupid's Bow* and as a member of this celestial family. The one thing guaranteed to make the matchmaking aspect of the job a breeze: The Sight, our ability to see threads and patterns in an astrological chart instantaneously. Why do we—Mercury, Venus, and I—use it for love? And not something more important? I blame the previous Mercury and Saturn, who lost a bet to Venus eons ago. I've read the Saturn notebook cover to cover, and I don't think The Sight is coming. This should worry me, but instead, it just pisses me off.

I am not good enough, thus everything about being in Boston, at *Cupid's Bow* HQ, pisses me off. Including the stereotypically romance-themed paint job.

The brightly lit, pink-walled room offers no stimulation, despite its garish color, and my brain enters low-energy mode as I click on the next two birth charts I've been assigned to evaluate for compatibility. Or, like my younger cousins—and technically my bosses—Venus and Mercury like to say, evaluating charts for true love. As if that exists.

The charts sit side by side, and the lines blur as the patterns evade me. In the five minutes I spend trying to determine if the pair are "soulmates," ten more enter my queue.

Fuck it.

I put the two nameless charts into the algorithm I created to increase my productivity.

A pop-up blinks, letting me know that the charts have been deemed "not soulmates." I click the red button on the *Cupid's Bow* interface and plug in the next pair. This algorithm has been the only thing allowing me to keep up with Merc and Vee.

Merc barges in with their locs pulled back into a braided ponytail and a navy-blue three-piece suit. The way their hair is styled and the fade on their sides make them look sleek, like the CEO they are.

"And what do you want?" I close out of the application and tilt down my computer screen. I can't risk prying eyes figuring out I've been faking it for over a year.

Merc smiles. "Weekly meeting, cuz."

My brows pull together and I check my phone, perplexed it's already the end of the day but happy because that means in an hour, I can leave this place and not worry about it till Monday.

"How's Uncle B?" Merc asks.

"Fine," I say, not offering anymore because I don't know much about my father's well-being, other than some photos he's sent.

Our walk to the soundproof, all-glass conference room in the middle of the office is made longer because Merc pauses to answer every question or comment from *Cupid's Bow* staffers on our way. I might not love working here, but my cousin, with their constant communication and friendly demeanor, is a great Mercury. I'll give them that.

I unlock my phone to show Merc the picture my dad posted online from Lagos two weeks ago. His dark skin is glowing in the bright sun and his blue shirt perfectly matches the ocean. The picture has no caption. Good to know silence is still his MO even across continents.

"He looks good," Merc says, and I agree. He hasn't aged a day since he left, and he's still very active. Why he decided to leave his beloved life behind and take me from my cozy software engineering life, I'll never understand.

"Yeah, he should be here," I say.

Merc pauses and places a hand on my shoulder. I look at their perfect manicure, confused by the gesture. "Trust me, you're the one who's supposed to be here."

I shrug off their hand, moving away from their pitying gaze. Despite the algorithm working well, I haven't fallen in love with being Saturn the way everyone else has with their roles.

Words from my childhood post-Mom come back to me.

You can't keep up the legacy like this. This is all I have to give to you. Dad's voice always got loud and shaky, his eyes enlarged by a dangerous mix of passion and fear, whenever he talked about my future and our "legacy." So much so, it turned me off. The old Niyi, previously proud and dedicated to astrology, faded away with each raised voice. Until it was time to leave for college and hatred occupied most of the space in my heart dedicated to my father.

Except a tiny portion. The part of me that still answers his calls and stares at his pictures for minutes at a time. My inner child, who simply wanted to be enough for his dad.

The *click-clack* of heels drags me out of my pitiful thoughts, and I put my phone away just in time for Vee's entrance. Her bouncy Afro is pulled back into one puff, and she's dressed in her signature purple.

"Niyi!" she squeals, using my given name after I sternly told her and Merc that calling me Saturn wouldn't fly, and runs to hug me. Her jasmine scent washes over me, providing much-needed calm.

Mercury is the people-person at *Cupid's Bow* in terms of communication; Venus is the people-person in terms of personality. Anything material, physical—heck, even emotional—Venus is right there, ensuring things are good for all parties. The both of them in charge of a dating app makes a lot of sense. After all, what's love without communication? The part that still confuses me is my involvement, both personally and in the grand scheme of things as Saturn. Saturn is known for rigidity, hardship, and time; it doesn't make sense to be roped in with the love crew.

"Sweet Vee," I mutter into my cousin's hair.

She pulls back and gives me an award-winning smile.

"How was your trip?" I ask. While Mercury is the CEO who keeps the business afloat on the human side of things—working with the board, keeping investors happy, that sort of thing—Venus, in addition to matchmaking, keeps us afloat on the celestial front. She travels across the world, keeping in touch with the other families that have been blessed (or cursed) with power like ours.

"Sun is always a riot," she laughs, and I nod. I haven't had the chance to visit Lagos as an adult and party with the matriarch, but it's one of my goals.

"Any word of her retirement?" Merc asks as they pull up the slides. A lot of the time, our weekly meetings are spent reviewing the chart pairings we can't decipher alone. In my first month here, the charts in question were mainly mine. But since implementing my trusty new algorithm method, I haven't brought a single confusing potential chart-pairing to the group.

"Sun's not ready to give it up," Vee says. I wish I could relate. Aside from The Sight, everyone talks about their powers giving them a newfound appreciation for life. For some gods, it creates a buzz in their blood they never want to relinquish. That happened to Merc's dad, who needed a lot of convincing to pass on his seat. Vee's mom gave up her seat at fifty, saying she wanted to live the second half of her life with her own beauty, instead of focusing on others. As for my dad? I'm not sure of his motive for abdicating Saturn.

Everyone in our family has turning points in their terms. Moments of reflection before their planet's next orbit where they can decide to either pave the way for the next generation or keep going. Except for Sun. As the center of the universe, the choice to let go is always present. Unlike the rest of us, Sun can abdicate without fear of illness or rapid aging because she doesn't have a specific orbit. I suspect, like the previous Sun, she will pass by natural causes and the next Sun will emerge from her bloodline.

Vee's next words bring me back to the moment. "I saw your dad." Her voice softens and pity transforms her playful tone into a melancholic lull.

"The life of the party?" I ask, even though the answer will annoy me.

"Not touching Sun, but close."

I take a deep breath, trying to ignore the urge to rationalize my father's illogical actions. The man didn't have time for his family when it mattered most.

Merc taps on the table. The rough sound forces me out of my thoughts. "Let's get started, shall we?"

·⁺✳ ♄ ✳⁺·

"I don't think so." Merc squints at the overlapping astrological charts, their pink-and-blue Corgi socks on the dark oak desk.

Vee, with her fingers deep in a bag of gummy worms, says, "I think the pair can work. The Scorpio Sun person did mention wanting something transformative."

"I agree with Merc," I say.

Both sets of brown eyes meet mine. Vee beams, and Merc raises a brow.

I clear my throat, adjusting to the attention. "The Scorpio and Aquarius pairing could either be transformative in the positive, all-consuming way, but it's more likely to be in the wreck-your-life way."

"He shows up!" Merc says, and I roll my eyes. They think I don't talk because I don't care, which is true. But mainly I keep quiet because those two go so fast I can't keep up.

"Two against three?" Merc asks, and we nod in agreement. Venus is more reluctant, but she goes with it because that's always been the protocol. When three are gathered, two dictate the flow in a blockage. Most of the time, the two are Vee and Merc, almost never Merc and me.

Merc clicks out of the charts, and I breathe a sigh of relief as I get ready to head out for my evening pottery session at Aaron's studio.

"Don't we have to talk about the mixer coming up?" Vee's question halts me. I completely forgot about that, and by the way Merc pauses in their cleanup, I guess they did too.

Merc winces and curses under their breath. "I forgot. Shit." They run their hands through their locs. "Okay, our first event as the core three. Vee, are the former couples ready?"

"The two people I previously coached, and their new partners, are all excited to share their stories." She beams. In the past, clients who haven't found a partner through our typical methods have done personal sessions with Venus, and after she works her magic, they find their person.

"The event planner is scheduled to come in on Monday to decorate the hall," Merc says.

"Caterer booked," Vee says.

"DJ playlist approved." Merc counts off item four with their fingers.

"Great. So, I'll be skipping out, if that's cool." I rock on my heels. That leaves me nothing to do for the event. Luckily for me, Vee and Merc had this gameplan set up from back when they worked with my dad.

"You have to be there," Merc emphasizes. Their eyes widen, shocking me with intensity. "Membership has taken a dip in the past year, and we need to put on a united front for the Board."

My eyes bulge. "Board members are coming?" That's never happened, at least to my knowledge. The stuffy white shirts have always been content in their ivory tower.

"When you drop from a ninety-nine percent success rate down to ninety percent in less than a year, they ask questions." Merc tries to keep their voice light and not look my way, but I know it's my fault. I am not my father, for better or worse, and in this business, it's definitely for worse.

"Guys—" I begin.

"No, don't worry, you're still finding your footing. It took me a while to adjust too." Merc sweeps aside my concern. That's a lie, but all right.

Vee places a pitying hand on my shoulder. I let her soothing touch linger for a second before shaking her off. I don't need any pity.

"On the bright side, your production is increasing. The Sight is coming in slowly but surely." Merc says.

A shaky laugh bubbles up from my throat. "Yeah, every day is easier," I lie.

As much as I detest this job, I don't want to be the reason why all of Merc and Vee's hard work goes down the drain. And deep down, as much as I dislike him, I want to make my dad proud. It's why I started reading up on astrology again. It's part of why I won't walk away, besides the fact that I literally can't stop being Saturn.

"Soon enough, we'll get *Cupid's Bow* back where we were." Vee rests her head on my shoulder. The weight of her belief crushes me. I gulp and give my cousins a shaky smile.

Two options run through my head as we say our goodbyes. One, fine-tune my algorithm to perfection and make sure they don't find out. Or two, unlock the full extent of my powers and retrieve The Sight.

I'm supposed to help Aaron out tonight by creating some novelty pieces for a client, but I can't...not with this hanging over my head. I'm a realist. I call Aaron to cancel my pottery session, head back to my office, and fire up the *Cupid's Bow* system backend.

3

Moyo

THE FAMILIAR VANILLA SCENT GREETS ME AS I STEP INTO Cole's empty apartment. Muscle memory carries me to his bedroom, and my brain succumbs to nervous excitement.

I never thought astrology would be my thing, but this past year with Cole has made me a believer. Standing in my boyfriend's house in a trench coat and sexy black lingerie, I'm glad I followed in the Three Wise Men's footsteps and let the stars lead me.

A satisfied smile forms on my lips as I take in my first-anniversary surprise. A royal blue bag holds the out-of-production perfume I spent months hunting down, and various sex toys are strewn across his silk sheets, waiting to be used. Even before he arrives, I know this pivot to something more intimate, more *us*, is the right decision. I can't wait to glimpse the lust on Cole's face when he sees me in this set.

After my inspection, I glance at the clock for the fifth time in thirty minutes. Initially, I checked to make sure my surprise would be ready for his arrival, but now my nervous excitement has morphed into full-blown anxiety because Cole *should* be home by now.

Was traffic worse than usual? I recall my own horror stories of driving in Boston.

Patience has never been one of my virtues, hence why I work with kids who move a mile a minute. This waiting is torture.

In my attempt to fend off restlessness, I turn my attention to the surround sound speakers, which immediately connect to my phone. Once I hit play, the passionate crooners of '80s and '90s R&B usher me into sensuality-flavored serenity. The music loosens my hips and the knot on my trench coat. With each twist and roll the coat begins to lose its hold on my body, and in a few short beats, it falls onto Cole's white rug.

The slight breeze from the perpetually stuck window makes me shiver. I notice my reflection in the mirror, and my breath hitches. Looking good is not new to me, never has been, but there are moments when everything aligns. The black lingerie complements my deep brown skin like no other. And yes, the body shimmer makes me shine when the light hits just right, but it's more than that. Waiting for my amazing boyfriend has me glowing all over. I look breathtaking and he'll agree. Cole's going to love this early surprise, the same way I loved his gesture with the key.

The night will be perfect, just like our meeting. We are written in the stars, soulmates, as *Cupid's Bow* put it, and tonight will be a new star in our ever-growing constellation.

Every minute increases my desire for him, and my jitters intensify. Should I call him? I squelch the urge. I refuse to ruin *this* surprise. Thankfully, "I Wanna Know" by Joe comes on and the nostalgic music takes center stage, displacing my worsening anxiety. God bless R&B. My eyes land on the toys, and I know what to do to get through the wait.

With long, manicured fingers, I caress my skin, and my tension dissipates. Each touch quickens my heartbeat as I shift my position to the bed.

As the R&B music picks up, the lead singer reaches an octave so impressive I imagine the crescendo loosening the knots in my stomach, and I cannot wait to be undone. Just before my stress evaporates completely, a piercing shriek stops me mid-movement.

My eyes spring open, and the sight freezes me.

Two sets of scorching blue eyes stare me down.

I wonder if this is how Medusa's victims felt under her stony gaze—

helpless and embarrassed. I lie there with taut nipples, legs spread, and mouth ajar.

"Moyo, what the actual fuck?" Cole's voice is the steel that pierces my trance. My hands retreat and my legs clamp shut, tightening so much I fear they'll never reopen.

I look at Cole.

My Cole.

His pink lips are twisted in an unfamiliar scowl, chiseled jaw stern below his dark blond hair. His arms shield a petite, blonde woman holding a small suitcase—a woman I have never seen before—whose eyes darken with disdain.

"I said, what the fuck?" Cole's unfamiliar rage spurs me into action, and I wrap the silk bed sheets, which I picked out, around myself.

"What?" I blurt, still in shock as I search for answers in the eyes I call home. Shame flashes across his features, and for a millisecond, I recognize the man I've been in love with for the last year. But it's not long before he returns to this new, foreign version of Cole.

He crosses arms over his chest, pushing his lickable pecs up on display. "There is no reason for my TA to be masturbating in my bed."

If not for the joint that holds a set of jaws together, mine would have literally dropped onto the sheets.

"Is she the one you were telling me about?" the woman beside him whispers, her ocean eyes stark and her lip upturned.

"Woah, woah, woah. Back the fuck up!" I yell, surprising myself with renewed confidence. "TA? I'm your TA now?"

At that, recognition seems to wash over the woman, and the disgust in her eyes give way to pity. What lies has he been feeding her?

"Moyo, please," Cole says, walking toward the bed.

He picks my trench coat off the floor and tosses it in my direction. I catch it with both hands and use it to shield myself from him and this trainwreck of a situation.

"I know I told you that you could come by whenever your family life became too hard to handle. I'm sorry if you misunderstood and thought

I was interested romantically." He keeps going, and I cannot believe his words. "You're a gorgeous woman, but I'm happily married."

For the first time, there's a silver wedding band on his left hand. In all our time together, he's never worn a ring of any sort. In fact, he told me he hates wearing jewelry.

My brain glitches and all I see is red. He has a wife? *I'm* the other woman?

This. Fucking. Asshole.

Hastily, I shove my arms through my trench coat, avoiding the Wife's eyes. But she turns away—bless her poor, unfortunate soul—probably feeling bad for the Black student who's fallen in love with her professor. Cole, on the other hand, has his gaze fixed on me. The lust in his eyes intensifies and his tongue darts out to wet his bottom lip, a movement I've become intimate with over the past year.

Unsurprisingly, his signature jaw tick shows up when I secure the belt around my waist. I hold his gaze, searching for something more than lust, but his eyes linger on my body with salacious longing, like a dehydrated man stumbling upon an oasis. There's no remorse, no sympathy, only an inspection of a body he wants to have.

My embarrassment transforms into searing anger, resulting in liquid pooling in my mouth faster than it did between my legs. I walk toward the devil and his wife in one swift movement and notice something else in his dead eyes—glee.

This fucker is...happy.

He's so thankful I didn't ruin his cover with the woman he plans to spend his life with. I can see it in the slight dip of his brows and the up-tick of his barely-there lip. He truly thinks I'll walk away and pretend this never happened.

Unlucky for him, he tried the wrong woman.

I propel the lava from my mouth, saliva mixed with disdain and hatred. When it hits him right between his eyes, I swear I hear a sizzle.

"Oh my god! Cole!" The Wife's incredulous, high-pitched voice makes my ears bleed. "We should press charges."

I turn my attention to her. "Madam, your husband here has been fucking me, a fully-licensed pediatrician, for over a year now."

Her eyes widen, and she looks at the man, who is growing redder by the moment. Lovely of him to match the colors; he'll fit right in when he gets to hell.

I dig inside my purse for his apartment key and throw it at his face. The metal hits Cole squarely in the left eye, a guttural groan erupting as his hands fly to his face.

"That was the key he gave me last week, lady. Enjoy married life with that piece of shit," I say with a tight-lipped smile.

On my way out, I slam his bedroom door.

Only then do I drop the bravado and feel my tears form.

· ✧ ✳ ♄ ✳ ✧ ·

Humiliation and anger grip my heart with superhuman strength. The only thing stronger is the urge to light Cole's dick on fire. My knuckles lose color as I release some aggression onto my steering wheel once I'm parked in my driveway.

How could I have missed this? How could I have been so oblivious?

The memories of all our good times in this car—from planning our first couple's vacation to stealing kisses at stoplights—make tonight even worse. With each thought, my anger builds, and the tears fall until my vision is as blurred as a window during a thunderstorm.

"Good thing tomorrow's the fucking weekend." My bitter words echo through my apartment as I saunter toward my bar cart, unscrew the cap off my favorite tequila, and take a hefty gulp. The earthy liquid goes down smooth, the warmth calming my nerves. An image of the last time I used tequila to get over being cheated on flashes through my mind. I shove the memory away, take another swig, and turn on my breakup playlist.

"Man Down" by Rihanna booms through the speakers, and I sing loudly. Tequila is the best dance partner I've ever had. My hips sway out of tempo as I imagine telling my parents I attempted first-degree murder, but couldn't go through with it, thanks to the whole doctor thing. Mrs. Adegbite might be harsh at first, but after I explain the circumstances, she'll privately pray God allows the judge to release me. The hard part will be ensuring Mr. Adegbite doesn't finish the job and end up in jail with me.

After I polish off the rest of the tequila bottle and three soju shots, Beyoncé's "Best Thing I Never Had" coats me in the truth: Cole lost *me. I* am the prize, and he lied, cheated, and strung me along. I can't believe he made me the other woman. He will live his life regretfully while I move on, because I'm funny, intelligent, and wicked sexy. I hope his wife leaves him. Not to mention, I'm becoming one of the most sought-after developmental-behavioral pediatricians in the country!

A little too much, my mind interjects.

"I'm becoming one of the best in the northeast!" I hiccup. I repeat the affirmations until I see new texts in my group chat with the girls.

> Anjie: How's it going? I'm sure he loved the gift.

> Sewa: Don't forget to gist us! We love the news! And we love this for you. Cupid's Bow coming in clutch!

I attempt to respond to them, but the end of Sewa's message reminds me of tonight's other villain. That stupid pink-and-purple astrology dating app that matched me with the blue-eyed devil himself. Soulmates, my ass! I haven't been in this much pain since I was in college. I avoided love to prevent this shit, and in eighteen months, *Cupid's Bow* ruined everything. Cole is to be blamed, but the people who sent him my way also deserve some smoke.

With glassy eyes, I struggle to navigate the bright app. "Stupid colors, stupid app, stupid cherub."

I stick out the tip of my tongue as I navigate to the complaints page on the *Cupid's Bow* website, and I try my hardest not to wobble off my sofa. After what feels like half an hour, my mind clears up enough for me to unleash my anger.

The big black letters stand out against the colorful app's complaints page. The first page reads:

What is the nature of your complaint?

"Fuck!" I scream when a drop-down menu with even more words appears. Instead of giving up—wouldn't *they* like that?—I take the time to scroll through the list of possible culprits.

App design...

I mean, yes, I have complaints, but they're not pressing. *No.*

Frequency of matches...

No.

Previous match...

Bingo.
I smile like a Cheshire cat when a complaint box appears.
"Let's do this," I say, words slurred. I crack my neck and squint at the miniature keyboard on the screen. I might be inebriated, but I have a lot to say, and they're gonna hear every last fucking word.

Moyo

I'VE ALWAYS BEEN BUILT DIFFERENT.

Another night of binge drinking without a single drop of vomit. Unfortunately, that's where my superior drinking powers end because as I've gotten older, a new alcohol-induced affliction has developed—a skull-splitting headache. Today's headache is confounded by a stream of sunlight through a crack in my blackout curtains. Clearly, drunk Moyo forgot to do hungover Moyo a solid. *Bitch*.

I slowly raise my pounding head from my couch and assess the damage. The room appears in order. My basket of horror movie Blu-rays sits untouched. And nothing's broken, unlike that one time in college that got me kicked out of school housing. The only things amiss are the empty bottles strewn on the floor, marking my journey from my bar cart to the couch like a treasure map.

I look down at my disheveled attire, and memories of last night come flooding back. Blue eyes stab me once more, for good measure, and I groan in accordance. The sound is heavy, prolonged, and almost loud enough to drown out the doorbell.

"Now, who the fuck?" I whisper as I get up and retighten the loose knot on my coat. I haven't had the chance to look at my face or hair, but I know

I look a mess. My fingers fly to my face—I should stop doing that—and the dryness confirms my hypothesis. I reach up to assess my hair, hoping to feel my bonnet. But, like forgetting to do my skincare routine, I also forgot to wear my bonnet. Honestly, what should I expect from someone who slept in a trench coat and last night's lingerie?

The *ding!* goes off again, and usually the sound amuses me, but with this headache, it's about as amusing as an awards show host. The ringing continues, increasing in frequency, while my patience nosedives. Now, I'm not a violent person, but vicious urges bubble in my core.

"I'll kill them." I yank the door open. "*What?*"

"Woah, anger management. Chill."

The quick retort from the familiar voice acts as a bucket of ice water, dousing my anger with a sizzle. Sewa's signature ginger braids swing past my eyes as she confidently walks into my space.

"Did you really text SOS to brag about your amazing night?" Sewa's eyes land on the empty bottles, and she gathers the evidence of my horrible night. The worry on her face almost makes me curse drunk Moyo again.

"Don't ask."

Sewa squints and tilts her head in pure confusion. She doesn't use any additional words, and I don't give any answers. We stand in the middle of the room while the cold winds nip at us.

"Let me lock the door," I whisper.

"Actually, wait a minute, don't lock it. Anjie is basically here, and you don't wanna have to get up again."

"What time did I text you guys?"

"Around 3 a.m. Woke up early this morning to work on some things and I saw it."

I swivel to face her. Sewa started her PhD in Linguistics almost two months ago and has been working every waking minute. If she's awake in the godforsaken hours of the morning, it shouldn't be to entertain my relationship bullshit.

"So why aren't you in class?" I ask, concerned.

Her eyes widen, and her perfectly shaped eyebrows raise. "Moyo, darling, do you know what time it is? Do you know what day it is?" she asks softly, coaxing me back to the velvet green couch I spent the night on.

"Uh, I don't know where my phone is, but I'm guessing eleven or twelve."

"This is why I've told you, repeatedly, to get a wall clock," she says.

I roll my eyes, patience thinning. Who in this day and age has a wall clock? "Are you gonna tell me the time, or are you just gonna be annoying?"

"Woah, again, anger management, chill," she repeats in the same tone as earlier, but louder.

"I don't need anger management classes."

"Yeah, and I don't need a car, so I can stop relying on the T," Anjie calls from the front door. "Do you know what those two statements have in common? They're both lies from the pit of hell."

· ✧ ✳ ℏ ✳ ✧ ·

You could've sworn Key and Peele were in the room with us the way these two are laughing. Tears stream down Anjie's face and Sewa kneels on the floor with half her body on the couch. If I had telekinesis, I would make the ground open up and swallow them because staying angry while they laugh is impossible.

"One more time, please." Anjie barely gets out the words.

I take a deep breath, roll my eyes, and take another look at the complaint on my phone, which I found between the couch cushions.

After a quick charge, I learned it was mid-afternoon and, more importantly, Saturday. Which explained Sewa's presence and why I hadn't woken to my work alarm but not why Anjie was here instead of at her restaurant. A *Cupid's Bow* notification popped up, and foolishly, I opened it.

The message read: *Complaint received. A Cupid's Bow representative will be in contact with you soon.*

To which the girls chorused, "What complaint?"

To which I said nothing at first, waiting for drunk Moyo to respond, but she'd left me yet another battle to fight sober.

I clear my throat and read the sixth complaint I left on the app last night, which I'd addressed to Saturn.

"...or better yet, shove one of your seven rings up your ass, experience an orgasm, and leave the rest of us alone." My attempt at a deadpan delivery instantly fails, and I bust out laughing with them. My laughter builds off of Sewa's, which builds off of Anjie's.

"That was wild," Anjie says, wiping tears from her face. "So, why the drinking and the numerous complaints?"

I look toward Sewa, who has taken a strong liking to her fingernails.

"No, don't look at her," Anjie says, commanding my attention. "She texted me something was wrong and said you weren't talking. So, now that we've had our laughs, let's have our chats."

Their eyes bore into my soul. Sewa's huge ones pleading, holding space for whatever I'm about to share. Anjie's smaller ones as calm as a tranquil lake, ready for whatever comes their way.

"I'm surprised neither of you mentioned the trench coat," I say. Then, I tell the story.

· ✦ ✳ ♄ ✳ ✦ ·

"So, I downed the rest of that bottle, along with some other things, and filed so many complaints I'm surprised the app didn't revoke my membership." The rawness in my throat from crying as I recalled last night's events ruins my attempt to infuse humor into the conversation.

My two best friends look at each other, grab their keys, and dash to the door. Sewa, the taller of the two, gets there first.

"Where are you going?" I reach them before they leave.

Once again, they look at each other.

"To murder a Caucasian. Why do you ask?" Anjie's soothing voice makes it sound pleasant, not like premeditated murder.

Sewa's voice is bland, like she's talking about the weather or the horrors of the Red Line. "I was just planning to break some kneecaps, but murder sounds more thorough."

"You don't have to do that?" It comes out as a question because I'm still unsure about my feelings. I'm hurt and infuriated, but the more I think about it, the more I want to let it go.

I try again. "You don't have to do that." This time it comes out firm, and they step away from the door.

"We can make it look like you had nothing to do with it," Anjie says sweetly.

Once again, the idea is tempting, but I took the Hippocratic Oath. Plus, getting revenge on a cheating ex is younger Moyo's thing. And although it felt good to see my college-ex lose a few on-campus positions as well as his stellar reputation after a series of complaints—that *I* had nothing to do with—another time would be overkill.

"The universe will deal with him," I say, eerily calm. I've never felt this way before, but it is incredibly welcome. Is this what happens when you're older and wiser?

"Same universe that sent him to you, but okay," Sewa mutters.

"Tell her, oh!" Anjie echoes.

I want to argue, but they're right, and it's hilarious. The success stories of *Cupid's Bow* are out of this world. Almost every match I've heard of ended up in marriage or a long-term partnership. It works, evidently. Maybe this year just isn't my time. Perhaps this disaster with Cole means I should take a hiatus to recoup and reassess my desires.

"The universe has shown me it's not my time," I say peacefully.

"Now, where did that come from?" Anjie's retort is swift.

"Like you said,"—I point at Sewa—"the universe sent him to me and look at that mistake. If there's anything I've learned recently, it's to accept lessons as they come, so I don't end up with a worse lesson one day." Sewa nods receptively, while Anjie looks like I zapped her with a taser.

"You know none of this is your fault, right?" Anjie asks.

My shoulders heave before drooping. I cradle Anjie's hands. "I know. But—"

"But nothing. It's not your fault," Anjie says. "I think you're using this to avoid your feelings. If that's what you want to do, that's okay."

I drop her hands with a frown. Here she goes again. Since we were clueless ten-year-olds, Anjie's spouted some version of this. Once she discovered therapy, it became "feel your feelings, Moyo."

"I complained to the app and cried while talking to you guys. I know my emotions, and I've felt them. I want to move on."

"You don't even remember those complaints," Anjie says. "But it's okay. Emotions demand to be felt. So, when the time comes—"

"Okay, spirit mama," Sewa cuts in, slicing the tension.

Anjie and I chuckle, taking the out and leaving the conversation for another time. We head to the kitchen, and Sewa makes herself at home, like always. She grabs a pack of chicken thighs and a jar of recently opened pesto from the fridge, then opens my top cabinet to retrieve the pasta.

"I'm going to shower to get last night off me." As I walk away, my mind casts back to the other dating apps I came across in my initial search. None of them have stellar ratings or reviews like *Cupid's Bow*, but I'm sure I'll find a decent one, *if* I try again.

"What will you do if they actually send someone to help?" Anjie's question stops me in my tracks. My stern restaurateur is a lover girl—always has been and probably always will be. Despite not being interested in dating, Anjie's the first one to remind us of the power of love.

And I get it, but the pursuit of love got me here, back to a hurt I never wanted to experience again. Maybe it's time to pursue something like companionship. If love happens, fine, it'll be a bonus.

Regardless of this new plan, I think about her *Cupid's Bow* question. Those apps never send anyone. Who has the manpower to individually visit everyone who complains? It's impossible.

"I'll send them right back," I respond, and Anjie shoots me a disturbed look. I laugh it off because she'll get over it, as will I. Taking my sights off love means I'll be okay. Most importantly, I won't get hurt again. I'll be fine because soulmates aren't even real. I won't be missing out on anything or anyone by not dating.

All I need in this life of sin is me and my girls.

Nothing more. Nothing less.

5

Niyi

WITH SMOOTH JAZZ IN MY EAR AND MY CLAY-SOILED APRON in my duffel bag, I'm at peace as I think of the hanging wall vases I threw at the pottery studio for Aaron's client. I've barely opened my front door when I jump out of my skin at the sight before me.

"Holy shit," I say instinctively, causing Merc and Vee to bust out laughing on my couch. My bag lands on the floor with a thud. I squint at the open bottle of 2021 Merlot from my collection and my open sketchbook. They always do this—come over and grab one of my Saturn-aged bottles from the wine shed and peruse my off-limits sketches—but afterwards they typically leave. Sometimes Vee stays, but never Merc.

"Why are you guys here?"

They don't stop laughing till I'm seated on the black leather couch. While they're distracted, I return my sketchbook to its safe place.

"You should've seen your face." Merc's words are scarcely audible, somewhere between a laugh and a wheeze as they struggle to catch their breath. Venus rubs their back and gestures for me to look in Merc's bag. I pull out their inhaler, and Merc's fingers find mine. After two puffs and slow drags, their breathing returns to normal. We might have the powers of celestial bodies, but they're still in a mortal case.

"Okay, seriously. What are you guys doing here?"

"There has been a complaint," Vee says, and I give her a look. "About you."

"What?" Different scenarios run through my mind. "An employee?" I don't talk to anyone in that office. I show up, do the minimum work, and leave.

"Oh, no," she clarifies. "A customer."

This alleviates some of my anxiety. "I'm not in a customer-facing role. Are you sure you have the right Niyi? I think there's another one in sales."

"There's only one Saturn," Merc says.

It's a Saturday. One of my only free days away from the wretched app. I try to leave Saturn in the office, and here they are bringing him into my home.

"Are you even listening?" Venus's acrylic nails clack in my face. "Did you just zone out on me?"

"Sorry," I say. "Just repeat everything you said." I smile and she kisses her teeth.

"The customer who complained was one of your first matches. You know, during the...week when..." Vee trails off. Her caution is appreciated but also makes me self-conscious. I don't remember the week I took over the role of Saturn in detail.

"What's the complaint?" I wince, bracing myself for the worst. The one thing Dad did tell me, during the transfer ceremony and via his notebook, is that Saturn is hated. People don't like delays or extra hardship. I don't like those either, so I get it.

"Just read him one," Merc says.

I expect to hear all the common complaints. Those I'm prepared for.

I can't find someone who's worth it. Not my problem.

I hate having you as the ruler of my 7th house. I wish I had Venus. It's all fun and games till they're prettier than you.

I am held hostage by my partners. The lesson here is boundaries.

The first part of the message is typical—how finding love with a Saturn placement is hard. But the second part makes me shift in my seat, clench my jaw, and stare blankly at the resin art on my walls.

Vee reads aloud, "'And why do you make it so hard for us, huh? Is it because you've never known love yourself?'"

My heart aches. Apparently, I approved this customer's match with my algorithm. They don't know me, but the words feel like a personal attack. The disgust in the complaint shames me.

"'You are some slimy, cobwebbed-dick, lonely-ass person,'" Vee continues, and the knots in my back develop their own knots. "'I know you have never had a love which is why *you* make it hard for *us*. I am literally over thirty, post-Saturn return. This shit was supposed to get better. That's what this stupid, fucking app said.'"

"Not my app," Mercury interjects.

Venus shoots them a heated glare. "'That's what all the astrology people say, and trust me, I did my research. But clearly, no one has ever spoken to big, boring bully Saturn who never wants anything good to happen to anyone. We're supposed to wait and wait and wait. What the *fuck* are we waiting for, huh? Absolutely nothing! I tell you because I am a grown woman with a great job and a great social life, but I am still struggling romantically. There is no world where that's supposed to happen, but clearly, it's this world because I got stuck with a sadist ruler of my love life. I have a Cancer Venus, so I know I'll be good eventually, but your delay is not cool. Next time you want to torture someone, skip me. Or better yet, shove one of your seven rings up your ass, experience an orgasm, and leave the rest of us alone.'"

This is my personal hell.

Vee nudges me, possibly to check if I'm still breathing. While she and Merc expected a reaction, I'm sure they didn't expect this reaction. *I* didn't expect this reaction.

Merc speaks first, as they typically do. "What are we gonna do about it? 'Cause if this gets out, it could be bad. Especially with everything happening with the Board."

Shit.

Words jumble around in my head, but a coherent response escapes me. My mouth opens and closes like a fish. Their stares pull me in and soon I'm stuck. Vee exchanges a look with Merc, and it dawns on me that they're waiting for me to say something. I'm about to ask why, but the answer reveals itself before the words form.

I should have a plan because I'm Saturn.

I finally understand why Saturn was paired with Mercury and Venus: for situations like this. Methodical, stickler-for-the-rules Saturn should lead the damage-control charge, but like every other thing related to this company, I'm useless. And at a loss for words.

"I'll handle it," Vee says. "I've offered the new coaching service to individual clients based on need, and I'd say this qualifies. I also recommend we throw in financial compensation. I usually do that for the most pissed-off folks."

I surprise myself. "But you should be focused on other clients and working on pairing charts. You're better at that than I am." The wheels in my brain spin and I hardly believe what I'm about to say, but it feels right. "I'll be the coach."

"What?" Vee says.

At the same time, Merc goes, "That might work."

I nod, feeling a bit better. I'll help this customer woman and—the idea pops into my head and it's perfect—use her as a test subject for my new algorithm. That way, I can keep something like this from ever happening again. I can keep pretending I'm a good Saturn.

"But he's just getting the hang of pairing people. Let his momentum build," Vee fires back.

Merc shifts their body to face her. "Couldn't working with someone individually be better then? To start slow? Probably what he should've been doing since the beginning."

I raise my voice. "*He* is right here, you know, and I'm capable of doing what I offered to do. The customer's Saturnian, right? Vee, you led me through the coaching course, so I know what I'm doing. There's no one better for the job than me." Conviction flows through my words and Merc smiles.

"There's our Saturn. First things first: getting the customer to agree." My conviction falters a little. How am I supposed to do that?

Vee smirks, and I wonder if I'll regret this. "Get ready for a field trip."

Niyi

WHEN VEE SAID "FIELD TRIP," I DIDN'T IMAGINE REVERTING to my primary school days. Why am I inside a hospital in a *Cupid's Bow* shirt as if I'm at risk of straying from the group? To make matters worse, this heavily starched shirt is the most uncomfortable thing I've worn since, coincidentally, my primary school field-trip days.

I fidget in the chilly reception area waiting for Dr. Moyo Adegbite, the complaining customer of the moment. The woman who could transform my career at *Cupid's Bow* if I can use her to fine-tune my algorithm. I pull up her file on my phone, looking over her astrological lines again.

I'm lost in the task of examining the relationship between Moyo Adegbite's Leo sun and Gemini moon when a voice calls my name.

"Niyi, right?" A woman—Moyo, I presume—walks up to me and I do a double take.

For the first time in a long while, I'm stunned. I stand to address her properly, and respectfully, but my knees falter. Like an oaf, I stumble before the absolute beauty in front of me.

The white of her doctor's coat provides a stark contrast to her rich brown skin. Loose spirals of hair frame her gorgeous face.

She clears her throat, startling me out of my trance. "Are you Niyi?" she asks, irritation audible in her voice.

"Yes, I am," I say breathlessly. Being rendered speechless was not part of the agenda. Especially not if I'm going to convince her to join the program so I can keep pretending I'm a capable Saturn.

She plasters on a smile, but it doesn't reach her eyes. "How can I help you?"

Words escape me, so I point to the embroidered logo on my chest. Her eyes scan the tiny words. They widen in recognition before forming murderous slits.

"Not interested," she says curtly.

"I'm here on behalf of Vinny Carr, Head of Operations at *Cupid's Bow.*" The words tumble out with the elegance of a newborn gazelle. She glares at me. "Mercury," I deadpan, and her mouth falls into an 'o.'

"Tell them thank you, but no thanks," she says and turns away. Before she can walk out of range, I touch her elbow, which sends a jolt through me. It takes two shakes of my palm to eliminate the spark. Once it's gone, I miss the feeling.

"Please," I say. She pauses and shoots a cynical look at her arm as if the appendage offended her. I take advantage of her hesitation and vomit the monologue Merc and Vee forced me to memorize.

"At *Cupid's Bow*, we pride ourselves on elite customer service. Therefore, we would like to offer you a monetary compensation package and a free dating consultant. The consultant will meet with you for up to three matches until you achieve a positive match."

Moyo's eyes could bore a hole directly into my face, so I stare at a patch of white wall beyond her to avoid forgetting my task or getting disintegrated by her venomous gaze.

The final stretch. "If your consultant is not up to standard, a new one will be assigned to you. All consultants are highly trained, as is the *Cupid's Bow* standard. You will not be disappointed by putting your trust in our establishment," I finish, and hold my breath in anticipation.

She cocks her hip and rests her pristine nails on her white coat. I can't help but wonder, what does she think of me? It can't be anything positive, thanks to this too-tight excuse for a Polo shirt, or the fact that I'm from *Cupid's Bow.*

Before she can respond, a young woman wearing pink scrubs bursts into the waiting room.

"Dr. Adegbite, consult in room seven," she calls.

Moyo lifts a shoulder in a half-shrug. "Again, thank you, but tell Mercury I'm done with *Cupid's Bow*'s services. Have a good day"—her eyes linger on mine—"Niyi."

For the first time in over a year, my heart feels alive. I'm captivated, and I can't explain it. I've seen beautiful women before, but somehow this meeting feels like a discovery. Fuck these powers. Aside from taking over my life, they now want to influence my attraction.

Without thinking, I touch her palm.

We both stare at the *Cupid's Bow* business card sitting there.

When did I grab that? When did I move? When did I touch her? Are my emotions enhancing my godly powers?

"Take some time to think about it. Call us about any part of the package if you change your mind. Have a good day, Dr. Adegbite."

Her nod is slight as she bids me farewell. I return the gesture and hope she calls. Because aside from how useful her case would be while I improve the *Cupid's Bow* matchmaking algorithm, I think I want to see her again.

Moyo

"MOYO, TURN ON YOUR CAMERA. ABI, ARE YOU HIDING OR what?" my mom calls out.

I turn towards the other participant on the group call, my dad, and stifle a laugh.

"Ah Moyosore, is everything okay? I can hear you, but I can't see you," my mom says, her voice switching from concern to mild annoyance. Technological difficulties happen semi-frequently during our weekly calls because my mom is often busy with her latest hobby and doesn't have the luxury of hopping on the phone with my dad.

"Darling, shey, your phone camera is not covered?" my dad asks, his normally gruff voice sweet and low.

I can't see my mom, but the change in her demeanor is apparent.

"Ọkọ mi, mi o mọ. Mi o ri nkankan," she says softly. Dad's sweetness transforms her annoyance from a bitter black coffee to a caramel macchiato. They are adorable, but currently, too much for my taste. I'll stick with efficient, stable, and dependable, like my daily plain matcha lattes.

My parents met in their early twenties during their National Youth Service Corps days. How they fell in love in the wilderness while marching in the hot sun, without great food or usable bathrooms, I'll never understand.

But I guess that's what love is. Something so potent, so mind-boggling, that it only makes sense to you and your lover.

Growing up around so much love made me think it would be easy to find, but after being chewed up and spat out twice by the jaws of infidelity, I'm done with it.

"Moyo!"

My mother's cheery voice brings me back. Her honey-brown skin is still radiant, and her pothos plants appear healthy despite the poor video quality. She needs to wipe her camera.

"Mommy..." My enthusiasm tapers. It's been over two weeks since the incident with Cole and the Wife. And not to give Anjie any credit, but the feelings eventually came and were indeed fully felt.

The first Sunday post-incident, I couldn't stop crying. Once the seal broke, the water came on with a vengeance. Before ten o'clock, I had bloodshot eyes and no energy to interact, so I canceled Sunday brunch with the girls and made up an excuse to get out of my weekly phone call with my parents.

After a week of forcing myself to smile at the hospital, including meeting someone from *Cupid's Bow*, I was exhausted. I made another excuse to my parents, told the girls I wanted more alone time, and spent the day binging all the *Scream* movies with a pint of ice cream and a shit-ton of Chinese food.

"My darling, what's wrong?" my mom asks softly, and the tears I thought were long gone threaten to return.

This is the reason I've avoided my parents these past two weeks. They see right through me, even when we're separated by three screens and a vast ocean.

Mom's eyebrows furrow and my dad leans in, as if getting right up to the camera will bring him closer to me. I wish it would.

"Oh, Mommy, I'm just tired." I yawn a little for effect. It's not a complete lie, and I can't have them worrying.

"Moyosore, you know you can tell us anything," Dad chimes in.

I want to take him up on it, but can I really tell my completely-in-love parents how messed up my love life is? How I don't think I'll ever have what they have? How, despite doing everything right, I can't hack this one thing?

I can't share any of that.

My lungs expand with the weight of the lie I'm about to tell. I scan my brain for the most appropriate one. Work has been the reason for my recent cancellations, so that's off the table. Maybe Anjie and the restaurant? Or how Sewa's getting on in her program? My parents love both those girls like they love me, their only daughter.

I settle on talking about Sewa when my dad breaks my train of thought. "Ehen, Moyo. How is Cole? Abi, that's his name, right?"

The dark eyes, which I inherited, are full of genuine wonder, his smile small and hopeful. He's probably mentioning Cole to put me in a good mood. I love that he wants to make me happy. Mr. Adegbite has always been the sweetest man I know. I told him about Cole before I told my mom because I knew he'd give me less flack for being with a white man.

When I did tell her, she laughed and said I'd make a great comedian before realizing I was serious. My dad just asked if I was happy and said that was good enough for him. He routinely asks about Cole on our group and biweekly individual calls, which Mom doesn't know about because she'll get insanely jealous. Despite his good intentions, hearing Cole's name opens the floodgates once more.

"Kola?" My mom calls for my dad, her voice delicate like she's traversing a minefield.

"Bisi, hold on," he responds in an equally hushed tone while I wail, the tears unstoppable.

I can't make out their features through the tears, but their concern is evident. Pity and worry are carved into the contours of their faces, the indentations so deep I don't need clear vision to know I'm scaring my parents.

Instead of acting normal, I cry harder.

"Moyo, please talk to us," Mom whispers.

I cry.

"Please," she tries again.

I sob.

"Do you want to talk to your dad alone?"

The sob catches in my throat.

I look up at her, tear-stained and hideous. I don't know how she can look at me with so much adoration. Tears have my vocal cords in a vice grip, so I just nod and wipe my cheek with the back of my hand.

"Okay," she says, smiling, but I recognize disappointment in her eyes. "Kolawole, over to you."

She hops off the call, and it's just my dad and me. We stare into each other's eyes, waiting for the other to begin.

He takes the leap. "Moyo, my only daughter. What's wrong?"

Still teary, I recount the story, the abridged version, of course. Dad is quiet all through except with the appropriate nods and *hmm*'s. When I'm done, he takes a deep breath, clasps his hands, and rests his chin on his knuckles. It's a simple act but a sign he's taking things seriously.

"Do you want me to come there?" he asks, and there's a sharp, unforgiving edge to his voice I haven't heard in years.

"And do what?"

"Talk to that irresponsible, useless boy," he spits, and the venom makes me smile. "You don't do that to a woman."

The increased tension in my dad's voice implores me to sit back. Many years of strict scoldings let me know exactly what's coming up: a rant.

"These new young boys are a disgrace and were not brought up properly. Haba! Is it not wickedness? It shall not be well with him," he says, looking to the heavens, and I shriek. "Ah, Moyo, don't shout. It is true, not a curse. Somebody like that cannot do well in life, especially in that marriage. Watch and see. Anyway, I'm happy you didn't marry him. If not, I would've booked my flight while you were talking. I will not stand for someone treating my angel like this. You are my wonderful girl who deserves someone even more wonderful, who will treat you better than I treat your mother."

"Oh, that's not happening, but it's all right," I mumble.

His anger is swift. "Moyosore, speak up. What do you mean that's not happening?"

"I know you see me as your little girl, but Dad, I'm thirty-four. Everything I do ends in ruin. I haven't experienced the love you and Mom have, and if I'm realistic, I never will." The words tumble out.

"Momo," he soothes, using his nickname for me and thus, melting my heart a little. "Never say that again."

"But Dad," I whine, transforming into his little girl.

"But nothing. Ah, ah, Moyo," he draws out my name in exasperation. "You want to give up because of this useless oyinbo? There is someone out there for you. I know it."

I wish I had his trust in the world. I did once, but look where that got me. I planned hard, loved hard, and still, here I am.

"Not everyone is lucky like you and Mom. Some people never marry, and they're fine."

"If it's that you don't want to marry, then we can talk about that one later—"

A chuckle escapes me involuntarily. As supportive as my dad is, he's still a Nigerian man who would love to walk his only kid down the aisle.

"But if you're saying this because of some ingrate, and now you think you'll never find someone, I won't have it," he says, shaking his head and his cheeks move in tow, similar to a chipmunk.

I have to let him down easy. "Daddy—"

He cuts me off. "Momo, before you start. I know your mother and I met early, and we knew immediately, but it was unexpected to find my soulmate at twenty-three—"

"And I'm thirty-four," I interject.

"I know. Now let me finish," he says with a laugh, and I signal for him to continue. "Some of our friends met their people at thirty-five. Even my close friend, Dayo. You know your Uncle Dayo, abi?"

He pauses to give me time to remember. It's laughable he thinks I would forget his best friend, who was a fixture at Christmas parties and held the best (and my only) sleepovers.

"Of course I remember Uncle Dayo."

"Ehen, see Dayo met Halima when he was forty and she was thirty-five. That's even older than you."

My eyes widen, but the more I think about it, the more sense it makes. My parents might've met early, but they didn't get married or have me till their mid-thirties. And Uncle D is older than them.

"See, I shocked you." He cackles, and I join in. "It wasn't too late for Dayo, and it's not too late for you, ọmọ mi. Just be brave."

His ear-to-ear smile is infectious. I smile back at him. My tears have dried up and the lump in my throat has dissolved. Talking to my wonderful dad always does the trick.

"In fact, maybe you can set those dating apps to a Nigerian man since you won't accept my proposal to set you up. You know Iya Faridah has a nephew about your age," he begins, and it's his typical monologue about all the people he knows with single sons or nephews. I tune him out. Although I love my dad, being set up by him is the last thing I'll do. It might take a while, but I'll figure something out.

"I'll think about it," I say when he's done, and he lights up.

Shit.

"So, I can send your number to Mama Tope?"

My brain conjures the image of the older woman with four sons who constantly terrorized the estate with marriage-minded comments. Her oldest two should be in their late thirties, but I think the one I had a crush on is already married.

"No!" I quickly lower my voice. "No." I can't yell at my dad. "I meant, I'll think about finding a Nigerian man over here. You don't have to do anything, and please do not send my number to anyone." I narrow my eyes at him. If I'm not firm, I'll get random messages from people I've never spoken to who are interested in making me their wife. Besides, I recently met a Nigerian man. The *Cupid's Bow* Niyi guy.

"Okay, O! If you change your mind, text me. Many people would love to meet you."

The doorbell rings, and my phone shows it's 2:30 p.m. The girls are right on time for brunch. Shocking.

"Are those my other daughters?" Dad cranes his head to the left as if he'll be able to see the door.

"Yes," I say before yelling towards the door, "It's open!"

Anjie walks in with a sheet pan, and the smell of jollof rice graces the room. The mixture of thyme, peppers, bay leaves, tomatoes, and goat meat stock always hits. Sewa, beside her, holds a bottle of champagne. They walk past me to drop the items off on the kitchen island.

"My girls!" Dad calls out.

Anjie plops down beside me while Sewa goes to lock the door. "Mr. A. Kilon poppin'?" she says, brandishing some hand signals she knows nothing about.

"Anjie-panjie." My dad mimics her movements. What is wrong with those two? "Nothing, oh. Just dealing with this crybaby."

"Dad!"

"Moyo, inside voice, please," Sewa says softly as she nestles into the space beside me. "Good aft–I mean, evening, Mr. A. How are you?"

Sewa's always been the polite one. And having only briefly met my dad in person during commencement weekend, she's never fully acclimated to his playfulness. Even though I've told her she can loosen the reins, she remains cautious. But I get it, because Nigerian elders.

"Sewa, sweetie, if this one can stop giving me a heart attack, I'll live to see my grandchildren—"

I gasp.

"Ignore her. Tell me how your PhD is going."

I extricate myself from the lovefest to set up the kitchen for brunch. On Sundays, it stops feeling like I live alone. And this Sunday, after spending the last several experiencing my entire emotional range, I appreciate the community I do have.

I grab several plates, champagne glasses, and the wings I made and set them on the counter beside Anjie's best-selling jollof. I return to the sappy scene right out of a Hallmark movie and hear them wrapping up with one final word from my dad.

"Moyo, remember what I said. And please call your mother so she knows you're okay."

"Will do!" I say, wiping my hands on my blue denim.

"Love you all. Daddy A, out!" He throws up a peace sign.

"Love you too," the girls reply in chorus.

"Please never say that again," I say to him, laughing before he hangs up.

Things are quiet for a second, per usual when a phone call with my parents overlaps with brunch, but pick back up when Anjie heads to the sedan for more food. Because brunch is a weekly occurrence and carrying trays of food on the train is tiresome, her head pastry chef, Mike, graciously allows Anjie to use his car. Sewa and I believe he's in love with her because why else would you hand off your car for an entire Sunday? But Anjie refuses to entertain the idea.

When she opens the tin foil, the decadent smell of asun sliders attacks my nose. The heavy scent of scotch bonnets hits first, making my eyes and mouth water. The smokiness of the goat meat comes through next, beautifully complementing the smell of jollof as it heats in the oven. The buns look freshly baked and fluffy, like cotton candy clouds. I cannot wait to get my hands on them. Sewa reaches for one, but Anjie swats her hand away.

"Before we dig in..." Anjie looks pointedly at Sewa. "I heard you're giving dating another try."

Can't my dad keep something to himself for five minutes?

I give them a shortened version of my conversation, wanting to get to the delicious food. I throw in the bit about Uncle D because Anjie knows him from growing up around our family. Anjie and I met at the bright age of ten in Junior Secondary School One, where we were bunkmates and became life mates.

"Mr. A and I"—she clasps her hands dramatically—"are like this. Always in sync."

I hit her with the big serving spoon and say, "My friend, let's sit down and eat."

We catch up over two sliders each, some wings, and two plates of rice between the three of us. Plus, half a champagne bottle.

"So...dating?" Anjie asks during the commercial break of *Only Murders in the Building.*

"Speaking of, did the *Cupid* people ever send any response?" Sewa asks, jogging my memory of the hottie with the stunned face and the too-tight shirt. I'm about to lovingly cuss them out for forgetting, but then I remember I chose not to tell them. I take another sip of my drink, looking away from their insistent gazes.

The show resumes, but Sewa pauses it. She squints at me for several long seconds. It's like watching a bloodhound.

"Yeah, she's hiding something," Sewa says matter-of-factly once she finishes her inspection.

"Oh, I know," Anjie says, taking another sip.

There's no use hiding anymore.

"Okay. They did send someone from *Cupid's Bow*. This guy, Niyi. He told me about monetary compensation and a dating consultant, or a coach, I forget," I say, sloshing my drink around. Niyi, the dark-skinned boy with the perfect smile and burning eyes who made the cool hospital waiting room feel blazing.

"See how she's smiling at her drink," Anjie jeers.

"I'm not smiling," I say, but my face betrays me with a cheesy grin made worse by their aww's and giggles. I hate these women so fucking much.

"Go on...tell us about him. You know you want to." Sewa's sing-song voice gives me the go-ahead.

"Okay, so imagine a guy about yay high." My hands go above my head a couple of inches. "Gorgeous, dark skin—"

"Damson-dark or Keke-dark?" Sewa cuts in.

I pause, thinking back to the moment in question. The stark white shirt was a breathtaking contrast to the richness of his skin. I'm sure he glistens right out of the shower and glimmers during the summer.

"Darker than Damson."

Sewa's eyes widen, and Anjie's head shoots back, accompanied by a low whistle.

I carry on. "His body also looked good. The white tee did wonders for his figure. I couldn't see everything, but the biceps were prominent. His smile was sweet, and he had perfect teeth. You know how I feel about good dentition—"

They nod.

"And the best part of the brief encounter was how he looked at me. He looked like he was gazing upon God."

"Reel it in, Leo," Sewa laughs.

I ignore her because his eyes—those mesmerizing, dark bronze eyes—are on my mind.

"It truly felt like I was the only girl in the world." I raise my palm to stop anyone from pointing out the cliché line, and Anjie's jaw closes. "It felt great to be looked at like that, with reverence. After everything..."

My energy dips, remembering the incident. My friends rub my back.

"And this will not be the last time, trust," Anjie coos.

· ✦ ✳ ♄ ✳ ✦ ·

We finish the episode. The killer's still at large and now someone's poisoned a dog. There's more to go, but it's getting late, and we all have early days tomorrow.

"So, before we go. About the offer from *Cupid's Bow*. You're gonna take the refund or what?" Sewa says, putting on her jacket.

"If you don't want it, you can give it to me," Anjie jokes.

I bite my lip, thinking of the grave error I made in telling these two about the offer. "I never even asked the amount..." I say and then cringe at their reactions. "I don't know if it's for the whole amount I paid or not. I was a little distracted at the time. It was in the middle of work."

"Sure..." Sewa rolls her eyes.

Anjie reaches for the business card. "Let's call and find out."

"It's a Sunday," I protest.

"We might get lucky," Sewa says.

Anjie waves the card in front of my eyes. It's a simple white card with pink-and-purple detailing alongside the company logo with a customer care number below. I don't know why I kept it in plain sight like that. I've had the chance to throw it out, but it stared at me every day, not as intensely as Niyi did, but close.

Fuck it. I have nothing to lose and only my money to gain back. I hand Sewa my phone, and she dials as Anjie reads the numbers aloud. She shoves the phone to my ear. It's ringing.

A moment later, a smooth voice I don't recognize picks up. "*Cupid's Bow*, Head of Operations. How can I help?"

"Hi, this is Moyo Adegbite. I received this number from the *Cupid's Bow* rep, Niyi, some weeks ago," I say, pretending I don't remember the exact day. It was precisely two Mondays ago.

"Oh, yes! Moyo," the voice says, becoming lighter and more familiar. "This is Vinny Carr or, better yet, Mercury. How can I help you this evening?"

My jaw drops, and I mouth "Mercury" for my audience. Their jaws also drop. Of course, I recognize the name. Mercury is one of the most prominent young business owners in the city. No one knows much about the internal structure of *Cupid's Bow*, but Mercury is a local celebrity in the young Black professionals' space.

"Hi, Mercury, sorry to interrupt your Sunday evening—"

"Not an issue. How can I help?"

"Your rep came by my office and said something about a monetary refund package?"

"Oh, yes. I can write the check right now. I'm so sorry things didn't work out with your previous match. But I'm curious, were you also interested in our personalized coaching service?"

My father's voice rings in my mind. I want someone that I am sure of. But to search for love? I don't know if I can handle another grand disappointment. I could use another app, but statistically, *Cupid's Bow* is the best. The numbers and reviews don't lie. And even though I lowkey want them to so I have a reason to give up, true love can't lie.

Sewa nudges my arm.

"What's happening?" Anjie whispers.

"I..." I peter out. I don't have an answer.

Mercury comes to my rescue. "You know what? Take some more time to think about it. I want to compensate you for that previous match and renew your faith in love and in *Cupid's Bow*. There's a mixer for current and previous app customers this Wednesday night at 6:30. If you have time, I'd love for you to join us." They pause for a response, but I have nothing to say as I digest the information. "Regardless, I've signed your check, and if you'd like, I can send someone right now to deliver it."

"Right now?"

"Yes. I know you haven't consented to the program yet, but I'll send the check with your prospective dating coach. You can get to know them, see if you're a good fit, and then decide after the mixer. How does that sound, Moyo?"

"Can they be here in less than an hour?" I ask, still wanting to get to bed on time.

"Why don't you give me your address, and I'll make sure they arrive in thirty minutes or less. And thank you for allowing *Cupid's Bow* the chance to make this right. Feel free to call if you have any other concerns. Hopefully, I'll see you on Wednesday."

I give them my address, and we say goodbye.

I'm stunned. I just spoke to one of the city's wealthiest people, and they were pleasantly chill.

"Who's coming in less than an hour? Mercury?" Anjie asks.

"My check and my prospective dating coach," I say. "Prospective coach because I haven't decided yet, but Mercury said I can see how I feel about him first," I quickly clarify.

Sewa smirks wickedly. "You said 'him.' That boy on your brain."

"And to think I was going to ask you guys to stay so I don't get murdered."

"You can admit you want it to be him," Anjie adds.

I herd them towards the door, shaking my head at their audacity. I wasn't thinking about Niyi. Why would it be him? There's no reason for it to be him. He wasn't even on my mind at all till Sewa mentioned him.

"Let me know when you get home," I say as they leave for the train station. Anjie will retrieve Mike's car tomorrow when she's sober, per brunch protocol.

After they leave, minutes pass as I lie on the couch, and I finally turn on *Ready or Not* to play in the background. I ignore the film as I think about the possibilities.

I could like my coach, or maybe I won't.

I could use *Cupid's Bow* again and find love. Or I might get my heart ripped out again.

This could be the worst idea. Or the best.

The doorbell rings. Either way, it's time to find out.

Niyi

I KNOW THAT SCENTS AND MUSIC CAN HOLD ASSOCIATIONS with another time and place, but I never thought working on a new algorithm would have me thinking about *her*.

First, it was the moment at the hospital when the *Cupid's Bow* card suddenly appeared in her hand. Now, two weeks of fine-tuning a process that typically drives me up the wall triggers a buzz in my veins now because I end up thinking about Moyo.

I don't know what these inexplicable power surges are or why Moyo appears to be a trigger. It's not on purpose, but if thinking about her makes my unsavory workload a little less tiresome, then so be it. Moyo is a means to an end. A potential client. Nothing more.

Regardless, every time Merc's phone rings, my ears perk up, hoping she's calling to accept the coaching proposal. And like a dog whose owner hasn't thrown the ball, I'm disappointed every time. Luckily, I hide my feelings well.

It's another Sunday without excitement, and we're at Merc's place because they wanted to try this fairly new Nigerian restaurant in the city. I'm lying on the couch, halfway to sleep, when Merc says, "You're gonna run a little errand."

I'm up, fatigue evaporating like mist. "Not your errand boy." I might still be getting my footing in the business, and this is their house, but I will not be spoken to like that. Merc stares me down. Their brown eyes glisten with gold flecks, and the corners crinkle a tiny bit. Merc always laughs with their eyes first. They're fucking with me.

"Thought you wanted to fix your mess with your Saturnian client, Moyo, but I guess not."

Are my Saturn powers malfunctioning again? All I can hear is my increased heart rate.

"She called?" I croak. I know I should be excited for an opportunity to get her help for my algorithm but that's the last thing on my mind. Her gorgeous face takes up every nook, cranny, and corner.

"Ten minutes ago—"

"You waited ten minutes?" I blurt out. I cough, clear my throat, and try again. "I mean, why didn't you come get me immediately?"

It's Vee who responds. "Are you gonna sit around, or—?"

I regret telling them anything at all, let alone accidentally gushing about Moyo's beauty when I got back from the hospital that day. The teasing that is still going on is insufferable. But on the bright side, it does bring me updates like this.

"Toss me my keys," I say, and she obliges.

Merc blocks my exit and hands me an envelope with the check inside. "Before you go, do you remember everything you need to say?"

I recite the script like a robot: "Hand the customer the envelope, explain the coaching process, answer any questions." It's not a long list, but they've mentioned it multiple times over the last two weeks. I couldn't forget if I wanted to. I couldn't forget anything concerning Moyo even if I tried, and trust me, I've tried.

Merc nods, satisfied.

"Okay, go get 'em, Tiger. I—we"—they gesture to Vee—"are counting on you."

I'm in my car when Merc texts me the address, and my buzzing optimism flickers to confusion for a moment. Moyo lives on my block. On the opposite side of the street but definitely the same block. How have I not met her before *Cupid's Bow?* I park my car in my driveway and walk to her house.

The question gnaws at me until the second I'm in front of her navy-blue door. I take one more calming breath, my finger hovering over the white doorbell.

I will not get carried away.

I will control myself and will not succumb to weird emotions.

I'm here to provide a service and figure out how to improve an algorithm I created.

I push the button and the door opens before I take my next breath.

Moyo Adegbite greets me in a pair of blue jeans that accentuate her curves and a white crop that highlights the fact she's clearly not wearing a bra. I stare a second too long before I remember why I'm here. I repeat my mantra in my head one more time.

"It's good to see you again, Dr. Adegbite." I extend a hand. I'm going to be the most professional person she's ever met. "I'll be your dating coach. May I please come in?"

· ⊹ ✳ ♄ ✳ ⊹ ·

"Once a month?" She repeats my statement with a slack jaw. It's been almost an hour, and we've gotten nowhere. This woman is insufferable and nothing like I expected. Don't get me wrong, she is beautiful and breathtaking, but she's also a pain in my ass.

"What's wrong with once a month?"

"I don't know what your dating life is like. Maybe you haven't been on a date in a minute. But when I'm actively dating—which I will be if I decide to go through with this—I see someone more often than once a month. I'd say every two weeks." She folds her arms and pushes her full tits up, letting some cleavage show. If this were another situation, I'd trail a finger along her collarbone and ask if I could feel more of her soft, delicate skin. Now, I just want to wring her neck.

Why is she commenting on my dating life?

I grit my teeth. "Next time, just say you think every two weeks would suffice."

"I'm trying to see if this arrangement will be worthwhile. Once a month wouldn't make sense," she scoffs.

"Fine."

The quicker I leave her house, the better.

It didn't start off like this. When I first arrived, we were cordial. She invited me over to a comfortable, green sofa. I handed her the white envelope and told her we'd discuss the initial details to see if we were a good coaching fit. Her smile was captivating, she invited me to use her lovely first name, and she radiated anxious, excited energy. I was the confident one. Everything was perfect...until I suggested that I sit in on dates.

She asked if I was dizzy. It was all downhill from there.

So far, we have agreed that I will *not* be sitting in on any dates. Supposing we do this—a prefix she never neglects to add—we'll meet in predetermined locations that will be communicated via Mercury. Yes, I suggested giving her my number or email to eliminate the extra step. Yes, she snapped at me. Throughout this debacle, one thing has rung clear: this woman is a Saturnian individual. Too many walls, not enough faith.

"Anything else, Dr.—"

"You called me Moyo before. Why are you calling me 'doctor'?"

I plaster on my fakest smile. "Yes, Moyo. Anything else you want to touch on?"

"To clarify, if I agree to this process, we'll only meet after each of the three dates. Yes?"

"Yes. Three dates with three separate matches. Unless you happen to be satisfied after the first, and then we're done."

Despite wanting to test my algorithm, I hope that's the case. I hope it will be perfect on the first try because I don't think I can last long with this woman.

"If you agree, we'll meet every two weeks, assuming that's the time between dates. We speak through Mercury and meet a maximum of three times," I recap.

Moyo sits with the words for a moment, her pretty face deep in thought, signified by the little crease in the middle of her forehead and a slight jut of a pink tongue. The tip adds even more color to the rich palette of her face. If I weren't so irritated, I might say she looks stunning. I can only wonder what pleasant things she can do with that tongue because being nice to me certainly isn't one of them.

"*If*," she over-emphasizes, "we do this, that sounds acceptable."

Acceptable? I literally just repeated her own words back to her. I forget to take a deep breath and jump to my feet. "Is this how you are with everyone?"

Her jaw ticks. "Thorough? Yes." She grins, and it is breathtaking.

"Not that. The light condescension."

Moyo also stands. She's only a few inches shorter than me but is still intimidating. "Condescending? Because I don't want you creeping all over my dates?" she asks.

"It was a suggestion, and it's worked for other people," I say, rubbing the back of my neck.

"Then you should've led with that evidence."

I clench my jaw to stifle a groan. She does work in medicine, after all. Being obsessed with numbers and evidence makes sense. Doesn't make this any less annoying, but it does make sense.

"Want to hear another strategy that's worked?" I ask, attempting to salvage this meeting. She nods receptively, and I think about the list I compiled. Here goes nothing.

· ✧ ✳ ♄ ✳ ✧ ·

"Role-play?" she shrieks, alarmingly loud for someone with neighbors. The reaction isn't as bad as some of her previous responses, but like the others, it leads to some bickering. I want to rip my hair out, but actually (and I'll never repeat this) it's kind of fun.

"After a date, you'll give me a rundown, yes?" I go over the process we agreed on one more time, and she nods. "Then, if need be, you'll tell me about a situation you're conflicted about, and we'll role-play it together. You'll play yourself, obviously, and I'll give you some feedback."

She nods warily.

"There's also role-playing that involves us going on a practice date so I can give you feedback on spontaneous scenarios," I expand, and the receptive vibe ends.

"Maybe not that second part. Can't have you falling for me." She takes a sip of water.

"Not in your wildest dreams."

Is she gorgeous? Yes.

Would I love to make her putty in my hands? Absolutely.

Am I seeing her in a purely professional capacity, and have I found that she grinds my gears? Yes, and yes. Therefore, romance is not an option. Plus, this attraction is just because of my powers. And I refuse to build a relationship based on powers I don't appreciate having.

I run a hand through my coils, and she laughs. It's the first time I've heard her laugh, and it sounds like angels.

Wow.

Dial it back, Niyi. I try to speak sense into my raging, god-influenced hormones.

"It's almost fun ruffling your feathers. If you could watch yourself, you'd do it too," she says, and I get quiet. This isn't news to me. Merc and Vee say it all the time. It hasn't even been two hours, and she reads me as well as people I've known much longer.

"Let's call it a night," I say. Best to stop before she reads into me even more.

"Yes. I'm still deciding, but I'll let Mercury know soon." Moyo rises and gives a big stretch that reveals a healthy amount of underboob.

I look away for both our sakes, depriving myself of the glorious angle. I remind myself she might become a coaching client, and if she does, she'll be the most important one. With her help, I'll figure out my algorithm once and for all and finally pull my weight as part of the upper management core trio.

"See you on Wednesday?" Moyo says, walking me towards her front door.

"Wednesday?"

"At the mixer?"

I need to stop forgetting about that. "Oh. Yes, I guess I'll be there."

My hand hovers above the doorknob as I take another look at her. Her brown eyes latch onto mine and everything in me pushes against leaving. But I must, because this is my job now.

True love isn't real, at least not for me and the Saturns who came before me. Plus, this woman drives me crazy.

"I gotta go," I say.

"Get home safe," she says, her voice soft as she opens the door for me.

"You actually can be nice," I say. It breaks some of the tension. The fire in her demeanor returns.

"I'm polite. There's a difference." She fights back a smile and then shuts the door in my face.

As I walk home with the cool, fall air caressing my face, I feel...different. Moyo's the most confusing person. And that was a trainwreck of a meeting. Nothing like I imagined, but it was fun in spite of the tension. This is the most stimulated, awake, and alive I've felt since before *Cupid's Bow*... maybe ever.

Do I feel this way because of my increasingly malfunctioning powers? Nothing can or will happen between us, but damn, it feels good. For the first time in forever, I feel good, and I want that to continue, despite common sense saying it's an anomaly. I don't know if Moyo'll do the coaching program, because I think she hates me now, but a selfish part of me hopes she does.

Moyo

I'M IN DEEP-FOCUS MODE AS I TYPE MY CONCLUDING NOTES from Danaya's final assessment session, with only the blue light from an archaic hospital computer to see by. For a hospital of this size, we should have better equipment. Then a notification startles me: *10 minutes to* Cupid's Bow *mixer*.

Shit.

I'm in a flurry, begging the old beast to shut down while putting sensitive documents in their rightful places. I rush to my car, still in my scrubs, and attempt to make it to a place twenty minutes away in five flat.

When I arrive seventeen minutes late, playing it cool while sneaking into the back of the hall, Mercury—who somehow looks better in person—spots me from the stage.

"And that's our final guest! The festivities can begin! Remember, eat, drink, get to know one another. Your soulmate might be in this room," they boom, and their voice reaches every corner of the packed room. They make a beeline to me, and all eyes turn to us. I want to shrink myself.

"Dr. Adegbite! It's lovely to meet you in person." Mercury smiles and graciously extends a hand.

I take it, scared of what the owners of those staring eyes will do to me if I don't.

"Same here," I say with a fake smile. "And please, it's Moyo."

Attention isn't foreign to me—a big, curvy, beautiful, Black woman—but I'm uncomfortable when it's not the attention I expect, and I don't look my best. My pink scrubs are cozy, but they're not the right outfit for this crowd. I wish I'd been in the mood to dress up today.

"Sorry I'm late. You didn't have to wait for me," I say quietly.

"Excuse me?" Mercury says, not hearing me over the chatter.

I'm about to repeat myself when another voice enters the conversation.

"Moyo, may I talk to you for a moment?" a steady, low-pitched voice says from above my head, and my body recognizes it before I do, sending a chill down my spine. Niyi.

I turn to face him, lifting my eyes to his face. I take in his set jaw and furrowed brows. Unsure of the reason for his presence, I tilt my head to the side and Niyi's eyes track to the empty section of the room, revealing no specifics.

Guess I'll see what he wants.

After excusing myself, Niyi and I walk to the back of the room, where it's much quieter.

"You're welcome," he says smugly.

My head whips so fast it almost falls off. "Excuse you?"

"I saved you from Merc. You're welcome," he repeats, leaning against the wall with a dramatic sigh and a stupid smile on his face. Niyi's casualness makes me do a double take. I came over because he looked worried. Not the other way around.

"No one *saved* me," I scoff.

"You looked uncomfortable."

"Still, no one saved me." I ignore his astute observation. "And who calls them 'Merc'?"

That makes him flounder. His mouth opens and closes repeatedly and starts multiple statements with "well," "you see," and "I," but they all fizzle out like water on a hot pan. I can't help but snicker, and he shoots me a look.

"It's a nickname," he finally gets out.

"I can tell."

Niyi's brown eyes fix on mine, shutting out the chatter around us. He can be smug and insufferable, but when he's quiet and looking at me like this...

One corner of his mouth lifts slightly as a stranger walks up to us. His brown skin is lighter than mine, and he looks at me with a nearly perfect smile. My attention moves from Niyi to the new man.

"Hello," he says coolly, leaning closer so the words land in my ear only.

"Hi," I respond, enamored by the sharp curve of his jaw. He's handsome.

"Maxwell." He opens his mouth as if he wants to say more, but Niyi's still standing here.

"Moyo," I say. "Nice to meet you, Maxwell—"

"Likewise, I'm Niyi," my prospective dating coach says, stretching a hand out to Maxwell.

"Oh, my bad. I thought y'all were done talking. I'll go chat with someone else." Pretty Maxwell gets through his words fast and evaporates from the vicinity before I can blink or stop him from going.

I call after him, but he's already out of sight, lost in the sea of people that has somehow only gotten larger.

Niyi watches me steadily. "He's not right for you," he finally says.

"And how would you know that? You didn't let him get a word in. I barely got to talk to him because of *your* interference." I push a finger into his chest, and it's rock solid. The sensation flusters me.

"He walked away from you just because I introduced myself. No man worth your time should feel that intimidated."

"He was polite. I would like a polite, kind man, someone who doesn't intimidate others just because he can."

Niyi's brows pinch together, eyes blanking before his face contorts into a scowl. "I didn't set out to intimidate him," he whispers as the crowd quiets down.

"You were enjoying it," I whisper-yell back.

"I don't want you to make a mistake." He lowers his voice even more, getting closer to me. His warm breath brushes against my cheek, and it's fresh and minty, as if he brushed his teeth or took a swig of mouthwash just before this thing started. Up close, I can see the details of his face even more clearly. I thought Maxwell had a jawline, but if I needed to open some mail, I'd call Niyi. His dark lips are sandwiched between his mustache and goatee. The facial hair doesn't connect, but it works. For him, it works.

His plump lips are moving, but I haven't heard a word.

"Répétez, s'il vous plaît," I blurt out in French.

"French?" Niyi gives me a puzzled look.

I don't have an explanation, so I go on the offensive. "You don't speak French?"

"Of course I do."

The smug look returns and his lovely brown eyes twinkle. "Je ne suis pas très doué dans mon travail, mais je sais que c'est un gars peu sûr de lui qui ne te mérite pas. Tu mérites quelqu'un qui t'honorera et te fera sentir aussi vivante que tu me fais sentir." He barrels through the words so fast, the only one I think I catch is "travail."

"You rushed through it."

"You don't understand French? Do you?" Niyi teases, his eyes bright.

"I shall not dignify that baseless accusation with a response," I bite back playfully, waving a hand in front of my lips to disguise my growing smile. My knowledge of the language comes from the five years I took it in secondary school in Nigeria, and all mastery is long gone, but Niyi doesn't need to know that.

I expect a retort, a comment of some sort, but instead, his lips repeat their earlier twitch—he's fighting back a laugh. I want to say something, to continue our lighthearted quippy exchange, but Mercury's voice fills the space once more and all heads turn to the stage.

"It's lovely to see you all mingling. Now we'll hear from some *Cupid's Bow* couples and from our first coached pair, for all of you interested in our dating consultation program." Some people take the stage and Mercury introduces them.

I'm almost at my seat before I notice I'm alone. I search for Niyi and find him pinned to the back wall. I shoot him a look that I hope conveys, "Why the fuck are you standing there? It's time to sit down."

He lifts off the wall and hurries to my side before the speakers begin. But when he gets to my side, he doesn't sit down. Instead, he squats, and my attention is pulled to the way his thighs stretch his simple black pants. He's so fi—*No.*

I refocus on the words coming from his lips.

"I have some other work to do, but this presentation will help you decide," Niyi says for my hearing only. "If you decide to work with me, I'll see you again. If not? It was lovely meeting you, Moyo. I wish you all the best, and I sincerely hope you find love." He squeezes my shoulder on his way out.

The first speaker, a chirpy brunette, sits and details her love story while a man holds her hand. His palm never leaves hers, and without knowing them, I can tell he longs to kiss the back of her hand, the urge eating him alive. Public performance must not be typical for them because her words shake more than mine did during my first year at the hospital's Foundation Gala. But when she stops paying attention to the sea of onlookers and focuses on her lover, her words gain clarity and strength. She finishes to thunderous applause, and he kisses her temple. The way her shoulders slump into his frame, the way he cradles her, tells me everything I need to know.

I don't even bother staying for the coaching presentation. My mind is made up.

I find Mercury standing among a group of people in impeccable suits and tell them I'll do it. Not because I want to work with Niyi, I don't care about him and his muscles, but because of the love I saw on that stage. I was kidding myself, pretending I would be fine with simply a companion. Or with someone who doesn't make my heart flutter simply by existing. Seeing those two on the stage reminds me that love is out there. It exists for others, and not just my parents.

Fear be damned. Cole and the Wife be damned.

I deserve to find someone, and I guess it starts now...again.

Moyo

EVERYTHING IS SO...PINK.

I mean, yes, it is a dating app called *Cupid's Bow*, but I didn't expect the boardroom to look straight out of Barbie Land.

This time—dressed in a pair of simple black slacks and a soft baby-blue turtleneck with my leather, shearling jacket—I'm prepared to enter the app's workspace. No scrubs, no rushing out of work. Ready to sign this agreement and get to work finding my life partner.

And see Niyi.

The thought is intrusive, making my heart flutter like a butterfly testing out its wings. My inner, secondary schoolteacher emerges, echoing a familiar refrain: "I will clip those wings."

This is not the time nor the place for a schoolgirl crush. I'm too old for it, especially over someone I have met less than a handful of times. Trusted methodology only. No experimentation.

As I prep my wing-cutting scissors, the double doors open and my efforts are sullied.

Mercury walks in first. Their locs bounce with their steps. They are effortless and chic in a monochrome, forest-green ensemble with gold jewelry to accentuate. Behind them holding a packet is Niyi, and damn, does he look good in navy pants and a light-blue crew neck, a few shades darker than my baby blue.

"Moyo." Mercury outstretches their hand. I take it and they pull me into a quick hug. "Thank you for giving us another chance."

"Thank your convincing clients," I say.

Mercury responds, "And you'll soon be one of them."

"That's the plan."

Mercury's bubbly demeanor switches to a more serious one in the blink of an eye. "I know we messed up last time, but like the couples you saw at the mixer, your matches will be handled by our most experienced match-maker. In addition, Niyi here will be listening to your post-date feedback and informing the process, so I am more than confident we can lead you to the love you desire."

Mercury's calm and collected expression is in stark contrast to Niyi's blank face.

"Now, I'll leave you to your introductory meeting. As always, feel free to contact me, but you're in great hands." Mercury flashes a smile in Niyi's direction, and the man in blue only shifts his eyes to acknowledge their words.

Soon it's just Niyi and me. Neither of us move for a second and then we move simultaneously.

"Sorry," we say in unison.

"No, you're fine." Also in unison.

I take a deep breath and gesture for him to go.

"Let's sit," Niyi says as he pulls out one of the office chairs. I move to his right, about to pull out my own chair, but his throat-clearing stops me in my tracks. "This chair is for you," he says.

"Oh."

As I take the seat, a wall of incense, cedar, and pepper hit me, mixed with some sweet elements that I desperately want to identify. I thought Cole had an impressive cologne taste, but Niyi's mix of woody tones with lighter aromatic and fruity ones is much more complex.

It's not until he speaks that I notice he has taken the seat to my right.

His captivating scent still lingers, and it takes everything in me to focus on why we're here.

"Ready to begin?" Niyi asks, not bothering to smile like Merc did during their introduction. Straight to business, I see.

"Yes." I follow suit.

"As much as our system works, there's nothing better than meeting the person involved; hence this meeting. I want to get to know you...to serve you, of course."

Before I can respond, Niyi opens up the packet he's been carrying. He takes out a document with an embossed *Cupid's Bow* logo on the side. "Take your time." He hands it over with a sophisticated, deep-purple fountain pen.

Years of scanning medical journals and patient charts make the contract a quick read. In my brief once-over, I note the details Niyi and I previously outlined.

Three dates. Three debrief sessions. A fat check. My personal coach—Niyi. A dedicated matchmaker, only written here as Saturn.

I imagine another Merc-like figure. The higher-ups must use astrological names to maintain business identity—I respect it. Plus, the Saturn individual being my matchmaker makes the most sense. My heart aches as I remember this Saturn person had the misfortune of reading Drunk Moyo's complaint.

Everything else looks good, so I sign and slide the contract back to Niyi. He extends his hand, sending another whiff my way. It takes me a second to register the appropriate response. Once I do, it's a firm handshake. Firm, but comfortable.

"Welcome to the *Cupid's Bow* coaching program." I expect a smile but his face remains straight. "Now, tell me a bit about yourself. How was your day? How was work?"

"Good. Long, busy day today, but that's normal." I repeat the typical polite reply I'm used to giving for small talk. My mind gives a little highlight reel of the day, and in the absence of doing a full shoulder roll to relieve tension—too conspicuous—I methodically pick at my nail beds.

Something flickers in Niyi's eyes. "Would you like to talk about it?"

Don't know if it's the ornate pink surroundings, but instead of brushing him off, I loosen up. First, with my preferred shoulder roll. And then with my words.

"Back-to-back sessions. I successfully got management to see one client pro bono, and it went great. Lovely kid, great family. I'm happy it all worked out. Now I'm trying to see another family, and management is giving me even more shit—" The words keep tumbling out. "It's like, despite everything I've done, and how successful the last pro bono work went, they still don't care. It's almost comical because in a few months, at the Foundation Gala, the CEO will rave about my work because it brings in good publicity. If only some of that money went into the pro bono work, instead of making me beg…"

Niyi nods slowly as I carry on, laying my frustration about hospital politics and red tape at his feet. It's not how I expected our first meeting to start, but he's a good listener. I'm comfortable sharing under his watchful eye and stoic expression, which is a good thing, seeing as he's my dating coach and all.

Soon I'm doing the thing the girls always jokingly chastise me for: responding to my own questions or dilemmas before my listener can answer. But somehow, Niyi remains calm. Nodding appropriately and littering well-fitting *hmms* as needed.

Once I'm done, I let out a weary sigh. Half-shy that I spoke uninterrupted for almost twenty minutes but also relieved to get things off my chest. "Sorry for the rambling. It's been a long day, and I haven't had time to talk to my girls."

"No problem at all," Niyi says. "Having a clear head before we dive in is best. And, Moyo," he pauses, and I'm forced to look into his warm brown eyes. "I asked you to share. Don't apologize."

Sheepishly, I say, "Thanks."

The air is thick for a moment, like right before heavy rain showers. Gloomy with a cooling quality that promotes watching a movie in bed.

I could bask in this, if this were a date and my relationship with Niyi weren't professional.

"Enough about me," I say, dispersing the rain clouds. "Tell me about your day."

"Oh, don't worry about me. We're here for you."

Niyi attempts to keep it moving, reopening the folder with numerous papers, but I stop his hurried movements by laying my fingers on the back of his palm.

His skin is quite smooth. My thoughts begin to wander, but Niyi's look of disbelief at the contact banishes them.

I withdraw my fingers. "One thing you'll quickly learn is I don't do well with solo vulnerability. I shared about my day, it's your turn." His brows furrow and before he can interject, I speak again. "Then we can get to work."

"*Cupid's Bow* work. Meetings," he says, giving in. "Just work. My life revolves around the company, so there's not much to say."

"Life revolving around work isn't great. There must be something or someone else."

"No one else. Just me."

"Nice," I say, and a second later my eyes widen, realizing how that must sound. "I don't mean it like that. I mean thanks for sharing." The words come out so fast. I must look like a deer in headlights.

"What about you? Any other things aside from work?" Niyi asks.

"Shouldn't we be getting back to work?" I raise a brow.

"Touché, mademoiselle. Rain check for our next meeting. Getting to know you will have to happen gradually." He speaks with an increasingly serene tone. I could listen to him on repeat.

Niyi picks up a page that looks like a printout of my current *Cupid's Bow* profile. "First, we're going to review your profile. And then"—he pulls out another piece of paper that reads *Cupid's Bow Questionnaire*—"we'll discuss your dating preferences in detail, I'll give you some time to fill out this questionnaire, and that'll be all for today."

My brows scrunch. "You have my profile right there. What more is there to know?"

"Just expanding on what you have. Some of the details are vague—"

"Like what?" I snap.

"Moving beyond the cliché mainly. For example, when describing your ideal man, you've primarily listed physical attributes. Which isn't inherently bad, but that doesn't give us much to work with when setting up a match."

"It wasn't a problem the last time I filled this out."

"I just want to make things better. How are we supposed to know what you want when you don't articulate it?"

I'm not sure if it's his words or how smoothly he says them, but I'm taken aback. I did articulate it. I know what I want, and I've expressed that. I took my time researching and filling out the app to maximize the potential of ending up with a good match. Who is he to tell me I don't know what I want?

"It's articulated. I know how to articulate—"

"I didn't mean it like tha—"

"Don't interrupt me." My sharp words act as a shield. "I spent a long time filling out the already extensive profile. And now you want me to repeat everything?"

"I believe it'll help."

"How about y'all do your job and we'll see after the first match? Does that work?"

Niyi nods, his stonewall of a face unchanged. I all but bolt out of *Cupid's Bow* HQ, my chest heaving with the ferocity of a dragon. Once I'm in my car, cooled down by air conditioning, I regret my childish outburst.

"You can't lash out because a guy questioned you, Moyo." I bury my head in my hands. God, what is wrong with me? If I can't even accept pushback from my dating coach, where does that leave me?

Why didn't this ever happen with Cole? It was easy, because he gave in to everything. I thought no conflict was a good thing, but maybe there were no clashes because we were hiding our true selves. Cole definitely was.

Did I do that too? No...at least I don't think so.

Ugh!

Thinking in circles will do me no good. I've signed the contract, and I promised my dad and my girls that I'd try dating again. I chose *Cupid's Bow* again, so I have to see it through. I also need to apologize to Niyi.

It's only three dates. And three meetings. I can handle that.

Niyi

VEE IS SPRAWLED OUT ON MY COUCH, WATCHING TV WHEN I walk in. With a weighted huff, I drop my bag, let out a tortured groan, and land in the only Vee-less spot.

That went even worse than our first meeting.

"Hey, keep it down. I'm watching here," she says, shoving me without a glance, eyes glued to a *Supernatural* rerun.

I flash back to Moyo's shocked face when I talked about her vague questionnaire responses.

Did I speak too bluntly? I worked on tone with Vee during the coaching crash course. I thought we were getting somewhere at the beginning. It was wonderful hearing more about her work and being a soundboard. Different from anything I've done, but comfortable. Practically natural.

But how am I supposed to keep faking that I'm a good Saturn if my major chance to fix my algorithm hates me? In every one-on-one encounter with Moyo, our personalities clash, leaving my heart racing like an Olympic show horse. Between arguing loud enough for her neighbors to hear, feeling genuinely happy afterward, pulling that little stunt with the French at the mixer—a language I haven't spoken in years but somehow managed to roll off my tongue because it was addressed to her—feeling so natural listening to her, and then freezing up when her fingers touched my palm, I am very confused. What a shit show.

I've been attracted to people before but nothing like this.

Over the past couple of days, I've struggled to forget the way her eyes twinkled when we spoke at the mixer. All her attempts to challenge me, plus her expectant look as she waited for me to return the challenge, lit a spark I don't know how to put out. This rapport makes me happy in a way I've never experienced in previous relationships. And honestly, in ways I didn't think I could feel as a Saturnian.

I inhale a deep breath. And then another.

"Either you share and I help, or you go freak out in your room and let me get back to my show," Vee says, muting the TV.

Her searching eyes wear me down. May as well tell her the truth. "I have a question. Hypothetical, of course."

Vee sits up. "Hit me."

I take another deep breath. How do I phrase this without sounding ridiculous or revealing that I think there's something else wrong with my powers, aside from not having The Sight?

"Let's say someone like us meets someone...normal. Is it common, as common as it can be, to develop attraction faster than we did before becoming pseudo-celestials?"

My cousin cocks her head, and her eyes squint as she assesses me. After a beat, her eyes widen before returning to normal. I know that reaction—Vee is a bloodhound for love. Not that what I'm feeling is love. But she can sense any strong emotional connections. I brace myself for her typical prying, but she subverts expectations.

"A lot is haywire at first," Vee says, and relief washes over me. "But after about a week or so, the emotions settle and it's business as usual."

Great.

"Another question. When you say a week, do you mean a week after meeting the person or a week after the transfer ceremony?"

"After the transfer ceremony," she answers, and my relief dries up.

I'm fucked then. Aside from not having The Sight, what little power I do have has gone haywire. Which explains a lot. At the mixer, I interrupted that guy trying to chat Moyo up, not only because I felt he was unsuitable for her but because I thought I'd do a better job. I, a Saturn, a sign notorious for weak relationships, thought I'd do better than a nice, probably decent guy actively searching for a partner. The jokes write themselves.

Vee continues. "Also, hypothetically, if you—" I cough and shake my head. She corrects herself. "If *someone* has such strong feelings that could be described as a crush, I'd tell them it's only a crush and not to worry. It doesn't have anything to do with The Sight or our godhood."

That's probably true for Vee, Merc, and anyone else who gained The Sight not long after the transfer ceremony. But I'm a late bloomer—coincidentally, another Saturn thing—so my path is different. It has to be. No regular crush is this consuming. I've only met Moyo a couple of times, and I already understand her in ways that both trouble and fascinate me. I pick up on her barely noticeable discomfort and make her laugh, and we share moments that stop all space and time. Every time I get caught in her eyes it feels like I'm in a cyclone, and I'm not sure I want to be rescued.

"I can feel you thinking," Vee says. "I don't want to pry but..."

I sigh. Better to get this over with. "Promise not to scream. Or to tell Merc. Or scream."

"You said scream twice."

"Exactly."

I run my fingers through my hair. "I think I might have a crush on her. My coaching client. It's not love," I add quickly, "but being around her does something I can't explain." Heightened emotions or not, the words are out in the world.

"You're just realizing this?" she deadpans and then bursts out laughing. "You've already gushed to me about her. And I haven't heard you gush about anyone since"—she pauses for dramatic effect—"ever."

I open my mouth to deny it, but nothing comes out. I do not gush, and in the rare moments I did gush, it was long before I met Moyo. Before Mom died and when Dad was still present. When I thought love was a possibility because of their relationship. Before I realized how much time Saturn stole from its vessels. But that illusion faded with time as Mom's health slowly declined, and Dad's devotion to Saturn over his family meant he wasn't present enough to intervene.

After Mom, all hope for true love died a slow death. Or so I thought. Maybe it didn't completely die off. If this isn't some wayward godly power thing, I suppose my heart could be stoking the embers. Regardless, I doubt what I'm feeling for Moyo is love. Having the powers I have and knowing what I know about the analytical way we assign matches, can I even say love exists?

"You can, and should, open your heart. If you were thinking about it," Vee says.

"But what good will that do? I'm Saturn. You know love isn't our thing."

Vee rolls her eyes. "There have been Saturns who've fallen in love."

"Name one besides my dad, who tried but ultimately failed." Aside from my dad, other Saturns never try to do the true love thing, clearly for a reason. Love requires dedication but so does Saturn, and it's impossible to marry the two. However, Dad thought he could do it. His hubris had to attempt the impossible and look where that brought us. Other Saturns accepted their fate, choosing their partnership to the planet above everything else. It's the entire reason the Saturn line jumps between multiple bloodlines. No love and fewer babies.

"First, your dad didn't fail. You know that," Vee says, and even though she's wrong, I don't correct her. "That doesn't matter. Behind the god stuff, you're a person. And she's a person. If you're really interested in her, I can take over her case, and you can work something out. Get to know her even."

I groan. Getting to know Moyo is the whole reason for my dilemma. Every moment spent in her presence makes me wish I was a regular *Cupid's Bow* user and not an employee on the backend.

"Niyi." Vee grabs my hand. "Most of the job is following our hearts. That's how we tap into our power and unlock The Sight. Follow yours and you'll make the right decisions. Whether that's pursuing this crush or not. Follow your heart. Trust me."

I hear the hidden message behind her spoken words: Follow your heart, listen to your crush. Typical Venus.

I wish I could, but with my Saturnian limitations, the biggest one in being my father's son, I'm not a regular guy who can follow through with a crush. It would ultimately lead to more pain for everyone involved.

My one wish of being completely Niyi fades. This, being Saturn, is my reality, and I need to start pulling my weight.

"Are you listening to me?" Vee says.

I nod.

"What did I just say?"

"'Are you listening to me?' Keep up, Vee," I joke, and she laughs.

"I said, if you need me to take over as her coach while you figure out what you want to do, that's fine with me."

"No. Don't worry about it, I'll be fine." I shrug. "Nothing will ever come of it. I'm sure things will subside. I can do my job."

Vee gives me a doe-eyed look and guilt eats at me. Here's my sweet cousin, trying to fix another one of my problems the same way she and Merc have done since I became Saturn. The least I can do for the both of them is figure out my algorithm. I can't quit being Saturn, so I might as well get decent at being a *Cupid's Bow* matchmaker, even without The Sight.

Vee narrows her eyes.

"Vee, I'm serious. I appreciate you, but I can do this. You taught me all your coaching tips, remember?" There had been three eight-hour long seminars, she'd better remember. "Like you said, it's a crush. Crushes are called crushes because they can be stamped out in a flash."

"I don't think that's correct."

"Trust me, it is." I make a dramatic show of stomping on the ground. "All done."

Vee laughs. "Listen to me, feelings don't work like that."

I know that deep down, and Moyo's pristine smile is still in my head, but Vee doesn't need to know that. I've never fallen in love, and I'll never act on these feelings. She's the key to figuring out my algorithm, so I have to see her. Becoming a better Saturn is a more important endeavor than a pointless crush.

"They do now. You forget that Saturn is also strong-willed and hard-headed. I'm fine to work with her. No need to interfere and definitely no need to tell Merc. The two of you do too much for me anyways."

"No need to thank us, we're family," she says. "Are you sure you're good? I can set her up with a match or help you come up with meeting points. Or I can take over the whole thing and you can get to know her like a normal person," she offers again.

Part of me wants to take that offer, but I know better. No point wishing on a dead star. Why waste both my time and Moyo's? I'm not selfish. This is my chance to figure things out and pull my weight at *Cupid's Bow*. I won't let Vee and Merc's hard work be for nothing because their Saturn was too busy trying—and most likely failing—to fall in love. There's too much at stake. The company. My family.

"If only we were normal people," I say. What might it have been like if I'd met Moyo before all this? But I never would've met Moyo if Dad hadn't retired and I wasn't forced to move to Boston. The futile dream fades to the background, letting me channel my energy into something productive. "Actually, Vee, tell me about those meeting points."

Her jaw drops, but she turns the TV off and pulls open her phone to show me some documents.

This is good. Having a set plan for the next time I see Moyo will be good.

This way I'll lead with logic and not ephemeral emotions.

Moyo

THE GROUP CALL COMES THROUGH, DESPITE MY PHONE BE-
ing on "do not disturb." The girls and my parents are the only ones who
can reach me when I've cut myself off from the world.

I apply clear gloss to my outlined lips and take a moment to marvel at
the difference a coat of gloss makes before accepting the call. Sewa and
Anjie's shouts, hollers, and squeals compete with Boistory's "Ore," forcing
me to turn down the music to hear them better.

"Wow! Maybe *we* should go out tonight," Anjie says, "'cause the way
you're looking, I'm sorry, I don't think whoever you've done all this for
deserves it."

"Unless it's that *Cupid's Bow* sales rep guy you were gushing about. Him,
I'll consider," Sewa says, her face out of frame so I can only see her green
bonnet.

I give them a deadpan stare at the mention of Niyi. I can't entertain the
thought. Do I find him attractive? Yes. But he doesn't fit into my new *Cupid's Bow*-specific plan. I'll be dating but only using matches from the app.
They've figured out the formula, and the couples from the mixer prove
that it works. Niyi—despite being one of the most stunning men I've ever
seen—isn't a *Cupid's Bow* match. Our astrology is untested. I'm not taking
that risk.

"So, what's the new plan?" Anjie reads my mind. "Don't look at me like that. I know your face when you have something on your mind. Share with the class."

"And what if I said there was no plan this time?"

"I'd call you a liar, but I don't like doing that," Sewa says, bringing her face into view. She's in bed, smiling, but the dark circles under her eyes are more prominent. Whenever we ask, she says that grad school is difficult and a PhD is more tiring than it looks. I believe her. Some of my med school peers were MD/PhD candidates, and most of the time, they walked through life like zombies. I don't want to see Sewa go through zombification.

"Share the plan," Anjie coos.

I sigh. "Okay, there *is* a plan," I begin. Because would I be myself without one? No. "I'll use *Cupid's Bow* and their coaching service exclusively. No dating anyone aside from the people matched by the app."

They're both quiet for a little too long.

"Well?" I prompt.

"It's..." Sewa begins.

"A little..." Anjie says.

"Limiting," Sewa concludes.

"I was literally going to say the same thing!" Anjie and Sewa try to high-five through the phone. These two are ridiculous.

I had a feeling they'd say this, and I don't blame them because they don't get it. They weren't at the mixer. They didn't feel the outpouring of authentic love from that couple on stage like a gush of water bursting through a dam.

"I'm going to trust the process. The couples I saw at the mixer were just too..." I groan, unable to describe the affection that flowed through the hall. "I'm trusting the process that gave those people their 'happily ever afters,' okay?"

"Okay," they chorus.

Cross-examination concluded, Sewa opens her big mouth. "Plus, you get to work with that Niyi."

I shut my eyes and take a deep breath. How many times am I going to explain this? After telling them about our initial meeting, our interaction at the mixer, and my pre-dates meeting, they think there's something there. Yes, he's attractive. But our interactions have consisted of mild irritation and bickering. I won't pretend the arguing isn't riveting, but it's ultimately not what I'm used to romantically.

"One, he's brash and he talks back a little too much. Two—"

"But you like it when we argue?" Sewa interjects.

"You guys are my friends. A man is meant to sit pretty, listen, and buy me things."

"Well, you're not wrong," Anjie says, and that causes us to laugh.

"And two, he's not part of the plan. *Cupid's Bow* vetted men for me already. Plus, he's going to be my coach. He literally cannot fit into the criteria," I say, hoping they understand and that this will be the last time I have to detail why I'm not interested in him that way.

"But he spoke French," Sewa says.

"And will you sell your soul for a baguette?" I ask with a poker face.

Anjie bursts out laughing, and then Sewa and I join in, cackling at varying decibels.

The conversation moves out of Niyi-territory for the rest of our time on the phone. I'm about to order my ride when Sewa says, "You sure you're ready to go on a date?" Her beautiful round eyes soften in a blend of concern and love.

I pause and present an assured smile. "Yeah. It's just a first date, and he seems nice."

My first match came three days after the *Cupid's Bow* HQ meeting with Niyi—Julian, a twenty-five-year-old Pisces man. His age and the Pisces of it all made me want to call Merc up and ask if they were joking, but after chatting with him online, I could see why we were paired. He's a straightforward, ambitious, bordering-on-successful marketing professional. He's been polite and flirtatious. Bonus, there've been no red flags.

"Where are you guys going again?" Anjie asks.

"The rooftop place we went to over the summer." I smile, reminiscing.

Boston doesn't have many fine things, but the proximity to the Atlantic Ocean is a winner.

"Their food was nice." Anjie nods.

"The DJ was my favorite part," Sewa says.

During the summer, they had an amazing DJ who played everything from Whitney Houston to Soca to Afrobeats. Granted, it was a Black event, hosted by a Black collective, but it was still at the bar with scenic ocean views. Now it's colder so I don't expect the same DJ, but I heard they had outdoor seating with heated inflatable igloos.

"I'll let y'all know how the food is this time around," I say.

"And call us after the date," Sewa says.

"Of course! I'm sure it'll be fine. Can't get cheated on at a bar," I joke, but it doesn't land. Instead, concern mars their faces, and I beat myself up. I can't keep giving them reasons to be concerned.

We're big texters who like an impromptu video call every once in a while, but the past three weeks have been unbelievable. I love them, but it's as if they hacked into my schedule and planned for someone to check in at regular intervals. In addition to their "Big Brother"-like hold on my life, Anjie's been dropping off more food. Not that I'm complaining, but she's acting like I no longer know how to cook. No longer know how to live since the Cole incident. I'm tired of it.

"Moyo, if you do—"

"Bye." I end the call mid-sentence, stopping Anjie from finishing whatever thought that would make me consider staying home. I'm committed to giving dating another go, so I just need to take that first-date leap. What's the worst that could happen?

Date #1

I SHOULD LEAVE.

It's been almost thirty minutes with no word from Julian.

What's the worst that could happen? I'd dared to wonder. Apparently, it's getting stood up by a fucking Pisces man.

But every time the urge to grab my purse and leave rises, the packed rooftop with its blue iridescent lights and transparent circular tents cools the fire of my growing annoyance.

I want to eat here, in one of these fake igloos, and have a nice night.

I want to stick to my plan. I *need* to stick to my plan. Use *Cupid's Bow*, go on the date, see the infuriating Niyi again, and find true love. It's an easy plan. And it should work in no time, barring the next *Cupid's Bow* man being a cheater like Cole...if I ever get to meet him. Despite my hesitance, I wait. If anything is going to ruin my chance at love, it won't be my impatience.

I'm silently seething—I said I'd wait, not that I wouldn't have an attitude about it—when a firm hand perches on my shoulder. I turn around, ready to cuss out the stranger infringing on my personal space, when I recognize him. It's the lightly tanned skin and gorgeous, hazel eyes that I've grown accustomed to over the past week though his *Cupid's Bow* profile picture—Julian.

Finally.

I'm about to comment on his tardiness when I notice his slight grimace and the beads of sweat collecting on his forehead. *Cut him some slack, Moyo.* I reluctantly chill as Julian's words tumble out with the grace of a hydroplaning vehicle.

"I'm so sorry I'm late," he says. His eyes are apologetic, but as he takes me in, they fill with desire, burning low, like a pot on simmer.

"I got you this." Julian pulls a rose bouquet from behind his back. I fight back my wince, replacing it with a tepid smile.

It's not his fault he got me roses. That's the default. It's a good gesture.

Julian's trying to make up for his undesirable start, and I should let him. The night is still young.

"It's okay. It's only been thirty minutes, not the end of the world," I say, attempting to reassure him, and myself, before calling for the waitress's attention.

"I accidentally spent a little too long making sure I look good for you. Fashionably late, as they say. How did I do?" Julian shoots me a cheeky grin as he gestures to his plain white- button down, Hermes belt holding up gray pants that are a few inches too short, thus revealing brown Fendi socks and black dress shoes.

I clench my teeth. "You look good."

"But you give me a run for my money."

On our walk towards one of the igloos, I force my smile to remain in place while my fist clenches and unclenches.

It's just a date, I remind myself. It's part of my plan. And it's a simple date that, despite the late start and interesting wardrobe choices, could still go well. The roses aren't indicative of anything. Julian isn't Cole.

But at least Cole dressed better.

I banish the thought as we sit, and Julian spends a moment admiring the blue lights around us.

"So, how was your day?" I ask, breaking the ice.

"Good," Julian says. "Spent the morning at the gym—leg day—and the rest of the day working on a personal project for my portfolio."

My ears prick up. Work is a safe topic, an easy gateway to getting to know someone. We had talked a little on the app, but nothing veering into real world topics.

I lean in. "I'd love to hear more."

"I love my job. It's great. But I've been there since I graduated college," he says, and I stiffen a little at the reminder of the age difference. College must've been not too long ago for him, while I barely remember my time. "And I want to move on soon. So, I've taken on some personal clients, and part of my Saturday goes to working on those."

"Working on the weekend isn't great, trust me I know," I say, finding congruence in our working habits, as I think back to weekends spent poring over Danaya's pro bono request. "But I hope you're at least enjoying the work."

Julian huffs. "It's work. SEO content writing and website copywriting for this gift shop brand."

"A gift shop brand? Like a chain of shops?"

I await his response, genuinely curious, but instead, his voice comes out soft.

"God, you're breathtaking," Julian exhales as if in a trance. He quickly snaps out of it. "Sorry, I got a little distracted. I don't think I've mentioned it, but you look amazing. Even more than on *Cupid's Bow*."

The appreciation makes me smile. "And you're not so bad yourself." I return the compliment even though the deep-blue lights aren't great on him.

"Coming from you? It feels like I've won the lottery," he jokes. "To answer your question, they curate and ship gift baskets. I don't understand it, but they pay well."

My mind goes to all the gift baskets my parents routinely receive during the Christmas holidays. Growing up, and till this moment, I suppose, I always imagined it to be a Herculean task to make and deliver those heavy baskets that housed vacation chocolates, pantry items, and other household goods.

"Is it an everything basket?" I ask. Now Julian looks confused, so I clarify. "Growing up, we had baskets with everything from chocolates to champagne to pasta and other pantry items."

"These are more curated from what I've seen," Julian says.

I give him a moment to explain further, but it never comes. He takes me in, smiling intently. The previous low simmer in his eyes burns brighter now, and in another circumstance, I might welcome it, but during a date where getting to know each other is the goal, it's too much. Not a pleasant simmer, but a scalding bath.

With my *Cupid's Bow* plan on my mind, I continue. "Any interesting examples you've seen? I imagine a chocolate basket is pretty typical."

Julian's smile tempers. "Nothing exciting. And honestly, I'd rather not think about work with someone as beautiful as you in front of me." He leans forward, breathing me in like a smoker savoring their last pull. His eyes roam, zeroing in on my chest.

Not to compare a date to a meeting with a *Cupid's Bow* worker, but when Niyi looked at me, it felt different. More tasteful than this. I want to be adored and lusted after, but not like this.

I redirect him with a noticeable throat clear.

"How about we look at the menu," I say, unable to keep the harsh edge out of my voice. As I scan our options, the tension loosens, and I remember why I picked this restaurant—the food.

"Oooh, churro fries," I coo.

"The chicken wings sound pretty good," Julian says, his excitement almost mirroring mine. The joy brings a boyish charm out of him.

I examine his soft features and growing beard. Despite the blue light, he is handsome. When he isn't staring at me like a hawk.

"Boy, they're glorified chicken nuggets, talmbout boneless chicken wings," I tease, feeling more comfortable.

"Hey! I don't like regular wings, so bring on the nuggets," he laughs, still scanning the menu.

I pause. "Wait, really?"

"One day, they just stopped being good. Haven't eaten them since," Julian explains, and I nod in understanding. Growing up, we always ate ogi and akara on Saturdays. Then one day, I stopped. It no longer smelled or tasted right.

"I also have my share of food I randomly stopped eating," I say.

"Good to hear I'm not the only weird person."

"Yeah, when I was seven, I stopped—" The sound of rippling plastic announces another presence in the now-cozy igloo. The soft beats of growing familiarity leave as a server in black leggings and a white shirt approaches us. Her oval face is made up simply, her hair pulled into a tight bun.

"Can I start you guys off with any drinks or appetizers?" she asks with an inviting smile. My mouth opens to order, but Julian gets there first.

He leans forward, menu choked between his forearm and the table. "I'd like the wings and a gin and tonic."

The server, whose name tag reads Jo, scribbles down his order, without sparing him a second glance. She shifts towards me, and I give her a courteous smile and open my mouth to order when Julian interrupts...again.

I take a quick breath, trying to quell my irritation.

"What else would you recommend?" he asks. Jo stiffens and pivots to face him once more, her previously welcoming smile replaced with a generic version.

"Customers typically enjoy the sliders, but if you're feeling very Bostonian, I recommend the clam chowder," she recites, as if reading from the menu's back matter.

"But what would *you*—" Julian leans forward and squints to read her name tag.

You've got to be kidding me.

"Jo—Jo, is it?" Julian gazes up at the waitress. "Your name can't be Jo. I mean, look at you."

And like he did to me, his eyes rake over her body. Unlike with me, he skips her face, automatically going to her chest and then spends considerable time looking at her legs.

I don't bother controlling my anger.

"Her name is none of your business, Julian," I say through a gritted smile, hoping to command his attention, while not making Jo feel even more uncomfortable.

Jo looks at me, and I wonder if I should even order anything, but her cool, brown eyes roll slightly, and I know she's unfazed by Julian's actions. Still, I give her an apologetic look before ordering a Paloma and churro fries.

Once Jo finishes taking my order, I turn to Julian, ready to confront him. But I have to wait, because instead of looking at me, he turns to follow Jo's movements, taking special interest in the sway of her hips.

When he's done ogling, he faces me like nothing happened.

"Can you imagine someone like that"—he points his thumb over his shoulder—"having a masculine name? I can't imagine what would make her parents choose such a name."

"Are you serious?"

"Would you choose a masculine name for a pretty girl?" he asks, chuckling.

Voice unshaken—surprising, with the earthquake bubbling inside me—I say, "My name is unisex."

Julian's retort dies in his throat. His lips stretch into a fine line before upticking into a smirk. He lifts a glass of water toward me. "Touché."

"No, not touché. That was uncalled for, you know."

Forget about *Cupid's Bow* and dating. There's no way I'm sitting here without correcting this pig. I might've ignored things about Cole, but even the promise of true love won't let me ignore this.

"It's one thing to ask for a recommendation, but it's another to make comments about her name and her body. It's disgusting."

"I didn't mean it to come off that way. I was curious about the menu, and the name stumped me. Honest." He places his hands up in mock surrender. "I'm sorry if I upset you, Gorgeous," Julian says with a degree of playfulness, but I'm not laughing.

"It's not about me. And I'm not your 'Gorgeous.' You have to apologize to her."

Julian sobers up with a hyperbolic deep breath. "Okay, okay, I'm sorry. I'll apologize to her. Sometimes I put my foot in my mouth when I'm in the presence of beautiful women, and with you in front of me, everything is chaos." He flashes a bright smile, but it does nothing for me. He can't possibly believe he'll coast through this evening on a dazzling smile.

"You don't get to blame me for your behavior."

Julian's smile fades. "I'm not blaming you," he sputters out, flabbergasted.

"Then don't deflect onto me."

He opens his mouth to say something but thinks otherwise. Smart—oh, he's starting up again. I guess not that smart.

"I think you're reading into things too much. I tried to make a joke, and it didn't resonate as intended. I already said I'll apologize to her. How about we continue getting to know each other, Beautiful?"

Even a set-up date from my dad would be better than this. At least Nigerian men are initially charming before their misogyny surfaces.

"You know what?" I ask, rhetorically. Lips curled into a snarl.

But Julian responds, blissfully ignorant. "What?"

"This"—I gesture to him—"isn't worth it." I push back my chair.

"Babe, c'mon. It was just a joke. Can't you take a joke?"

Ignoring him, I grab my bag from the chair. He quickly mirrors my actions, blocking my exit.

"You can't leave yet. Are you jealous of the server? I could never choose someone like her over you."

That stops me in my tracks. Unfortunately, giving him more room to continue.

"I'm sorry I'm making so many mistakes, Beautiful. No need to be insecure. You're the one I'm on a date with. I'll apologize to her, we'll request another server, and start over. How does that sound, Gorgeous?" He ends with another bright, lopsided smile.

I'm almost amused by his audacity. But it wears off faster than a toddler reaching for a knife.

My next words explode with frustration.

"Why is every other word out your mouth a compliment? 'Gorgeous' this, 'Beautiful' that—" Then it dawns on me. "Do you even remember my name?"

A creeping redness tints his cheeks and ears.

"Beautif—I'm not the best with names. C'mon, we can still have a great night. I promise. I know how to treat a woman," he says, his salacious stare burning into me. He attempts to grab my wrist, but I easily yank it from his grip.

"Don't touch me," I spit.

He takes a step back, momentarily stunned, before quickly recovering.

"I promise. We can turn it around. You've been great to talk to. You're beautiful, I'm hot, let's start over," he pleads, but I walk out.

I don't know how he got into *Cupid's Bow*, but there's no way that man will become my soulmate—or anyone else's.

On my way out, I see Jo on her way to serve another table. She raises a brow.

"I had to," I whisper.

"Girl, I would've done the same thing," she says with a smile and then continues towards the back of the restaurant.

The next thing I hear is my name followed by a clatter of dishes.

I turn to the sight of Jo shrugging with an unapologetic, blank face; Julian wiping a creamy liquid from his eyes with a loud groan. It makes me want to give clam chowder—which is my guess to the mystery dish—a shot.

I catch Jo's eye once more and recognize her glee. It reminds me of the delight I felt spitting in Cole's face.

I give her my realest smile of the night.

People always say revenge is best served cold but, as I watch Julian deal with chowder in places where chowder should never be, I think it's best served hot.

13

Moyo

THE GIANT T-REX IN MY OFFICE ALWAYS DRIVES DARKNESS away.

Patients and their guardians come here with apprehension, fear, or even tears, but it's hard to stay gloomy around Sandra, with her tiny arms and big feet. The way she stumbles through a scenic jungle with a clear-blue lake and a volcano in the background reminds me that my patients can handle any terrain, even when their adults think otherwise.

Today, I need that same reassurance.

I rest my head against the tree that connects one wall to another. Thoughts of the catastrophic date with Julian plague my mind.

Am I cursed? I've not had a date that piss-poor since college when I saw a drunk rando peeing in the parking lot on my way back to my dorm, after a lackluster date with a cute Econ major who turned out to be an anti-vaxxer.

Did I make the wrong decision getting back onboard with *Cupid's Bow?* Will I get another bad match? What if *Cupid's Bow* asked that couple to lie? What if they were hired actors? I should have just talked to that Maxwell guy at the mixer.

My 10 a.m. spiral, sponsored by a last-minute cancellation, ends when the best nurse in the whole hospital drops by.

"Aren't you meant to be doing paperwork or something?" Yaz's hair enters the room before she does; it always does. Her puffy hair sits high in a pineapple bun, and her face sports minimal makeup and a quizzical look. She enters the room in her soft pink scrubs, matching shoes, and terrifyingly calm energy.

Yaz joined the hospital almost two years ago and has been a blessing ever since. When I joined, fresh out of my fellowship, I was one of a handful of Black people in the building. Another reason why Sunday brunch and my relationship with the girls is so important; I was lonely. I'd come to work, be "presentable," then return home exhausted, only to do it again the next day. Community means everything to me, so when I noticed Yaz's coily bun in the lunchroom for the first time, I almost screamed. I ran up and tapped her on the shoulder. She turned around with a scowl, but when her eyes landed on my Black face, her smile grew. We spent lunch together, and the rest is history.

I cross my arms and lean back in my chair. "You're chill today. What's up?"

Yaz is the most organized person, always no-nonsense in the office, but a completely different person outside the four walls of professionalism. She currently has outside energy, and it's throwing me off.

Yaz finally looks at me and it's accusatory. Her eyes are wide and searching. She scans me like I'm at the airport, and my confusion grows. I lift my eyebrows and shake my head. She cocks her head to the side, giving me a deadpan look.

"Are you forgetting something?" she asks.

Did I forget something? I turn to my computer, a gigantic, stone-age device throwing off heat. There are tons of new emails but nothing urgent. And no changes to my schedule.

Yaz hops off the table. "It's nothing in your email," she says and tries to cover her laughter with a cough.

I'm still reeling. My eyes dart around the room, ensuring I have all my materials. I rummage through my bag to see if I left anything at home.

"I'm lost," I say finally, throwing my arms in the air.

"Imagine my surprise hearing from Anjie about you going on a date with some customer service guy from that dating app!" Her tone is playful but has some annoyance behind it. Yaz hates being out of the loop. She got close to Anjie after I took her to the restaurant. She tasted Nigerian food, became Anjie's number-one fan, and now she talks to my best friend without me.

"I don't know what kind of game of 'Telephone' this is, but I did not go on a date with any customer service guy," I say. Will I be able to go one day without thinking about that vexing Niyi and how his voice scratched an itch I didn't know I had?

"So, there was no date?" Yaz asks.

"Not with any customer service guy."

"Why not? Anjie seems to be rooting for him."

"He's cute, but mildly aggravating if you ask me. Most importantly, he's my dating coach, and after seeing the couples at the *Cupid's Bow* mixer, I want to trust the system. Which means waiting for matches and not pursuing some annoying guy just because he looks good. Simple. Plus, he's not my type," I huff.

Yaz smirks. "Oh, I see why she's rooting for him. He riles you up," she says with a shimmy.

Instead of answering, I turn to my email. I am not rehashing this Niyi conversation with someone else. I can't keep thinking about him, especially not at work.

"Wait, before you go back to work mode. How was the date with whomever it was you went out with, then?"

"He was a misogynistic ass. Completely unworthy of my time," I say, signaling the end of the conversation with my sharp tone.

Yaz shrugs and stretches. "Well, I tried. Anjie still owes me a week's worth of meat pie," she says giddily.

That Anjola Kuti will get a stern talking-to when I get home. The gall she has, offering someone else free pastries! I would've given her all the mind-numbing details of the lackluster date if she'd asked me.

"Heard about this year's gala date?" Yaz asks as she heads for the door.

The Boston Hospital's Foundation Gala is our annual charity event that always falls just before New Year's Eve—a time for staff to parade ourselves to donors like beauty pageant contestants. This little act of self-exploitation goes a long way toward job security.

Aside from working hard, staff like me have to bring in either good money or publicity. Something to make the administration recognize our hard work because they wouldn't otherwise. Typically, Black employees aren't the ones considered for the Clinical Excellence award given out at the ceremony. But we earn them a lot of money. Last year, I raked in a few thousand dollars with my winning smile and charming personality. This year, I plan to go big. Not for the hospital per se, but for my clients. More money equals better services, and hopefully, more support for critical pro bono work for my patients.

Ever since Yaz joined, there have been more diverse hires at the hospital. Instead of five of us, we're now ten. A better number—double digits, baby—but not enough. This is another reason the gala is so important to me. If I cement my place as an influential staff member, I'll be listened to more often, and with less pushback. Medicine is too important for only one demographic to be in charge. My patients are too important.

"Yep! It's the 29th this year. Praying the weather is good," I say.

Yaz opens her mouth to say something, but her pager goes off. "Pray I'm not working that night." She waves the black pager. "I'll catch you later, girl," she calls, jogging out the door.

My pager goes off as well, and I groan.

They couldn't even let me do mindless, menial tasks for my entire free hour, huh? I roll my ankles as I rise from the ergonomic chair and make my way to Dr. Whitney's office. She's an older Black woman who has been on the team since long before I joined.

"Oh, look who's here, Darrell." Dr. Whitney's pitch is high as she tries to coax out a boy hidden somewhere inside the room. An unofficial part of my job description as a developmental behaviorist is helping with shy kids.

I sit on the floor, crisscrossing my legs as much as my thighs allow. I pull out one of the blue toy sports cars I always carry in my pocket.

"I have a cool race car but no one to play with," I say. A dark head of loc'd hair emerges from behind a chair, and Dr. Whitney gives me a nod of appreciation. I let her have the race car—I have plenty—and I leave them to their appointment.

Sometimes, I love my job.

$$\cdot \diamond \ast \, \text{\scriptsize h} \, \ast \diamond \cdot$$

As I leave work, I check my personal email.

The first email that catches my eye is from *Cupid's Bow*.

Mercury@CupidsBow.org: Update! [RESPONSE REQUIRED]

I completely forgot—okay, that's a lie—I neglected to give the app or my coach an update on last night. I didn't see the point in setting up an entire meeting to tell Niyi my date was a weirdo who, rightfully, got chowder everywhere by the time I'd left early.

Dear Moyo,

I hope you are doing well.

I wanted to personally check in with you about your date with Julian. I see you have not yet logged in an update to the app. Is everything all right?

Oh, that's sweet.

Mercury's been a delight in all my interactions with them. They present a chill, down-to-earth vibe in the media, but for that to be their real personality makes me feel more secure in my decision to remain with *Cupid's Bow*.

95

However, we did receive an update from Julian, and we are sad to hear this wasn't a perfect match. I have taken the initiative to schedule your first post-date debrief with your coach, Niyi. Please find attached the date, time, and location. Niyi, cc'd here, will be expecting you. Please confirm your availability with him in case of a schedule conflict.

Once again, thank you for being a part of the *Cupid's Bow* family.

Yours Sincerely,

Vinny "Mercury" Carr

I finish reading the message, and my face sours. To say I'm pissed off is an understatement. I can't even begin to imagine the bullshit that pig Julian reported. From his behavior at the table, I know he's somehow spun this to make himself look good. Boys like Julian are why I chose *Cupid's Bow* in the first place—to eliminate them from my dating pool.

What happened to the exclusivity and the vetting process? I'll have to ask Niyi and see what he has to say. He seems like a thorough person. Similar to me in that regard. Exactly the type of person, I should be matche—

No. Too much. He's not an option. Curse those girls, and Yaz, for making me think about him so much.

I shut down the thoughts. Instead, I take a screenshot of the email, send it to the group chat with an annoyed comment, and then chuck my phone into the glove compartment of my car.

Moyo

ANJIE WASN'T KIDDING WHEN SHE SAID THIS HALLOWEEN masquerade party was secret. Usually the location of these events, with their viral advertising videos and generic passcodes, is obvious to anyone remotely trying. But this? This was like finding a needle in a haystack.

On this North End road full of various people, locals and tourists alike, it's easy to move undetected—if you're white. But being three Black women, we get the usual stares.

"This is why I hate coming here," Sewa grumbles under her breath, her words barely intelligible above the street chatter and increasing winds.

Hugging my coat tighter, I silently curse myself for wearing regular black lace tights instead of my heat tech ones. My need to feel sexy post-Cole and that disaster of a date with Julian might be my downfall.

"Almost there," Anjie says for, easily, the thirtieth time tonight.

"We've been walking up and down the same stretch for hours," Sewa says.

I reply, "It's been fifteen minutes."

"That's what I said," Sewa deadpans.

Our chuckles synchronize, cutting through the discomfort.

"Babes, you sure that customer was legit?" I ask.

"Lionel? Absolutely. He's a regular at the restaurant and is always inviting me to these seasonal events. Between your bad date, my recipe testing mishaps, and Sewa's fuck-ass professor, we need a girls' night out."

"Amen to that!" Sewa practically screams, turning even more heads in our direction.

I lock arms with her, pulling her in for a side hug. This semester of her PhD program has been rough. She's so tired from her long days that it's hard to drag her out of the house.

My head nuzzles into her neck, breathing in her rosy scent. Sewa rests her head on mine and we hang a few paces back, letting Anjie continue her failed Dora the Explorer cosplay.

"You good, babes?" I ask.

Sewa takes a second. "Yeah, I'll be fine."

"I didn't ask if you'll be fine. I asked if you are currently good?"

"Don't get semantic with me," she jokingly chastises.

I nudge her shoulder. "If you'd just answer..."

Sewa's soft groan permeates the air. "It's hard. Harder than I thought it'd be. I feel like I'm drowning with no end in sight."

Having gone through med school, residency, and my fellowship, I know a thing or twenty about academia breaking souls.

"What do you need?"

"Nothing. It's only the beginning, but I can't think of anything except wanting it to end." Sewa says this softly, as if the wind will carry her words to Anjie who is five feet ahead, squinting at buildings, looking for the entrance to this party.

I look up at Sewa. Her face is perfect, as per usual. With her ginger braids in a half-up, half-down style and immaculate makeup, she looks unbothered. But as someone who's known her for over a decade, I see the fatigue, even beneath the concealer. How did I miss it these past few weeks?

Guilt washes over me.

I've been too caught up in myself. In dating. In Cole. In *Cupid's Bow* to notice my best friend is trudging through quicksand and sinking fast.

"Have you—"

"Moyo please. Not tonight," Sewa cuts me off. "Tonight is for drinking some rich guy's liquor, dancing without a care, and having fun. I don't want to talk about it any further."

"Sewa—"

But before I can string together a coherent thought, Anjie yells, "Found it!"

"Later," I whisper to Sewa.

Anjie stands akimbo. "Pick it up, slow pokes! A night is about to be had."

She leads us to a dark burgundy door dangerously close to a dark alley we had passed multiple times. Standing in front of it, it's no wonder we missed it. You wouldn't imagine a door being there, and in the dark night, it blends right in.

Anjie gives a hard knock. The viewing door opens.

"Code?" a gruff voice demands.

Anjie clears her throat. "The owls are not what they seem."

"Welcome to the masquerade."

For what looks like an old door, it doesn't make a sound as it's opened.

"You can leave your coats here." The man who let us in opens a small coat room. "And remember, no photography or videography once inside. Keep your masks on and enjoy."

He disappears through another door, and we put the finishing touches on our outfits. Sewa's in a blood-red, v-neck, flapper-esque dress; Anjie's wearing a white lace dress cinched with a detailed black-and-white corset she thrifted during the summer; and I'm in a black handkerchief dress paired with my lace tights because my ass always makes skirts shorter than they should be.

For the finishing touch, we put on our masks. Sewa's is red and sequined, concealing just the area around her eyes, Anjie's white mask is Phantom of the Opera-esque, covering half her face, and mine is black lace, with a flower kissing my temple and a piece of lace dangling towards my collarbone.

"Anj, are you sure this isn't a sex party?" Sewa asks. I laugh, but Anjie only shrugs.

"I thought about it. Honestly, I'm not sure. Lionel only shared it was an invitation-only party."

"And you trust Lionel?" I ask.

"I barely know the gu—"

"Anjola!" Sewa raises her voice, but the humor underneath is palpable.

"Hold on nau, let me land," Anjie cautions us. "I barely know him, but he's my most loyal customer. He won't do anything dangerous to his favorite restaurant's owner."

The logic is mostly sound. I also wouldn't fuck with my Nigerian food supplier.

"Let's take a risk and succeed. We haven't done something like this since college."

"For good reason," I add.

"Abegi, we'll have fun. If it's a sex party, we can watch or joi—I mean leave." Anjie backtracks when she sees our faces. "I didn't know this wasn't a safe space."

I shake my head. "You're not a serious person."

"As long as we're together, everything will be fine, right?" Anjie asks seriously.

I look to Sewa, and for the first time in weeks, there's some light in her eyes. I clasp hands with her and Anjie.

"Us against the world. Always," I say, and we follow the arrows into another dimly lit hallway, adrenaline buzzing between us.

Anjie was right. This feels just like college. Fun, possibly idiotic, but exhilarating. And like college, I know it'll be a great night with these two by my side.

Moyo

IT TAKES MY EYES A SECOND TO ADJUST TO THE LIGHTING, or lack thereof.

Like children drawn to the hypnotic melodies of ice cream trucks, we follow the path of the music to a dimly lit, smoke-filled room littered with masked individuals dancing without a care. The DJ, also masked, is on a balcony strewn with intricate asymmetrical sculptures. The faint lights change color and bounce off the sculptures, giving the room a psychedelic feel.

It isn't a sex party. It's a dance party.

Of course, people are chatting at the bar and on the sidelines. But most people are dancing to the DJ's Russian roulette of songs. Currently, it's a salsa song, but when we first entered it was bachata.

A dance party with music birthed from all over the diaspora. And privacy is maintained and freedom guaranteed due to anonymity and lack of cell phones.

This is amazing!

"Ta-da!" Anjie twirls around, her white dress blending in with the smoke.

"You knew what it was?" I ask.

Anjie replies, "No, but yes. But no."

"Thanks for the illuminating explanation," Sewa deadpans.

Anjie rolls her eyes. "I didn't know explicitly, but Lionel and I some-times dance together in salsa class. So, I guessed it'd be dance-related. The masks initially threw me off, hence why I was reluctant to share."

"But you still trusted your gut?" I confirm, remembering how she cautioned against excessively high heels.

Anjie nods, her mouth opening to say something else when it turns into an excited shriek.

"Mi amor!" A masked man's words stand out from the music.

Anjie and a man I'm guessing is Lionel embrace and trade cheek kisses.

"You finally came!" Lionel says.

"In the flesh." Anjie outstretches her hands in a faux curtsey. "Here are my girls, who you've heard so much about."

Anjie passes quick introductions, and Lionel gives us courteous nods. A loc'd man comes up to Lionel, the creasing in his forehead communicating what we can't hear over the music.

Lionel apologizes for the interruption. "Love," he says to Anjie, "here is the artist that created all these amazing pieces." The loc'd man gives a wry smile.

"Actually, I can't take all the credit. My friend..." He waves over a man with such an impeccable jawline, I practically do a double take. His loose-ly buttoned white shirt shows off his muscles.

Stop it.

Before the artist can introduce his handsome friend, the music chang-es and the crowd—including Anjie and Lionel—goes wild. Soon my best friend is whisked away.

I turn to Sewa to discuss Anjie's betrayal, but a woman's stunning nail set is trailing her collarbone. For a split second, Sewa directs her attention to me and mouths "sorry," before focusing on the woman twirling her gin-ger braids in one hand, a firm grip on her waist with the other.

I don't want to stand around, so I ask the two men before me, "Dance?"

"I'm sorry, I have to make sure all the art is still in one piece," the loc'd artist says, excusing himself.

The handsome man says something, but his voice is drowned out by the crowd. His extended hand tells me everything I need to know.

I accept his invitation and soon we join the dancers.

On the dance floor, there's no need for words, as our bodies move in sync to the salsa song. He moves backwards, I step forward into the space. I'm not well-versed in salsa, but his delicate yet commanding touch makes following a no-brainer. I'm surprised how fluidly we move. Mystery Man isn't a professional, but he's more experienced than me.

Just as I'm getting used to the fast-paced salsa, the DJ takes it to my comfort zone—kizomba.

Mystery Man looks at the other dancers, trying to decipher the footwork and tempo.

"Follow my lead," I say directly into his ear. "It's the same basic steps."

Where salsa is fast paced and energetic, kizomba is slower and sensual. Despite both being partnered dances, kizomba focuses on connection.

I press my chest against his, our faces mere inches apart. His brown eyes are pretty behind the mask. Focusing on the basics, I lead us through a simple side-to-side four count. Once he adjusts to the tempo, it's smooth sailing.

"I'm going to show you something," I whisper.

"Got it," he responds. There's something familiar about his voice, but I can't place it.

Momentarily letting go, I demonstrate the slight repetition in the clock step until he nods and we return to the kizomba hold.

His warmth envelopes me as we do the basic side steps, and when I whisper, "Now," we attempt the clock step.

Our hips align, his left leg resting firmly between my thighs. Maintaining eye contact, not that I could look away if I tried, I keep count. For the first three counts, we move forward and backward. The next three, I step out at an angle, back in, and out again. Our first trial is just that, a trial. But for our second round, Mystery Man bends his knees a little more and adds more hip rotation.

We grind into one another, pressing closer with each repetition.

If I wasn't so dedicated to my *Cupid's Bow* plan, I could see myself enjoying a different kind of dance with this guy.

Following the tempo, we move faster or slower as needed, but always stay just inches apart. Close enough to hear each other's breathing and feel each other's sweat, but nothing inappropriate.

As the kizomba music slowly comes to an end, I attempt a saida. My sexy dance partner sticks to the basics, watching me step to the side to complete the three-count.

Too caught up in the burning sensation from Mystery Man's hands on my hips, I collide with another pair of dancers.

One of them falls, snagging the hanging black lace of my mask and taking it down with them.

Grabbing onto Mystery Man is the only thing that preserves my balance.

"Are you alr—Moyo?" he asks.

I finally place the deep, husky voice.

"Niyi?" I ask, secretly hoping I'm wrong.

It's one thing to dance with a complete stranger at a party and entertain thoughts of hooking up with them. It's another thing to dance with my not-part-of-the-plan dating coach.

The sexy Mystery Man takes off his mask, and yep, it's Niyi.

I do what any self-respecting individual would do after sharing an intimate dance with the one person they absolutely shouldn't be rolling hips with—I scurry away, leaving him standing in the middle of the dance floor.

Not my finest moment...but it is better than standing there, making awkward small talk as I take in his toned, sweaty body. Now *that* would be detrimental to the plan.

And who am I if I abandon my plan?

Niyi

WAITING FOR MOYO FOR OUR POST-DATE DEBRIEF IS fucking with me. Even the busy, late-afternoon coffee shop atmosphere fails to distract and I find myself zoning out even more.

After the events of two nights ago, in every spare moment, I recall the sensation of Moyo's body against mine. Dancing kizomba together, with our bodies melting into each other, was bliss.

I'm constantly transported to that night. Her hands draped across my neck, her hips in harmony with mine, heavy breaths exchanged in the space between us. Conversation was not on the menu, just whispered minor instructions that I readily complied with.

But despite that lovely moment, I need to remain focused on *Cupid's Bow*, not the feeling of Moyo's soft skin.

My fingers run through the questionnaire that wrecked our last meeting. Maybe second time's the charm? After all, she is still willing to meet with me. From the way she sprinted away when she learned I was the man behind the mask the other night, I thought she'd request another coach.

Thankfully, that didn't happen because I need to fix my algorithm.

I go over my checklist to chronicle what went so wrong with her first match. Based on her initial profile, Julian should've adored Moyo, and she should've eaten it up. Even working without The Sight, I felt good about that one. But alas, I messed up...again.

Isn't that good? I hush the inner voice that has gotten even louder since the night at the party. I cannot be with Moyo. She has a plan to use *Cupid's Bow* to find love and I have a plan to succeed at work. We're soulmates in our aligned wishes. I can't mess that up just because I find myself hooked onto her every word, think about her constantly, and her waistline elicits dormant physical reactions.

The coffee shop door opens and a gust of cold air attacks my face.

I suck in a short breath, and then I see her.

Her hair is pulled back in a low bun, drawing attention to her face. This is the first time I've seen her hair up, and somehow, she's even more stunning. She scans the room, her piercing eyes focused on finding her target. It's interesting, seeing this side of her. It's clear she's still in work mode because she's more like the Moyo I met in the hospital than the one I've seen since then. Nothing like the carefree Moyo I met a couple nights ago.

She pivots in my direction and her face blooms, her eyes softening in tandem with a sheepish smile, but as quickly as her expression arrived, it disappears.

"So, so sorry I'm late," she says. The urgency in her tone is a mismatch with her steady pace.

"No worries." I stand to welcome her, hastily pulling out her chair before she gets the chance. First, she looks at me, then the chair, and then back at my face. I raise my eyebrows and nod at the seat. Our gaze locks. Moyo squints, while my eyes widen.

This is as intense as our stares on the dance floor, maybe even more so. Moyo blinks first. "Fuck."

The unexpected expletive tugs up the corner of my lip. It's cute. She's cute.

"It smiles!" Moyo says dramatically as she takes the seat.

I push her in. "Good?" Her nod is my reply, then I take my seat opposite hers. "I do smile."

"Between our first meeting, the mixer, meeting in your offices," Moyo counts on her fingers. "Even the other night..." Her tone borders on hesitation.

I wasn't going to bring it up if she didn't, but here we are.

"The dance was very different."

"I didn't know it was you," Moyo says.

"Me neither. If I did, I would've just said hello."

Moyo lets out a weighted exhale. "So, we good? Do we need to report this to Merc or anyone?"

Considering the employee handbook and my selfish goal, I say, "We didn't go beyond dancing, and we didn't know it was each other. If your mask didn't fall off, this would be any other meeting. Therefore, we don't need to, but if you feel more comfortable or would rather change coaches, I completely understand."

"Oh, I'm fine. Just didn't want to put you in an uncomfortable situation."

"I'm very comfortable from where I'm sitting. Are you?"

"As I could ever be, *Coach.*" Her eyes sparkle with mischief and amusement. I can't look away. Like I'm being consumed by a black hole, the pull is intense and out of my control. It takes everything to force myself back into reality.

I clear my throat in a semblance of professionalism. "Before we get into the specifics of the date, I'd like to get to know you and your interests more. Sounds good?" I ask cautiously. She stormed out the last time I tried to dig deeper.

"I actually wanted to apologize for our last meeting. It was a little unnerving to be told that my meticulously put-together profile wasn't good enough." Moyo picks at her fingernails.

I stretch my hand towards her. Not touching, of course. But holding space. "Dating profiles are hard. Distilling yourself and your wants into a few hundred words is near impossible. Especially because we rarely think about what we want. We just go with the flow until something clicks, but that doesn't happen for everyone. And it's not just in dating, but almost every facet of life. We hardly ever sit down to reflect on what we truly want." My mind drifts away from dating to my life, my role as Saturn.

Ever since I took on this role, I haven't had a minute to examine how I want my life to go. Do I even have a life to direct when I'm beholden to my family and godly duties?

"Sounds like you can relate." Moyo's voice softens.

"Can't we all?"

"Touché," Moyo says. Her eyes light up again. "I have an idea. I know you have questions for me. How about when I answer, you do the same."

"Moyo..."

"Remember? I don't do well with solo vulnerability. Plus, a conversation is better for follow-up questions. You can dig deeper. You get to know me, I get to know and trust you. It's a win-win."

I shake my head. "I really shouldn't. Everything should be focused on you."

"And it will be. Unless you don't want to share. It's okay if you can't handle it." She shrugs, but her lowered pitch makes her tone the furthest thing from nonchalant.

Succumbing to the moment, I drop my pitch to match hers. "Moyo, I can handle whatever you give me."

The entire room melts away and the late fall weather evaporates along with it. I thought Saturn was cold and unfeeling, but I feel a foreign, burgeoning heat.

If this is a sign I'm not good at this job, I accept it. I'd rather be warm, my blood rushing at a probably unhealthy rate, than cold and measured like my father.

Neither of us say a word, and my eyes fall on her parting plump, gorgeous lips.

In another world, I'd make a move, but Moyo deserves more than that. I am beholden to an unforgiving, isolating duty. And I refuse to be like my father.

Despite every fiber of my being screaming at me to stop, I sit back and give a piss-poor attempt at laughter. It's stiff and undeniably awkward, but it brings us back to some air of normalcy.

Moyo sits back as well. She clears her throat. "So, what's your first question?"

Moyo

I DIDN'T EXPECT NIYI'S FIRST QUESTION TO BE "WHAT DO you like to do for fun?"

Without thinking, I answer, "Movies, trying out new restaurants, hanging with my girls, and I guess, dancing but that is primarily when I'm with friends."

Niyi listens intently, his eyes not leaving mine as he scribbles down my response.

"What kind of movies?"

"Horror, mainly."

His writing stops. "Really?"

The miniscule indent in his brows makes me smirk. People are usually thrown off by my blood-and-gore fascination because of my job with kids.

"Shocked?" I ask.

"Honestly, a little. But it makes sense. After all, you *are* a doctor. Any favorite subgenres?"

"Slashers have my heart."

"Would be a shame if they did that literally," Niyi says. He puts the pen down.

"Is that so?"

"And lose an amazing doctor who cares about her clients and doing pro bono work? Absolutely."

It's been weeks since our meeting at *Cupid's Bow* HQ. "You remember that?"

"That and everything else you've said to me."

Heat creeps up the back of my neck. He's my dating coach. Of course, he has to remember things I've said in order to help me find my soulmate. I shouldn't project fantasies onto someone showing a modicum of attention. That's how unsavory situationships and one-sided attractions form.

"Um, yeah...uh...what about you? Your hobbies outside work?" I change the subject.

"Haven't gotten into much since I moved here, almost...two years ago now. I've been too preoccupied with work, but I enjoy pottery and collecting wine."

I'm a connoisseur of delicious food, so an equally exquisite drink is never far away.

"What's your favorite wine?" I ask.

Niyi answers almost instantly, "I love a Cabernet. You?"

"I have a Tignanello at home I've been saving. Should've guessed you were a fellow red wine fan, seeing as I knew you were a man of taste."

"That obvious?"

"Unfortunately, so."

"What gave it away?" Niyi asks.

"You—" I'm about to mention his open-buttoned, buttery shirt from the dance. From what I felt as our chests pressed together, I know it's an expensive, well-made shirt. But mentioning that would be delving too deep into flirtation. The beautiful art pieces that night return to mind, helping me pivot. "You helped with the party pieces, right?"

"Indeed. My friend, Aaron, owns an amazing art studio. He was contracted to create some sculptures for the event. He asked me to create some clay vases and whatnot."

"What else do you make?" Fascination gives life to my words.

"We should really get back to you. There are a lot of questions," he says softly, his shoulders tensing.

"C'mon, humor me. Remember we're having a conversation. I want to get to know you too," I remind him.

"Mugs, bowls, plates, the cross between a bowl and a plate—"

"The perfect eating vessel," I interject.

"Exactly," Niyi snickers, and it feels like a mini reward. "And honestly, anything else. I've been at it for a while, so experimentation is a big part of the process."

"Must be nice to make things with your hands."

"It is. As I'm sure it's nice to help people."

"Indeed. Have you ever thought about selling some of your artwork?" I ask.

He brushes this aside. "I'm not a real artist, so no, never."

"According to who?"

"I already have a job," Niyi replies. "Don't have time to make a career out of a hobby. Now, can we go back to you, so I can do my current job?"

"Fine...what's next in your master list of personal questions?" I ask.

The air around us lightens as the conversation flows. We end up talking about everything but *Cupid's Bow*-related topics. Niyi isn't a horror fan, but he's really into crime dramas. Where my favorite Nigerian food is rice and ayamase, he is obsessed with asaro—something I don't eat because of texture.

We talk, laugh, rinse and repeat until a server tells us closing time is near. The sun's soft orange glow filters in, alerting us to how late it is.

"Don't forget to drop any cups and plates on your way out," the brunette says. She smiles, but the unspoken message is clear. We're the last two customers in the cafe. When did everyone clear out?

"Of course. We'll be right out," Niyi says. We toss our empty cups in the trash as we leave.

"Have a great night," I say to the staff as I slip on my coat.

Niyi walks ahead of me and opens the door.

"You know you don't have to do that?" I say as we wander around the block. No destination in mind, only the desire to continue our conversation.

"I know. I do it 'cause I want to. Does it make you uncomfortable?"

The question gives me pause. The simple answer is no. Why would it be a problem? It's the quintessential romantic thing.

"I'm just not used to it."

"Previous partners haven't done that?"

Considering my only recent partner has been Cole, it doesn't take me long to think. "No. Wasn't a thing."

"And you were okay with that?"

My brows scrunch. "I never thought about it. I'm used to being the helper, so it wasn't amiss that I was playing that role in my relationship."

"So...what do you want in a partner now? More of the same?"

"I...I still need to think. All I know is I don't want anyone like my previous matches."

"That's a good place to start. Tell me what you didn't like about them?"

I launch into the story of the date with Julian, which I've dubbed *The Trainwreck*.

When I'm done, my irritation is once again palpable, a marked difference between the calm I've experienced over the past hour and a half with Niyi.

"I'm so sorry," Niyi apologizes.

"Thanks, but it's not really your fault. You just work there," I say, and he looks even more apologetic. I sometimes feel responsible for messes at the hospital, but I know better than to blame an employee. "In fact, I was wondering how such a grade-A loser got into *Cupid's Bow*. I was on the waitlist for months."

Niyi chuckles slightly. "That's a great question that, unfortunately, I don't have the answer to. But it leads me to wonder...why *Cupid's Bow* for you?"

I swallow. "Well, I knew I wanted to date again, and I did some research and your app was the best one. Great reviews, great numbers. All foolproof stats."

"The app might have glowing reviews, but remember, dating is still all about people. And people can be different in person, regardless of their compatibility on paper," Niyi says.

"I wanted to give myself the best chance, and it worked for a while."

"Did it though?" he challenges me. "You mentioned being the constant helper. Doesn't sound like fair emotional labor to me."

He's right.

With Cole, I was basically on autopilot. Dating because I wanted to be in a relationship, and not because I cared about my partner. I remember all our arguments. The common string was me wanting him to do more, plan more, *be* more, and sometimes he would. Only for the cycle to repeat itself. But despite my discomfort, Cole was there, and that was somehow enough.

"So, again I ask, why *Cupid's Bow?* Why did you come back?" Niyi asks in rapid succession.

This makes me snicker. "Believe it or not, it was my dad. He convinced me that it wasn't too late for me to find someone."

"Wise man. I'm taking it you're close?"

"Extremely." I beam. Some people find it weird, but my dad and I are genuine friends. "What about you and your parents?" I ask.

"Mom passed a while back—"

"I'm sorry."

"Thanks, but it is what it is. And my dad and I don't get along."

I think about my relationship with my mom. It's not bad, but once I became a teen, I gravitated towards my easygoing, personable dad, and moved farther away from my stricter mom.

"Was it always like that?" I ask cautiously, expecting him to push back. However, under the soft moonlight, Niyi's shoulders relax and his voice becomes quiet.

He takes a deep breath. "Not always. We were close when I was younger. I wanted to be just like my dad. But after my mom died, things changed. He got colder, his expectations became more stringent, and I became my own person, much to his dismay."

I've seen Niyi serious at work, flirtatious on the dance floor, but this is the first time I've seen him look...tired.

"Relationships with parents can be hard," I say.

"But we gotta do it." Niyi shrugs. I don't know the specifics of the relationship with his dad, but it's evident it bothers him.

"There's always a different option," I say.

"For others, definitely. For me, unfortunately not."

Part of me wants to push, but I barely know him. It wouldn't be right.

Instead, I relish in the silence. Even walking quietly with bated breaths in the cold, I'm having a better time than I did with Julian. A low bar, but still.

"Sorry for being a downer," Niyi says after we've been walking in circles for a while.

"Heavy topics elicit heavy reactions. It's okay, I understand."

"This should be your time, and I took too much of it talking about myself."

"Am I complaining?" I retort.

Niyi falters. "No..."

"Then we're all good. Besides, this has given me time to think about what I want in a partner and why I'm dating."

"Great!" Niyi perks up. "Ready to share?"

It's my turn to hesitate. The thoughts are still forming. And there are other things I need to consider that I'd rather do alone.

As if reading my mind, Niyi says, "How about we call it a night? I can give you the questionnaire and you can let Merc know when you want another meeting to discuss."

"How about I just email you when I'm done?"

"Are you changing our rules?" Niyi teases.

"Yeah, yeah, yeah." I playfully hit his well-defined bicep. The contact reminds me of my physical attraction to him. A fact I had shockingly forgotten about while we'd been talking.

"It's more convenient cutting out the middleman," I clarify, putting on an air of nonchalance.

"If you say so," Niyi says, and then stretches out a palm. I look at it, confused. "Your phone, so I can put in my email."

Oh, yeah.

He puts in his email *and* number, saving it under Niyi-Cupid's Bow.

"If you wanted to give me your number, you could've just said so," I tease.

"I'll keep that in mind," he plays along. "But seriously, if you'd rather call to talk about your responses versus setting up a whole meeting, I'm down. I'd love to hear your responses before you have your second date. Wouldn't want it to be like the first."

The mention of the second date brings me back to reality. He is helping me with my love life. I can't get that twisted, even if things feel natural.

"Goodnight, Moyo," Niyi says, extending his hand for a professional goodbye.

"Night, Niyi," I mirror his actions. When his hand meets mine, it fits like a glove. Our fingers glide against each other, my subtle callouses pairing well with his smoother skin. When we part, a jolt of electricity hits me. I jerk back, while Niyi stares at his palm.

As I walk to my T-stop, I can't believe a simple conversation with someone contractually obligated to talk to me is making me feel this way. Niyi's only doing his job, and I need to get it together. To remember the plan: Use *Cupid's Bow*, get a perfect match, and fall in love in the most risk-averse manner.

I can't find true love if I'm crushing on my off-limits coach.

Niyi

"WHO'S MOYO'S NEXT DATE?"

Vee's words ring in my head as I work at Aaron's studio. The spin of the wheel and soft clay in my hands aren't enough to reduce my Moyo-related anxiety. This anxiety has been vicious—practically taking on a life of its own because I know I'll need to choose Moyo's next match from one of the viable candidates, but I don't want to.

After our coffee shop meeting, I changed some of her answers and re-wrote some lines of code, which reduced her dating pool, and most of the people changed. All except one—Maxwell, the guy from the *Cupid's Bow* mixer. Maybe he was right to approach her that night. Perhaps it was destined by the stars, and I need to put myself out of my misery and be the cupid that ordains their love. But I'm stubborn and, evidently, selfish.

Luckily, I still have some time before I have to lock things in because Moyo hasn't gotten back to me with the questionnaire. Or initiated any contact since our last meeting almost a week ago. Not that I expected her to, but a foolish part of me thought I'd hear from her.

"'Bout to set up for the class," Aaron says. "Wanna stay?"

I slowly lift the bowl I've been crafting for a few weeks and put it away. I used to attend Aaron's 10 a.m. class till I got to know him and we became friends. Now I join him in the early mornings for some silent work time—and whenever I need a break and he's available, really. A welcome departure from my talkative *Cupid's Bow* reality.

"Thanks," I say, joining him by the sink to get the clay off my fingers.

"You don't have to thank me every time," he scoffs, and I smile. Not because of his words, but because they remind me of what I say to Moyo. I try to push the smile away, but her megawatt personality fills my mind and, like my growing attraction to her, I'm unable to stop.

"Who got you smiling like that?" Aaron asks.

"Oh, nobody. Just work."

"I like my job"—he looks at the quaint studio—"but it's never made me *that* happy. So, who's the lucky person?"

I wipe my hands with a towel. "It's one of my clients. She's making great progress, and I'm sure we'll find her soulmate soon. She's one of the girls from the party."

"The one you danced with?"

"Yeah."

"You've fallen for her, huh?" Aaron chuckles.

"I-I-I..." I stutter, trying to find the words to deny it, but it's impossible. I wouldn't say I've fallen, but I can feel my heart beginning its descent. The lie is in my mind, but my lips want no part of it.

Instead, I tell another truth. "It doesn't matter if I have. She wants true love, and I can't give her that."

Aaron's smile fades, and the older man examines me. "Why? You just want sex?"

"Fuck, no." It's more than that.

"You don't love her?"

Love. A basic four-letter word and the bane of my existence. How am I supposed to know what love is if I've never experienced it? My only example of a Saturn experiencing love is my father, and see how that turned out? Mom was withering away and Dad never noticed till the inevitable happened. I know I care for Moyo, but love? I'm unsure.

"But you like her?" Aaron asks.

"Very much."

"So, what's holding you back? The job? You can quit a job if you really want to. Shit, I never told you, but I ended up here 'cause I quit my lackluster banking job and drained most of my savings to fund my cross country move for a woman I no longer speak to." Aaron laughs, and I expect to hear underlying pain, but there isn't any.

"And you don't regret it?"

"Listen, there's only a few things worth living for, and love is one of them. I had seven glorious years with her before I messed up." Aaron winces. "What I'm tryna say is, if you care about her, don't set her up with another guy and then be sad wondering what might've been."

"But the job is family. I can't quit family."

"I'm not saying you should, but there's always that option." Aaron shrugs. "I got a job for you, if you're down."

"Serious?"

"Decided to partner with the event planner to make more custom pieces. You'd be an asset."

I enjoy making my ceramics, but becoming a full-time artist? How would that work practically?

Aaron picks up on my slight hesitation. "No pressure at all. If you ever decide to leave the family business and go for your girl, let me know."

"I don't know..."

"I'm just saying, think about it, 'cause with love, everything's possible. Next time you're with her, just be yourself. Ignore work for a second and see how you feel." He pats me on the shoulder and turns to head to the back room.

"Thanks, man."

If only it were that easy. I doubt quitting Saturn is possible. Also, the next time I see Moyo, it'll be for a coaching session. There's no room to play pretend, even if I want to.

With my stuff in my navy-blue duffel bag, I walk out of the building towards the car park, ready to head home for a lackluster Saturday, when I spot her.

She's in a casual beige sweat set with a dark-brown, knit coat over it. Her hair sits pretty on top of her head in a loose bun.

What are the odds?

Before I can stop myself, I yell, "Moyo!"

Her head whips around, searching for the sound.

I jog over. "Hey, Moyo."

She places a hand on her forehead to block the sun as she takes me in. Her eyes linger on my body before she reaches my face. Recognition dawns, and she smiles.

"Niyi!" she gasps. "What are you doing here?"

"Pottery." I hold up my bag. "Why are you here?"

Moyo lifts her plain, white tote bag. "Retail therapy."

"What kind?"

She opens the bag and lets me peek. It's filled with numerous DVDs, but the few that catch my eye are *The Shining*, *Blacula*, and *Eve's Bayou*.

"Movie marathon?" I ask.

"I wish." She looks to the side and the wind lifts her hair, making her look ethereal. "Been a rough week. Still working on some things, but I needed a pick-me-up."

Is that why she hasn't gotten back to me?

My ears perk up. "What happened?"

"Same management shit. I think I've almost worn them out, but actually, they're the ones wearing me out." She laughs, though it's less bright than usual. "Sorry I haven't sent the questionnaire back. I haven't been able to find the words."

"No worries. How can I help?" I ask.

"With the questionnaire?"

"With anything."

"Oh, that's sweet, but don't worry about it. In fact, I need to go so I can catch the train. Car's also out of commission."

"Let me give you a ride," I say, and she pauses.

"Niyi, thank you. But don't worry about it, I don't want to take you out of your way."

If she sounded like her cheery self, I might've let her stick to her plan. But she sounds exhausted, and even without explicitly saying it, I know not having a car must be salt in the wound. Boston is walkable to some extent, but where we are, it is not. The closest station is thirteen minutes away on foot, and I'll be damned if I let her do that.

"Actually, we live on the same block. So, no trouble at all." I smile, and somehow it makes her smile.

Mission accomplished.

"Why didn't you ever mention? I'd—"

"You'd invite me over?" I know I'm being forward, but it's Saturday. I'm not working. Not being Saturn of *Cupid's Bow*. Right now, I'm Niyi, and I'm enjoying the moment with her. No thoughts of love, matches, or a future. Just living in the moment.

"We could've had meetings close to home." She tips her head. "And you could've been helping me with menial tasks while I finish work and we talk."

"Tasks like?"

"Laundry," she says after a beat.

"Washing or drying?"

"Ironing and folding."

"Good thing I went to the African Mother's School of Ironing."

She chuckles, and then her smile drops. "I was joking."

"I wasn't." I hold her gaze. "Let me help you. I have skills other than asking probing, dating questions."

"Like what?"

"I'm very good with my hands," I say softly.

"Is that so?" She raises a brow and a dangerous glint appears in her eyes.

"You'd have to take me up on my offer to find out."

We stand there, looking at each other. Our breaths are becoming more laborious, but I doubt it's because of the weather.

"Let me take care of you. Just today," I say, and without overthinking, I extend a hand.

"Just today." Like it's a normal occurrence, she takes my hand, and the contact sends a hum through my veins.

Unlike our previous handshake, this one lacks firmness. I can barely call it a handshake. We're simply holding hands.

Maybe Aaron had a point. This will probably never happen again, but being myself with her feels good.

· ✦ ✳ ♄ ✳ ✦ ·

"Where do you want this?" I ask, as I fold the last scrub shirt and place it on the pile. Moyo attempts to get up from the couch, but I stop her. "Just tell me where, and I'll do it."

"Leave it on the board," she groans, and her heavy sigh of defeat is music to my ears. Despite agreeing to let me help, Moyo still tried to complete part of the ironing. Maybe she thought I was joking and that when I got to her house, I'd take back my word. She only agreed after providing a demo and closely inspecting the first shirt I ironed.

"Anything el..." My question tapers off when I walk back towards her couch to find her sprawled on the ground, arranging stacks of papers into different folders.

She moves to stand, but I place a hand on her shoulder as I lower myself and sit beside her.

"What are you doing?"

"Helping you..."

Moyo yanks the empty, green file folder from my hands. "You've done more than enough. You're lucky I let you iron."

"You 'let' me? I volunteered."

"Same difference. You've helped enough."

"You were supposed to be resting while I ironed," I remind her, "not working on something else."

"I have a lot to do. I'm meeting with upper management this week. The Foundation Gala is inching closer, and after the event, I plan to ask them for additional funds to continue my pro bono work. Everything needs to be perf—"

I still her hand. "You also need to rest. It's Saturday."

"And I will, once this is done. Don't worry about it." She smiles, but it doesn't reach her eyes.

"Can I hel—I want to help."

Moyo looks up at me. The light seeping in from her curtain hits the side of her face perfectly, giving her an angelic glow.

"This is work, so, no. Thank you. HIPPA, you know. But thank you for the ironing. You've saved me some hours this weekend." She looks around. "I think that's all you can help with. In exchange, I'll get the questionnaire back to you ASAP."

I sigh, not wanting to leave her like this, working alone on a weekend. Surveying the room for anything I can do, my eyes land on the white tote and the DVDs from earlier.

"How about I sort these for you? Save you more hours."

"I'll do those during the week. I have a system."

"So, explain the system."

"Niyi." It sounds like a warning.

"Moyo." I smile. It takes her a second, but she eventually releases the smile she was fighting back.

"I have a way of doing things. Don't worry, you can go. Everything will get done eventually." We've had numerous back-and-forths, but those were slightly different. I thought her resistance was only towards *Cupid's Bow*, not all help in general.

My voice softens. "You don't have to do everything alone, even though I'm sure you're used to it. I have nothing better to do today."

"Really? You wouldn't rather be at home, or out with friends, or out with—doing whatever it is you do?"

"And give up a chance to iron and arrange DVDs? Never."

"Blu-rays. Well, I have a couple of DVDs, but most of these are Blu-rays."

"There's a difference?"

Moyo looks at me like I'm a lost puppy. "You have so much to learn if you want to be of any help."

"Teach me."

She bites on her lip for a moment, and the image sears into my mind before I focus on her spiel about the differences in video quality.

"I'm still hearing it's a DVD," I tease, sifting through her storage basket to find new spots for her most recent purchases.

"Well, then you're a horrible student," she says.

"I did get a little distracted." I catch her eye, but she looks away.

"I know. My collection can do that." She beams at the almost-full basket. After work and her girls, it's an easy bet that her film collection is the next big thing in her life. When she said she liked horror movies, I wasn't expecting this. It reminds me of my wine collection.

"It's arranged by genre, subgenre, last name, and then by color." She hands me a list of subgenres.

Our fingers linger for a second as I take note of the feel of her hands. "I'll get to work."

We work in silence for a few minutes, the sorting and rearranging becoming easy after adding the three new movies to her collection. So easy, it affords me time to glance at Moyo's stern work face. She looks so much like the passionate, no-nonsense woman I first met, and as hot as she is, I wish she'd take a break.

"Does it make that much of a difference?" I ask when I'm done sorting.

"Huh?" she asks, looking up from work.

"Blu-rays and DVDs. Is the quality that different?"

Moyo smiles. "Trust me. It is."

"You'll have to show me one day."

"I can send you a YouTube video showing the differences." She reaches for her phone, but I place a hand on her shoulder.

"I meant a movie marathon. One DVD and one Blu-ray, and I'll tell you if I can spot the quality difference."

"Two movies don't make a marathon."

"Okay, four movies then."

She pauses and a crinkle forms on her forehead. "You don't ha—"

"I don't have to, but I want to. You work extremely hard, so I'm sure you'll need a marathon soon. Plus, I want to see what the fuss is all about."

"But—"

"Unless you know there isn't that much of a difference, and you don't want to admit it."

"First of all, I do admit when I'm wrong," she says. I laugh, and she almost looks annoyed, but her eyes surprisingly soften.

"You couldn't even admit I volunteered to iron."

"Whatever." She rolls her eyes and nudges my shoulder, closing the distance between us. "Second, I'm always right, and you'll see. Not today, but you'll see. If you're sure about watching four horror movies with me..." she repeats with a downcast expression.

"Why do you keep asking for clarification?" I ask, turning my head toward her. She doesn't move, so my jaw rests on the top of her thick head of hair. "I've said I want to be here, and I'm suggesting this."

"You don't even like horror."

"Maybe your superior quality and taste will change my mind."

"You think I have great taste?" she asks, moving her head back to meet my eyes. Somehow, our thighs touch.

I can't help it, my eyes lower to her lips. "Moyo, you know your taste is perfect."

"Is that so?" She tilts her head, giving me a full view of her neck. I use all my strength not to use my tongue to explore her lines. It takes everything to soften my heavy breathing.

I clear my throat but despite my attempts, my voice is still thick with desire. "Tell me when you're available and I can confirm it."

"I wish I had time, but..." She gestures to the mostly arranged files I forgot about. Their presence brings me back to my senses.

"I'll leave you to it," I say, getting up, hoping my arousal isn't on display. Moyo gets off the floor with me.

"Thank you for your help today. It means a lot."

"It's no big deal. You're my favorite client."

"Am I your only client?"

"Does that make a difference?"

Moyo kisses her teeth. "But really, thank you."

"I never thought you'd be this nice to me," I joke.

"Guess you're growing on me," she says, and the way she looks at me, I get the urge to step closer. To feel her skin against my fingertips. To have her lips on mine. But I can't. I'm not her goal. She isn't mine.

"I'll see you later then," I say, stepping away.

"Have a good rest of your day. And I'll send the questionnaire tomorrow."

"There's no rush. Take your time."

"You sure?"

"Absolutely." I smile because it's true. There's no rush. I'm not ready for her to fall in love with someone, even if that'll help me as Saturn.

The door shuts behind me and I release a deep breath. I can't keep doing this—working against her wishes to steal these little moments of selfish joy. Between our meeting and today, one thing is clear: Moyo's not used to the support she deserves. She works day and night helping others, but refuses help in her personal life. Even in the most minute ways. Today, I managed to connect with her, but she needs someone who can be there for her at all times.

The answer is clear.

Her happiness is the most important thing, and I can't not be Saturn. It's impossible to quit. Right? Therefore, I need to stop kidding myself, schedule her second date, and play Cupid.

Moyo

ANJOLA KUTI IS A HORRIBLE PERSON WHEN SHE THINKS she's right. Her laughter echoes over the phone and through my apartment.

"And you wanted to give up on love" was the first thing she said after I let her and Sewa know about recent Niyi-shaped developments. After our first debrief, I avoided thinking about dating—which went swimmingly, thanks to work—until I ran into him earlier today.

"You're doing too much," I respond with a vacant glare. Love? I'd only conceded to having a little crush and possibly wanting to kiss Niyi after our afternoon together. Tangling tongues does not equal melding lives. Love is out of the picture. Unimportant to this entire conversation. Niyi isn't part of the permanent equation, and he'll never be. When I said I'd use *Cupid's Bow*, I meant trusting the app, listening to my coach, going on dates, and finding true love. Not falling for my *Cupid's Bow* coach. Attraction is one thing, but he's not vetted, and I need someone who is. Someone I can be sure won't hurt me.

"And *you're* not doing enough," Anjie retorts, folding her arms.

"What does that mean?" I snap.

She softens her voice, approaching me with the same caution one would use if they stumbled upon a skunk. "It means I want you to go for what you want and not only what's on your grand list. I want you to be yourself. The Moyo we know and love."

"I am going for what I want. I am being myself. That includes having a plan, and you know that. I'm open to the dates from the app. I went to the mixer, and I'm even talking to the infuriating, assigned dating coach. What more is there to do? How else can I be more Moyo?" I swing my arms in the air.

Silence falls, leaving only the rhythmic sound of my clothes swishing in the washer. My breathing settles, and I wait for one of my friends to speak. Anjie and Sewa share glances, so clearly, there's more to say.

"Babes, are you okay?" Sewa asks in an attempt to break the ice. Nothing is melting.

"You know we love and care about you," Anjie adds.

Sometimes when they tag team, it feels like an intervention. I hate it.

"Get this over with," I say, and Sewa's lips form a line. Anjie takes a deep breath.

"You know you've never really spoken about the whole C-word situation," Anjie says, and I almost laugh her off the phone. Cole? I haven't spoken about him because there's nothing to say. It happened, I cried and wallowed, and it's done.

"And yes, I know we urged you to get back out there, but you haven't seemed excited by any of it," she concludes.

"Till now," Sewa interjects with a smile.

"Till now." Anjie nods. "Till this customer service guy, or dating coach, or whatever he is, popped up. Now you're smiling as you tell us—in heavy detail, mind you—about how he ironed your clothes. You're back to spontaneously calling us, and you look happy. Not apathetic like you did when you were getting ready the other night."

"I was excited," I protest.

"You were excited about how you looked, which anyone would be," Sewa says. "But you were very so-so about the date. We know you, babes, and that wasn't you."

"I'd even say the way you talk about this 'infuriating consultant,'" Anjie says, using my words, which does force a smile, "sounds more exciting than whenever you told us anything about Cole."

"I agree," Sewa cuts in. "Since getting back into dating, you've approached it like a process, which is all good and fine. But for the first time since college, you're open and less methodical. You're being the Moyo who, while yes, plans a lot, also embraces her feelings. When was the last time you felt the overwhelming desire to kiss someone?"

I hope it's a rhetorical question because the answer escapes me.

When did I last feel an all-consuming romantic urge? Unable to pinpoint a specific moment, I turn their soft words over again until they lose shape and become mush. I sit there silently. Words on the tip of my tongue threaten to escape, but I'm not ready to let the girls know they're right.

My moments with Niyi, whether at the dance party, at the mixer, in the coffee shop, or in my own living room have been fun—different, but fun.

Unplanned. Spontaneous. Too much fun. Which is probably why I'm overthinking.

How can a man who's been nothing but professional and is not even my match from the stupid app have me developing a schoolgirl crush?

What is wrong with me?

Moments with Niyi play in my head like a movie montage, making me smile with the same unfiltered joy I experience when the theater's lights dim.

"This, Moyo babe!" Anjie exclaims. "See how you're smiling?"

"Shining all her thirty-two," Sewa chimes in.

The urge to shut everything down with Niyi overtakes my emotions.

"He's my dating coach. I can't. He's just doing his job," I say in quick succession. Trying to convince them and myself.

"You think he'd be at your house doing manual labor if he wasn't interested?" Sewa asks.

"He's been nothing but polite," I counter. "I can't take politeness as interest."

Anjie says, "Maybe you should..."

"You're so used to doing everything, maybe accepting someone being polite and helpful is a welcome change," Sewa adds.

"Exactly!" Anjie cosigns. "Thinking about Cole, and hell, let's take it back to Isaac," she continues, dredging up the Ghanaian junior I was obsessed with sophomore year—and my first experience of being cheated on after I walked in on him with his "best friend."

"Take what back to them?" I ask.

"They weren't the sweet kind. In fact, they were guys you always had to chase. Now here's someone doing the same thing for you," Anjie explains, and Sewa nods in agreement.

"And what if Niyi's not interested? Wh-what if this is all in my head?" While I'm beginning to recognize the type of partner I want, I don't simply want to project onto my dating coach.

The girls sport matching pouts. "Then you try again," Sewa says, at the same time Anjie says, "Then he's misguided," resulting in much-needed laughter.

"But for real," Anjie says. "It'll be okay. Things don't have to be perfect."

I understand where they're coming from. I really do. But uncertainty breeds so much confusion and fear. And for the first time, I'm scared. Of being alone. Of being with the wrong person. Of heartbreak.

"Things won't end up like Cole or Isaac," Sewa says. "Even if it's not with the dating coach, you can't live forever in fear crafted by those douchebags."

"Yeah, fuck them!" Anjie says, making us laugh once more. "Really, open your heart. You're blossoming again, and we think you should hold onto that."

"And as cliché as it sounds, keep following your heart. It's moving you to a new place. A place where you're excited to talk about dating. A place where you're not stuck on plans," Sewa says.

"So, as you get to that place, we're here if you need to talk about those two assholes who should consider witness protection before I finish my Muay Thai classes," Anjie jokes again, and I almost laugh, but memories of my time with Isaac and Cole hit me like a freight train. A new wave of embarrassment washes over me.

I'm not embarrassed of who I was with them; I refuse to be ashamed of my loving nature. I'm embarrassed because even when the red flags resembled red sirens, I shut my ears and allowed myself to be lulled by sweet nothings. I'm embarrassed that I let them change my loving nature.

Never again.

My mind flashes to the extensive *Cupid's Bow* questionnaire in my bag. My girls and Niyi are right. I need to figure out what *I* want from a partner. Not what I'm used to accepting or what is handed to me or what I think I need to have. I need to realize what I, Moyo Adegbite, actually want and value in a romantic partner. Fears and all.

Looking at my platonic soulmates, Anjie and Sewa, I know exactly where to start.

"I love you guys," I say, choked up by their care. I should be used to their love by now, but I'm beginning to think it's impossible. Real love renews every morning like fresh dew.

"We love you too," my girls say in unison.

I exhale a refreshing breath. "I think I'm ready to fill out the *Cupid's Bow* questionnaire."

Anjie raises a brow. "Not going for the dating coach?"

I shake my head. "I'm going to figure out what *I* want first. And, I'm still going ahead with my remaining two dates."

Sewa opens her mouth to protest, but I continue talking. "If I'm going to be me, then I still need to have some semblance of a plan. I don't know if Niyi likes me. He might simply be doing his job, but that doesn't matter because I don't want to throw all my emotions into one guy like I've done before. I want to date, with an open mind, and see what I actually like. No more hanging onto one guy for dear life just because he's available and I'm afraid of rejection."

When I'm done, I receive thunderous applause.

"That's what I like to hear," Anjie says.

"Guess we'll leave you to it," Sewa says.

We sign off with blown kisses and even more *I love yous*.

I retrieve the questionnaire from my bag, throw my laundry in the dryer, and head to bed.

Soft pillows cushion my back, but still, knots form as I read the first question.

"Why am I dating?"

Despite the realization I had with my friends, the immediate response that races forward is clinical. I want to find love because I'm supposed to. It's the next logical step in my life. After wading through the hard, self-defining years that are the late twenties to early thirties, I should be rewarded with a partner for all my trouble. But that's not all it is. That was mainly my fear and anxiety talking.

Right now, I'm dating because I'm ready to bring someone along on my journey. I'm ready to share a life with someone. I *want* to share a life with someone. I have my girls and always will, but they have their own lives. We'll always have brunch, but during the week, I come home to white noise and leave to white noise. I'm looking to fill the silence.

I might throw up as I admit it, but that year with Cole was one of my happiest. Having someone right there to share my wins, especially when Anjie was stuck at the restaurant or Sewa was buried in applications or her research job, was life-changing. Even though the focal point of our relationship was physical and the rest highly superficial.

In the passive excuse of my relationship with Cole, companionship was the silver lining. Recounting our days to one another against the soft background noise of a low-budget movie while he plastered me with kisses, walking the cobblestoned streets of the North End under starry skies, with clasped hands I thought would never untangle.

Even when I was upset at him or discontent with his distance, I thought we would never come undone because he was there. Not always mentally present, but he was there physically, and that gave me hope.

That made it okay.

I was ready to live below the standards set by my parents and the love I've received from my best friends because he was there, and I wasn't ready to be truly vulnerable. I thought I was searching for true love, but it demands an openness I hadn't accessed.

Aside from the true love testimonials, this is why I gravitated towards *Cupid's Bow*. Approaching love with detachment was my way of not getting hurt, but instead that left me with Cole, which was even worse. Instead of going with my gut, like when I became friends with both Anjie and Sewa, I treated love like it was another thing on my checklist.

Love isn't algorithmic. It's dynamic. And dependent on people ready to make it work. Not one person, not just me asking for signs of commitment so I can feel less lonely, but *people*—a team.

The words I need to answer the first question graciously reveal themselves.

I pick up the pen.

"Why am I dating?" I repeat. "To find the one who makes me feel like my community does—loved, appreciated, and most importantly, supported. To find someone I'm ready to grow with and vice versa." I write, and the words flow, full of affirmations and hopes and dreams. It's long and beautiful. Like love should be.

Niyi

RETURNING FROM MY WINE SHED, VEE PLACES A NEWER Riesling on the table. Merc uncorks it, expertly pouring us three glasses.

I swirl the glass to release the aroma, and a hint of butter wafts up to my nose. But when I take a sip, the sweet pear flavor jumps out. Not dry enough.

Merc smacks their lips. "How long did you spend on it?"

"Was concentrating for an hour."

"Any thoughts on why white wines are harder than red for you?" Vee asks, taking another sip, even though I didn't reach the desired effect. She loves a sweet wine.

"Minus not having The Sight?" I ask.

She cocks her head to the side, giving me a dead stare. "Well, duh."

"Probably your affinity for reds makes you subconsciously put in more effort," Merc answers for me. "It's why a lot of submersibles break down in the Caribbean Ocean."

Seeing my confused look, they explain further. "Uncle Hashim, Neptune, lives in Jamaica and despises them, especially the billionaire- or corporation-owned vessels."

"Evidently, feelings *do* affect powers?" I ask, giving Vee a pointed stare.

"What you were thinking was wrong, though. I literally told you following our hearts is how we unlock The Sight." Vee throws a cushion my way. It hits me smack-dab in the face.

"Venus!" I'm ready to return the cushion back to sender.

"It wasn't supposed to hit your face," she says, already raising her arms and darting her eyes towards the only escape route—the door to the kitchen.

Merc watches us with amusement in their eyes. I track Vee's hesitant movements, trying to predict her direction to ensure the cushion collides. I aim to the best of my abilities, narrowly missing her but hitting Merc.

Shit.

Out of everyone in the family, Merc has always been the most mischievous, even before receiving the power of the trickster planet.

For the next few minutes, we're simply cousins again. Not pseudo-gods. Just a good ol' fashioned family engaging in extremely childish, violent play-fighting.

The three-way battle continues until my phone rings.

"Hello?" I say, out of breath.

"Um, is this Niyi?" the other person says, and I recognize it's Moyo. "Is this a good time?" she asks, just as Merc hits a distracted Vee.

I stifle a laugh. "No, no. I mean yes! it's a good time. It's always a good time to talk to you."

Vee, with murder in her eyes, begins chasing Merc around the living room.

"Are you sure?" Moyo asks, clearly hearing Merc's cross between laughter and a shriek.

"How about I come to yours, and we take a walk? My place is too chaotic for a phone call."

"I can tell." Moyo laughs softly. "See you in a bit?"

"Of course."

I shiver when I get to Moyo's front door. Wearing only a fleece jacket was a mistake. The initial adrenaline and sweat from playing around with Vee and Merc made everything warmer.

It'd be too much of a hassle to go change, so I knock on the door.

"Coming," Moyo calls out. She opens the door in a matching green sweatsuit and a blue puffer jacket. She takes in my simpler outfit. "You're not cold?"

"Had to rush out the house. I'll survive."

"Sure? We could go inside?" Moyo offers.

It puts a smile on my face. "A walk would be good. Also, you have gotten nicer to me."

"Don't make me regret it."

"You can admit we're developing a good rel—working relationship." I catch myself. Moyo has a goal. I have a goal. Get it together, *Saturn*.

Moyo's expression is unchanged. She must not have heard my blunder.

"So, what did you want to talk about?" I ask.

Moyo pulls out a carefully folded paper from her jacket pocket. "I completed the questionnaire."

Reality sucker punches me harder than Merc hit Vee with the throw pillow.

"That's amazing." I infuse as much pep into my words as I can to disguise my disappointment. "I'll take that and make sure everything is taken into consideration for your second date."

Moyo withholds the document. "Remember, this is a reciprocal relationship. You don't get to read my deep thoughts without sharing as well."

Wanting to be in her company a little longer before our working relationship ends, I give in. "Sure, ask away."

It takes Moyo a moment to read the first question and her response. Her voice is velvety as she reads. It's no wonder she works with children. Her response is well thought-out, a proper exploration of both her wants and needs.

I know exactly how to fix the algorithm to incorporate her desires, and my Saturn-side rejoices, but Niyi harbors bittersweet feelings.

"Thank you for sharing," I say when she's done.

"What about you? Are you dating? Wait, can I ask that?"

Knowing there's no future between us, I say, "It's technically outside work hours. I won't tell, if you won't."

"Deal."

"To answer your question, I am *not* dating right now. Maybe never, if I'm candid."

"Why not?"

Simplifying the truth, I say, "Work, family, there's just so much going on. I don't have the space to be a good partner."

Moyo's brows crinkle and I anticipate a question. "But do you want to?"

"Doesn't matter what I want."

"Coming from the guy who pushed me to think beyond the generic and reflect on what I'm looking for."

"Do as I say, not as I do." I shrug.

"Hypocrisy doesn't look good on you, Niyi," Moyo says. " I know you believe there's no different path for you, but you'd be surprised by what a strongheaded, iron-willed personality can do."

"Speaking from experience?"

"You have to ask? I'm Saturnian, baby." Moyo does a 360, making me laugh. If this is the last night before she meets her soulmate, it's a good one for me. "What are you? I don't think I ever asked?" Moyo follows up.

"Also Saturnian. Aquarius sun and moon." Another reason why my dad made me his successor.

"You're a stubborn Saturnian *and* a new moon baby, but you're rolling over and letting your life be dictated by external powers?" Moyo huffs, aghast. "Niyi, not to tell you how to live your life, but come on. You definitely know more astrology than me, but Aquarians go against the grain and new moons are literally new beginnings."

Coming from Moyo, this familiar information sounds new. For the first time, my placements aren't spoken in reference to being Saturn for my father or the family business. I might not have The Sight, but I have the Saturnian iron will that helped me maintain my distance from my dad for years.

"You're right," I mumble. "Thank you."

"Simply returning the favor," Moyo says softly, looking away.

I pause and stand in front of her, not letting the moment simply pass by. "You helped me realize some things, so I mean it, thank you. There's no need to brush it off. You want to be with someone who will appreciate you? Then it's time to start accepting others' gratitude."

Moyo looks at me, her lips slightly parted. For once, I'm unable to read her expression. The air feels supercharged, or it might just be the cold and my improper jacket.

"Once again, thank you, Moyo," I say, trying to read her brown eyes to no avail.

She watches me for a beat before responding, "You're welcome, Niyi."

"Great job."

"Do I at least get a sticker?" Moyo jokes, breaking the tension. "I always have stickers on deck for my clients."

"They're kids."

"All I hear are excuses," she smirks. We haven't moved but have somehow moved closer.

"What would satisfy you?"

"Well, what are my options?"

"You know you shouldn't answer a question with a question," is all I can say to avoid going even further downhill.

"And what are you gonna do about it?"

The moonlight illuminates half of her face and shadows shield the rest. Almost as if Moyo's wearing a mask, like she was at the party. The only time we've met where she wasn't a *Cupid's Bow* client and I wasn't Saturn.

I wish I could return to that night. I wish it were that night because I want to kiss her. Right now—staring at her round cheeks, losing their luscious color in the cold, and the coily hair I'd like to dig my hands in to caress her scalp—all I can think about is kissing Moyo.

"Moyo," I say, breathlessly.

"Niyi," she responds.

"It's pretty late. Let's call it a night." The words exit through gritted teeth.

"Uh, you're right." Moyo clears her throat. "It's cold and late and it's bedtime."

We walk back in silence. There's not much to say, at least on my end, because every cell in my body is begging to embrace her. In another world I would, but despite Moyo's pep talk, I'm still Saturn. And with that comes impossible responsibilities that make me the kind of partner I wouldn't wish on anyone, especially not on Moyo.

"Night, Coach," she says once we arrive at her door.

"Night, Moyo," I reply. "We'll get your second date on the books."

"Looking forward to it."

I rock on my heels. "Likewise."

Moyo looks at me, one hand on her doorknob. "You're not..."

"Want to make sure you're inside before I head home," I explain.

"I'm already at the door."

"Humor me."

Moyo rolls her eyes slightly, opening the door. I watch her go in, waiting for the oak door to close, but it opens once more.

She hurries out and hands me the completed questionnaire. "Forgot to hand it in. Don't want to be a bad client," she jokes.

"Impossible." I smile.

"Uh, this is goodnight, for real. Text me when you're home?" Moyo heads back to her door.

"You'll be the first to know. Have a good night."

The door closes with a *thud* that oddly mimics the aching sound of my heart. Without Moyo's presence, the cold permeates deeper than expected. I really should've worn a proper jacket.

Perusing her thoughtful responses, I know exactly who to pair her with for her second date. As much as it pains me to do so, giving Moyo the best chance at a long-lasting, present, meaningful lover is more important than my feelings.

I should've rejected Dad's inheritance. I shouldn't have shown up to the transfer ceremony. But I did. Out of cowardice, resignation, and oddly, the childish desire to gain his approval. Instead, the man barely spoke to me afterwards and was on the next flight out.

I gave up everything. I am giving up something I genuinely want because there's no way to be just Niyi, not Saturn. Like an anointed priest, I am chained to my vows. But unlike the clergy, I didn't choose this life. I don't want this life. I don't like this life.

There must be a way. It's too late for a chance with Moyo, since her next date will likely be her soulmate. But there must be a way for myself.

Gods can live indefinitely as long as the commitment to serve is renewed. But I don't need eternity to know I am not committed to this role.

I want one life. My life.

And once I say goodbye to Moyo and get the algorithm in place, I'll figure out a way. Like Moyo reminded me, I am Saturn and of the New Moon—if change is possible, it's my job to find it.

Date #2

I STEP INTO THE QUAINT, RETRO DINER WITH CHECKERED linoleum floors and red booths and am transported to the '50s. In the corner sits a jukebox that ties the aesthetic together, but music plays from the overhead speakers.

A doorbell chime announces my presence, and a tall, handsome figure turns to the sound.

"Moyo, right?"

"Maxwell?" I confirm.

"In the flesh." He beams, and I linger on his features. Just like at the *Cupid's Bow* mixer, his chiseled jaw, light brown skin, perfect teeth, and inviting warm, brown eyes draw out my smile. The monochromatic black pants and turtleneck he's wearing make his skin pop. He's as handsome as I remember.

Guess that listening to Niyi and my girls worked, 'cause this pairing might be it.

I remember Niyi standing in my driveway as he waited for me to open the door. The contentment on his face as he savored the silence with eyes fixed on me. Like he had nothing better to do with his time. My smile threatens to widen, but I temper it, deciding to focus more on the present.

My date. Someone who fits into the plan.

"Shall we?" Maxwell extends a hand.

I take it, pleased by his gentlemanly manners.

Unlike my abysmal first date, Maxwell planned the entire night. Dinner and an old movie—perfection.

He gestures for me to enter the booth ahead of him, and a sharp whiff of cedar hits me. He not only looks good, but he smells great.

An older, white lady in blue wearing a white apron approaches our booth.

"Evenin'. I'm Jan, and I'll be taking care of y'all today," she says with a prominent Texan drawl. She provides a run-through of the complicated menu, outlining tonight's specials before giving us a few minutes to think.

The name Chelle's Shakes n Sides is written in the same '50s script font as the brightly colored sign on the door. The laminated mini booklet features an extensive list of alcoholic and alcohol-free milkshakes, burgers, fries, sandwiches, steaks, all quintessentially American.

"Ever been here before?" I ask, hoping to find a topic to settle my uneasy stomach.

Maxwell lowers the menu to give me his full attention. *Another Brownie point.*

"Never. Been planning to for a while but with this being out of the city and the theater only playing once a month, my schedule hasn't made it easy."

"And things aligned this weekend?"

"When you're involved, the stars make a way," he says, flirting unabashedly.

"As a faithful Saturnian, I'd hope so."

"The stars would be foolish not to help me out."

My heart flutters, only slightly, but I feel the quick movement. To hide my blush, not like my dark skin doesn't already do so, I bury my face in the menu. Soon after, Jan comes by to take our orders.

For my drink, I choose "The Campfire Killer," a s'mores milkshake with mezcal and marshmallow vodka. Maxwell chooses "Grown-ups' Table," a Baileys-dominant drink with birthday-cake flavored vanilla vodka. We also get a side of crinkle-cut fries to start.

"Sure you don't want anything else?" Maxwell asks after Jan leaves.

"I ate not too long ago," I say. Anjie made me taste-test desserts before driving up here. After my first *Cupid's Bow* date, I welcomed the pre-dinner dessert. But sitting here with Maxwell makes me regret that decision.

"No worries," he says, with a calming smile. "So, are you excited for the movie?"

"I've never seen it, but I've always wanted to."

"Neither have I, but it's a pioneer in the genre—" he begins, but he's cut off by the arrival of two hefty milkshakes and a basket of salty, aromatic fries.

The smoky mezcal of "The Campfire Killer" warms my insides, and I quickly take another sip.

Fuck. This is good.

Maxwell takes a sip of his drink topped with whipped cream. He also goes back for seconds and shakes his head fervently. "This is too good."

"I know, right?" I say, my lips never leaving the straw.

He slides his drink towards me. "Want a taste?"

"Oh, no," I protest. "Please enjoy your drink. I'm happy with mine."

Maxwell raises a brow, and the change in his body language brings Niyi to mind.

"You sure?" he asks, his hand already poised to take the drink back.

I promptly take Niyi out of my mind. Not the time or place. "I'm sure."

We spend the next couple of minutes conversing about the slasher sub-genre of horror, which tonight's movie birthed.

As my spirit-forward milkshake glass reaches empty, my uncontrollable chatterbox—or as it's commonly known, my mouth—comes to life to discuss one of my favorite topics—*Scream.*

"What's your favorite one?" I ask.

Maxwell leans back into the scarlet booth and throws his napkin onto the table. He folds his arms, flexing his biceps. My eyes are drawn to the movement. I know it's cold, and that's why he has on long sleeves, but I wish I could see his arms. He and Niyi have roughly the same build. Do they have similar musculature? I wonder what Niyi would look like in a turtl—

"Moyo." Maxwell's husky tone snaps me out of it.

"Sorry, spaced out. What were you saying?" I'm slightly annoyed with myself. I can handle my liquor. There's no reason for me to be disassociating like this.

He doesn't miss a beat. "It's cool. I said *Scream 2* is my favorite."

"And here I thought things were going well."

Maxwell laughs, and it's a hearty sound.

"What is *your* favorite, then?" He leans in.

I do the same. "It's the original *Scream*, and let me tell you why..."

I go on, mentioning the major talking points I've shared with the girls, and anyone who'd listen. I touch on the brilliance of the opening scene, the homoeroticism of our dual killers, having the killer be someone we meet before the final reveal, the humor, the party scene! The party scene!! And so much more.

"...and that's why the original is superior." I conclude my passionate monologue, heart racing as the movie plays in my head—lines of dialogue and line delivery, especially anything Stu Macher said.

I await Maxwell's opinion with bated breath. I feel a little vulnerable after sharing my interests so openly like that.

He takes a final sip of his drink. I watch his throat bob and his tongue swipe his lip.

Down girl.

"You know what?" he begins, and I sit up, hoping for a contrary perspective so I can delve deeper into my points or hear him out on his opinion. I doubt I'd change my mind, but it's still worth hearing something new.

"I agree," Maxwell says instead. "I'll have to rewatch it when I get home, or we could watch it together sometime," he adds, leaning in.

As soon as the words leave his lips, I deflate. Luckily, the light on his phone flashes, allowing me to not respond.

"Shit," he mutters, "we gotta get walking. The drive-in is about ten minutes away." He reaches into his pockets and brings out a leather wallet.

"Walking? We're leaving our cars here?"

"Oh, yeah. I called earlier, and whoever was on the phone, now I'm guessing Jan, mentioned that some moviegoers park here and then walk to the screening."

"That doesn't answer how we're gonna hear the sound of the movie," I point out, confused.

Maxwell sits back down. "Sorry, I didn't explain that well enough. My car is already parked there, the entry fee and everything settled. I also have blankets and pillows for maximum comfort," he says with a wide grin. "You can leave your car here and pick it up after the movie. Does that make sense?"

I bite my inner lip a little. "Yeah, that's okay," I say quietly. He runs to the counter to pay for our dinner.

I spend most of the walk to the drive-in parking lot staring at my white sneakers, wishing I had chosen either a longer coat or longer pants as the wind nips at my ankles, while Maxwell admires the starry night.

"Do you do any stargazing?" he asks, stopping to admire a planet in the clear sky.

"Umm...honestly? Not really. Occasionally I look at the moon, but nothing deep."

"You're a Cancer rising, right?" he asks, and I nod. He remembers that? "Seeing the moon makes sense, but you can see something else right now." The marvel in his voice forces me to look up. The navy-blue sky is populated with bright dots I can barely make out.

"If you look over there..." He points to the left. I try to follow his lead, but I'm met with only a dark, starless sky. Maxwell places a cool hand on my shoulder, inching me slightly to the right. His other hand rests on my waist, the contact sending a thrum of energy through me.

Moving his hand from my shoulder, Maxwell points toward a bright dot larger than the rest. His breath lingers by my ear as he whispers, "You can see Saturn."

I'm so distracted by the goosebumps and Maxwell's deep voice that it takes me a moment to realize he mentioned Saturn—the planet that kick-started this entire journey with *Cupid's Bow*...and Niyi.

I need to stop thinking about him.

"How did you get into stargazing?" I turn and focus on my date.

"It started before the astrology bit," Maxwell says, brushing the side of his thick coils with his palm. "Astronomy has always been an interest, hence the aerospace engineer day job." My mouth falls open. I can't believe I forgot that. Shit.

Maxwell, the gentleman, laughs it off and continues. "Yeah, I decided to look more into the planets and found it quite interesting, which was surprising."

"Why was it surprising?"

"I didn't expect it to make sense, but it somehow does. And I think it's a fun little thing you can share at parties or when you meet new people." He nudges my shoulder gently. "So when I found this dating app, I wanted to try it out."

"How's it going?"

Before he can answer, an attendant's voice rings out, informing the large crowd of the movie's imminent start. I follow Maxwell into the field of cars, towards his Volkswagen Atlas. As mentioned, the car is filled with blankets and various pillows, ranging from down to memory foam to throw pillows. There are also different candy brands in the glove compartment. I grab one of the mini fruit snacks once I'm in the passenger seat.

"Comfy enough?" Maxwell asks.

"Oh, of course. This is all fantastic, and beautifully decorated, I might add."

"Thank you! Wasn't sure, couldn't read your face." He rubs the back of his neck.

Like Niyi, my mind supplies. No matter how hard I've tried to shake away the thoughts, they keep coming back, like a hydra.

"Sorry. I've been told I have a very unreadable resting face. It's not you," I say.

"Hopefully, with time, I'll get to read you better."

I pretend not to hear him as he dials the radio to the movie's frequency, and the countdown begins.

"Wait, before I forget, how's your *Cupid's Bow* experience been?" I ask, wanting to end our pre-movie conversation with the present, not talking about future dates.

Maxwell's gone all out but I'm not in love with it. At the start, I thought this—he—might be it, but now I'm not sure. The worst part is I can't pinpoint why.

"After the mixer, it took a while to match me, so you're my first date," he says with an infectious, megawatt smile. I know I'm meant to smile, but it gives me pause.

His first? Oh.

He places his hand close to mine, near the gearshift. Not open to hand-holding and not wanting to be suspicious, I reach for a pack of sour gummies, taking my hand away from his.

He begins to say something else, but the countdown ends, and the title card introduces Alfred Hitchcock's *Psycho*.

Saved by the slasher.

21

Moyo

"DID YOU LIKE THE MOVIE?" ANJIE ASKS AS SHE PUTS TO-
gether a special, post-Thanksgiving Day brunch. She only treats us to
"soup and swallow" for brunch when it's a special occasion or after sig-
nificant time apart. With Sewa returning from visiting family in DC, it
counts.

"I did," I respond.

"And he was nice?" Sewa follows up.

"Yeah, he was respectful and didn't try any nonsense."

"Moyo," Anjie says above the sound of rummaging through cabinets, "he
doesn't sound boring to me. Abi Sewa?" She looks at our copper-haired
friend, who for the first time in weeks, looks refreshed.

"Someone that showed you a whole planet. I don't know if boring is a
word I'd use," Sewa agrees.

"Exactly. I don't get the problem," Anjie reiterates.

I resist the urge to roll my eyes. This response is not entirely unexpected
because, even while thinking about it and retelling the story, I have to admit that it was an okay time. It wasn't a knock-your-socks-off, run-to-gos-
sip-with-your-friends kind of date. But it was all things I should've been
obsessed with. That diner—when I remember the name—is a perfect girls'
night option. The drive-in would be fun to revisit on a solo movie date.

I enjoyed both things, but there's something about Maxwell that didn't click.

Anjie reappears, holding a tray with three bowls, and Sewa and I watch intently, waiting to see the food combo she's blessed us with this time. Anjie sets the tray down, and the yellow soup with green flecks and various cuts of meat stares back at us. My stomach grumbles in approval. It's been a while since Anjie made ègúsí and eba, but it smells perfect. The earthy, roasted-nut scent wafts into my nose, and my stomach roars to life.

Before we dig in, Anjie dips back into the kitchen to retrieve a bowl of water to cleanse our hands. We each wet our right hands and dig into the eba Anjie made to accompany the soup.

Mid-scoop, Anjie says, "You still haven't shared the problem with this Maxwell."

"Oh yeah, I forgot about that. Was it the driving distance?" Sewa inquires.

The thirty-minute drive wasn't a nuisance, and I respond accordingly.

"The diner food wasn't good?" Anjie prods.

"The fries were regular fries," I begin, and Anjie is about to leap. "But! Their milkshakes were superb. Best I've ever had."

"They're lucky I don't make milkshakes," she grumbles.

"You're so unserious," Sewa cackles. "You can't even drink them, professional Pepto Bismol consumer."

Anjie huffs. "Lactose intolerance is a real thing."

"It wasn't the food," I say, still laughing a little. "I'll take you guys to the diner once I remember the name. It was—" I pause, words evading me as I try to articulate my issues with Maxwell. Then a lightbulb goes off in my head. "Okay, I'm explaining why the original Scream is the best one, yeah?"

They both nod. Red palm oil from the soup coats their fingers, creating a stark contrast to the white balls of eba halfway to their mouths.

"And he agreed. He simply agreed," I proclaim.

After that first incident, on our walk back to the diner after the movie, we shared our differing opinions on Psycho. Every time, regardless of what

I said, Maxwell readily agreed with my rebuttals. I'm always right, and I admire when people know that. But having it just accepted felt like a cheap date cop-out.

Opinions always differ and I love hearing varying perspectives. With nonconfrontational Maxwell, as sweet as he was, it felt like he was saying things to appease me. It made me wonder, did I get through to him with my crystal-clear opinions, or was he looking through a crystal ball and agreeing with whatever he thought I wanted him to say?

Anjie pivots towards me and touches my hand with her clean one. "I'm still lost, darling."

I draw a deep breath. "There wasn't any chemistry."

Anjie furiously shakes her head. "If it was chemistry, you would've said that."

"I think I get her point," Sewa says, coming to my rescue. "You know, Moyo likes to fight—"

"Ignore her," I say.

Sewa kisses her teeth. "As I was saying, she likes to fight. Therefore, this guy going with her every whim must've been exhausting. Poor Moyo, finding a man who listens and admits where he's wrong." Her sarcasm could fill a dam.

"It's not the admitting part. You guys aren't understanding me," I lament.

"It's the mental battle—the engagement—the discussion you like," Anjie summarizes.

"Exactly!"

"We got you, babe. We just like to have a little laugh," Sewa says.

I muster as much faux solemnity as I can. "One day, by the grace of God, you guys will become serious."

"You first," they say simultaneously, and then high-five. Despite the fact that I've known Anjie longer, she and Sewa have this incredible ability to gang up on me as if they share one brain cell—sometimes, I fear they do.

"As I was saying before I was rudely interrupted," I say, giving Sewa a pointed look, "I didn't get the intellectual stimulation I like. So, to me, there was no spark." I shrug.

Anjie stands up dramatically. "Breaking news, a Yoruba woman wants a man to be able to fight her before she can fall in love with him."

"I'm going to eat in my room," I say, lifting my bowl.

Their whines and objections make me sit back down.

Sewa says, "It's okay. We get it. Everyone has a thing that gets them going. Yours is needing to get into a verbal grudge match, and that's okay."

"I'm never disclosing anything ever again," I mumble.

"See you next week for Moyo's date rundown?" Anjie asks Sewa, and she nods dramatically, causing braids to fly in her face. She sputters when one sticks to her glossed lip, and I cackle as I watch her try to dislodge it without using her hands. My enemies always experience turmoil.

"When are you going to tell the app?" Anjie asks when things quiet down.

The question catches me as I'm halfway through conquering a piece of meat, so I put up a finger. "Already did. I also told Maxwell I didn't feel the same when he asked for a second date," I respond after chewing.

"Oh, you weren't feeling him at all," Sewa says.

I almost feel bad, but after writing down the things I want in a partner, it was clear that, even though Maxwell ticked most of the boxes, he would never scratch the itch I desperately need, and that's okay. He's a great, thoughtful guy who'll find someone more his speed.

"All they have to do is find someone you can spar with who'll eventually give in. Piece of cake," Anjie says.

The reluctant smile of my latest sparring partner flashes through my head.

"Yeah, I'm sure there's someone out there..." I trail off in deep thought. I hope there's someone on the app who gives me the level of stimulation and care I've come to enjoy. Someone other than Niyi.

Why can't I be with him again? I think.

He's my coach, and he's not part of the plan, I answer myself.

But he makes me feel more alive than any part of the plan has, and he doesn't have to be my coach. I can always screw the plan or ask for a new coach. My mind fights back, trashing my excuses.

The last time I completely disregarded a plan, I was young, idealistic, and hopeful. Now I'm not as young and slightly less idealistic, but am I hopeful? Taking another risk in the name of love scares me, but Niyi's unwavering presence makes me want to be brave.

His unsolicited acts of kindness, basically bullying me to accept help, make him different from any man I've known. Cole certainly never volunteered to help with anything, and at the time I was okay with that, because I'm the one who takes care of people, not the other way around. Well, my parents and my girls look out for me, but maybe I should expand that list to one more person. The Saturday he spent here ticking two items off my list—reorganizing my movie collection and ironing—gave me more time to prep for my successful meeting with management. The meeting was all me, and I'm one step closer to my funding now, but Niyi's help reduced my sleepless nights that week. That partnership is something I could get used to.

He is something I could get used to.

New plan: Fire Niyi as my coach and take another leap. Hopefully, this time it goes my way.

Niyi

I'M SEATED IN THE RESTAURANT'S PRIVATE ROOM AS I AWAIT my cousins, the Saturn book Dad gave me burning a hole in my pocket.

After Moyo's thought-provoking words on our walk, my quest for autonomy began. However, since my family is secretive and my legacy-crazed father would have a conniption if he learned I was searching for an out, I resorted to the only place with Saturn-specific information: the notebook.

Before Merc and Vee arrive—and I possibly change the trajectory of all of our lives—I look it over one final time.

The old book has maintained its shape and quality due to our powers, the same power that preserves a Saturn's body and mind for the duration of their tenure. An everlasting companion of sorts. Mercuries gain technology that transforms with the times, while we get paper. Figures.

After speaking with Moyo, I once again read the notebook from cover to cover, combing through the entries for each of the previous Saturns. Previous Holder Name, Tenure Length, Date of Relinquishment, Current Holder Name, Date of Transfer Ceremony.

A majority of the entries were similar, listing twenty-nine years—one Saturn orbit—as the tenure length. A few overachievers, like my great-great grandfather, completed two orbits, bringing their tenures to a lengthy fifty-eight years.

It was only when I returned to the beginning that I noticed a discrepancy I had somehow always glossed over, the first entry, which was peculiar since it was a member of the Jakande family instead of a Bankole. The Tenure line snagged my eye: five years.

Five? It shouldn't be possible. Yet there it was. Written in word, bound in time and history.

A Saturn who didn't complete their orbit. A Saturn who abandoned their post.

I scoured the book once more, hoping for some sort of explanation, or, better yet, an instruction manual for how it came to be. I looked in the "How the Bankole-Saturn Lineage Came to Be" written on the final page; sadly, it was only the written version of the story Dad always told me when I was growing up. No hidden messages about the means of gaining the power, just a simple line: "The Jakande family, no longer able to serve as the Saturn-incarnate, bequeathed the mantle to us, the Bankole family."

My only hope of learning more would be to find a member of the Jakande family who could provide more information about the process. Maybe one of them would even be willing to take up the mantle. However, unlike other celestial families, the Jakandes haven't kept in touch. Therefore, to find them and find my way out of this, I need the help of the Master of Networks and Information themself, Merc. Hence booking the coveted private room of Merc's favorite Nigerian restaurant.

The person of the hour and Vee both stroll in, shopping bags in tow.

Vee sits down, handing me one of the bags. "This is for you."

"For?"

"We're attending a charity gala within the next month, I forget exactly when. I'll check my calendar and let you know," Merc fills in, taking their seat beside Vee and opposite me.

"Okay...I guess."

The waiter, a young teen, comes in to see if we want appetizers or anything else to drink besides water. Ordering for the table, Merc asks for a small chops platter, Scotch eggs, yagi wings, and a pitcher of Chapman.

"If I had known I wouldn't be recognized here, I would've done more sit-down meals versus ordering in," Merc comments once the boy leaves.

Vee shakes her head. "You love eating at home, except when it's a business meeting."

"You hardly ever eat at my place," I chime in.

"Or mine," Vee says.

Merc puts their hands in the air in defeat. "I've heard you. I don't like sitting in restaurants during my leisure time after spending a portion of my day in restaurants for meetings. Is it a crime?" they say, making Vee laugh. They look over at me. "You should actually take it as an honor that I'm seated here instead of asking you to bring the food over."

"I needed the atmosphere and possibly the threat of a crowd to discuss something," I say.

Merc's lazy demeanor turns serious. Venus looks concerned.

Here goes nothing.

"I want to quit *Cupid's Bow* and the role of Saturn."

Like scratched DVDs, it takes them a while to unfreeze.

"Clearly, I should've worn a meeting tie," Merc sighs, just as the waiter brings our appetizers.

"How about you explain further," Vee says.

I pull out the book, show them my findings, and launch into my hypothesis: If it has been done once, it can be done again.

A plate of asaro for me, jollof rice for Merc, and spicy creamy pasta for Vee arrive as I finish my explanation.

"The Jakandes don't like us, especially not your family," Merc says, which annoys me. "Even if we do find someone, how are you sure they'll help?"

"I'm not," I admit. "It's a shot in the dark, but it'd be even worse if I don't try."

Vee cuts in. "Wait, you've shared *how* this could hypothetically happen, but *why*? Do you want to quit because of Moyo?" she asks softly. I know she cares, but I wish she hadn't said anything, especially that.

Merc's mischievous smile comes out. "Are you doing this for your crush?" They ask with a dramatic pout. "As you know, I'm a sucker for love. But you can have love and be Saturn. Your dad did it, and clearly the line has carried on, so other Saturns did as well."

"Firstly, my dad wasn't great. Secondly, it's not simply because of Moyo. Saturn...living Dad's legacy is not for me. I'm not like either of you. Not everyone can be the perfect Mercury or Venus. We're approaching two full years, and I still haven't achieved The Sight. If I could do my own thing and an actual Saturn takes over, it'll be a win-win for everyone, right?"

Vee brushes over the chunk of my words. "Wait, Uncle B wasn't great?" she asks, even more concerned than before.

I exhale. "He had his issues. I know it seems like our estrangement happened in adulthood, but that's far from the truth."

No one knows the truth because Dad won't talk about it, and—despite being celestials—like any other Nigerian household, when a child distances themselves from family, it's assumed to be the child's fault.

Merc doesn't say anything for a moment. "Would you still make this choice if you got The Sight?"

"It's been two years, it's not coming."

"But what if?" Merc asks pointedly. "It makes things easier, quicker, more comfortable."

I fire back, my voice rising, "I don't want to continue being miserable on a 'what if.' This might not work, but it's worth a shot."

"You expect me to find people who clearly don't want to be found? Based on a flimsy guess?" Merc's volume rises to match mine.

"Isn't that your job?"

"It was your job to stay in the job, but now you want to abandon Vee and me."

Before our egos overflow, Vee jumps in. "How about we calm down? Take a walk, and we can talk about this later. No one is being abandoned."

"Fine," Merc and I both huff.

"I'll walk." I stand up, not bothering to listen for a response.

I'm on my way to the bathroom to splash some water on my face when a woman with familiar curls emerges from the kitchen doors, holding a takeout box.

"Moyo?"

"Oh, Niyi," she says, shocked. "What are you doing here?"

My tension dissolves. "Getting something to eat. What about you?"

I ask, then remember the outcome of her second date. "Also, I'm sorry about the date. I thought that one would work out."

I won't deny it. When I got the notification and saw they weren't a match, I might've done a sly fist pump under my work desk. Before the crushing realization that I'd have to find her another date hit me like a freight train.

"Oh, don't worry about that. He was a great guy, just not for me."

"We should schedule a meeting to talk about this in detail, but is there anything you want me to reevaluate ahead of your third, and final, *Cupid's Bow* date?" I ask. The earlier I can start prepping myself, the better.

Moyo breaks our eye contact. She tugs on her bottom lip.

"Everything all right?"

"Yeah...um...I actually wanted to...uh."

"Moyo, it's okay. I can take whatever it is."

Moyo tilts her head and crosses her arms.

"I don't bite, unless requested," I say. Now that makes her relax a little.

Her arms fall by her side. "I'd like to cancel the third date—"

"Oh...okay."

"And stop working with you, as my dating coach."

"Oh." My heart sinks. I always knew the relationship would come to an end, but I was banking on having time to prepare myself, not having it yanked away like a rotting tooth.

"Instead, I'd like to go on a da—practice date. You know, like you initially mentioned way back when?" She chuckles awkwardly. Maybe she's trying to let me down easy.

Honestly? I'm fine with it. One more time in Moyo's presence. I'll take it versus quitting cold turkey.

"Sounds good to me. I'll set it up and forward you the details," I say, using an over-exaggerated smile to conceal my disappointment.

"Perfect," Moyo says.

"Great," I reply.

"Sweet."

"Nice."

"Cool. Gotta get these to a friend." Moyo holds up the takeaway pack.

I move out of her way. "Yeah, I should get back to my friends."

She looks back at me on her way out, giving me a final wave and smile.

Calmer, I return to the private dining room, expecting to reach an agreement or get into a proper screaming match with Merc. Instead, Vee sits alone, sipping on the rest of our Chapman.

"Merc left."

"I can see that," I say.

"Y'all need to talk it out later," she says. "I can't have you fighting."

I nod, keeping quiet to avoid rehashing the topic. The last thing I need right now is a Venus-scolding. In fact, I need the opposite.

"Vee..." I say, thinking about where to take Moyo for our last meeting.

"Yeah."

"Any restaurant recommendations? I need somewhere delicious, cozy, and impressive."

"I'm not asking for details to maintain plausible deniability, but I'm very excited for you," she squeals. "There's a master list Merc and I've been working through in the hopes to find something for a *Cupid's Bow* partnership. I'll forward it to you."

"You're the best," I say.

"Never forget," Vee replies, scrolling through her phone.

My email notification chimes a moment later. Looking through the list, I mentally sort them into *no*, *maybe*, and *yes* piles based on the feedback Vee and Merc wrote beside each one.

This has to be perfect. Saying goodbye to Moyo is inevitable. The least I can do is give her a date she'll never forget.

Moyo

WHY DID I SUGGEST A PRACTICE DATE?

Replaying our run-in at Anjie's restaurant, I can't believe I was too chicken to propose going on an actual date with Niyi. Guess old avoidant habits die hard.

This is not a date. This is not a real date.

I commit the sacred words to memory and bring them to the surface every few minutes on the drive to the restaurant where I'm meeting Niyi, but it does nothing for my nerves.

Do I actually have nerves over a man? At my age? Evidently the giddiness of a crush doesn't give a fuck about age. Luckily, or unluckily, today is Niyi's last time coaching me. After this little sit-down meal, I'll never have to be in his presence in a professional setting again. Hopefully, I can muster up the bravery to go for what I really want: seeing Niyi in highly unprofessional settings.

It's almost poetic that after attempting the hands-off, report-back approach—which helped—our final meeting is the hands-on approach I was against earlier. I thought he'd hinder my dates by being nearby. Little did I know that simply being around Niyi would feel better than any date has in my entire life.

This is not a real date, I remind myself. Unfortunately, that crucial piece of information doesn't stop my hands from fidgeting. They move so much, I shove them between my equally jittering thighs to keep them still and warm.

Niyi ordered the ride from my place to the date and kept the location a surprise—which pissed me off a little because it didn't give me much to work with for my outfit choice. But I went with simple because, again, *this is not a date.* I chose sage-green cargo pants and a white button-down top with loose feathers at the bottom and on the cuffs, layered with an almond-colored sweater. For more color, I added a silk scarf of greens, yellows, and reds around my head, allowing my blown-out hair to billow behind me. It isn't snowing, so I picked a fur-lined, leather coat and a pair of simple white-and-green sneakers.

Once the driver stops outside the restaurant, I know exactly where we are. I hop out of the car, thank the driver, and spot Niyi in front of the building. He's also dressed casually in a green shirt under a black jacket; his pants and shoes are all black as well, but he has little, gold accessories that make his dark-brown skin pop. The gold necklace sits on the green, providing a sexy contrast. I'm a Yoruba woman; we go crazy for a gold-chain moment. It's in the Bible.

I give him a tempered smile and point to my pants. "We're matching a little," I say once he can hear me.

He doesn't laugh or smile, but he looks amused.

"You're the better-dressed one," he says as he surveys my outfit. The look is blatant but not sleazy. When he's done, his attention goes to my eyes, holding me in place, not allowing me to look away. His tongue wets his lips a little before he returns to his composed self. He probably forgot to apply lip balm. Nothing worse than chapped lips in the cold.

"Shall we?" Niyi says, and when I nod, he gestures for me to go first.

We bypass the regular indoor seating and go straight to the patio with three yurts. I hear voices coming from two of them, so I move towards the silent one. I'm about to open the flap when Niyi stills my hand. The slight contact sends my internal temperature skyrocketing. Like a child experiencing the tinge of a hot burner, I yank my hand away.

He doesn't seem to notice. He just pulls the flap back, welcoming me into the warm interior filled with wreaths, fairy lights, and a table for two. I shrug my coat off and hang it on the rack, then rub my arms for warmth, but the heat soon envelops me. I'm still taking in the interior—pine garlands line the inside, white-and-gold decorative stars dangling from them and mixing with the lights beautifully; above the table is a hanging planter with eucalyptus overflowing—when Niyi pulls out a seat for me.

My lips turn downwards and my eyebrows raise. He shakes his head and looks away. I'm transported back to the first time he pulled back my seat at Cupid's Bow HQ.

"Thank you," I say. He pushes me closer to the table before taking his seat.

"You know you don't have to do that every time we hang out." My words come out in pieces, broken up by a forced chuckle.

"I know," he says. "It's my choice."

This whole thing is beautiful, from planning a surprise to ordering my ride to making a reservation at one of the city's most sought-after winter dining experiences. I'm impressed. A grin takes over my face as I browse the classic American menu.

"Okay, so any thoughts or observations?" Niyi captures my attention.

"Um, it's...beautiful," I offer, unsure.

"Oh, sorry, that wasn't clear." He shakes his head as if chastising himself. He always does that. "I meant my behavior as a good date. That's what I was modeling for you," he clarifies. The room feels like winter again and my muscles freeze up.

"Oh, that..." my voice trails off.

It's not a real date, Moyo. Don't forget that.

I infuse pep back into my voice. "You're being a lovely gentleman. No notes." I force a laugh.

"That's the kind of treatment you deserve, Moyo," he says, and the room is now dryer than the Sahara. His gaze is so intense, so piercing. I want to look away, but it's arresting.

"How did you find out about this place?" I ask. It's not exactly a hole-in-the-wall, but I need to say something to distract from the intensity he's directing toward me. What's he doing? Trying to imprint my image in his brain?

"Merc's doing a restaurant tour for a new *Cupid's Bow* partnership, and this was on the list, so I offered to check it out." He slides the menu to his left.

Oh, this is an additional work trip. A wave of nausea hits me. He's not even here for me...

Hurt coats my vocal cords with pain and rejection. "Wow, so you can't even pretend like you chose this place for me. I always knew Mercury had great taste but thank them for me," I chirp, trying to create a sarcastic, jokey moment to hide behind.

Niyi's eyes fill with remorse. "Moyo, this was for you," he pleads. "You mentioned visiting restaurants as one of your favorite things, so I asked Merc for the list of top restaurants and chose this one for *you*."

It's weird having someone other than the girls or my parents understand my discomfort when I hide it with humor. It feels even stranger that he remembered a comment from our first coaching session, despite this not being the first time. Am I so used to my hyper-independence that I can't fathom someone putting in the same effort that I do for others?.

I'm again embarrassed by my reaction to a perceived slight that triggered my insecurities. At our first meeting at *Cupid's Bow*, it was that I didn't know what I wanted from dating. Now it's because I know what I want, and the object of my desire isn't acting according to the perfect scenario in my head.

"Moyo, what's going on?" Niyi stretches his hand towards mine.

"I'm sorry. That was passive-aggressive and an overreaction."

"Yes, you're right. But that doesn't answer my question. What's wrong? You've been fidgety all evening."

Guess it's time to spill my guts.

I take a deep breath and, on the exhale, I spiral into what can only be described as word-vomit.

"I thought this was just another work add-on for you," I begin. Niyi hums, his intense gaze not leaving mine. "And that made me upset because

I've started to have feelings for you and was secretly hoping you were seeing this as a real date, not a practice one. I know I've gotten ahead of myself, and you don't feel similarly because I'm a client, but our working relationship ends after today, so despite this being wildly unprofessional, bear with me and let's enjoy this extremely hard-to-get-into restaurant."

"You...have feelings for *me?*" Niyi looks dazed.

Great, I've broken him. I should've just canceled this entire thing. And started afresh with someone other than my dating coach.

"Like I said, no worries. You can ignore that, and we can have dinner. Or, if you're uncomfortable, we can end things here."

"Moyo." His voice is firm. "Breathe. Can I get a word in?"

I nod. If I talk, I'll just keep self-sabotaging.

Niyi rubs the back of his neck. "I am proud of you for sharing what you want, even if you do need to work on your delivery. I shouldn't have mentioned Merc and made this sound like just another job. I apologize."

Again, I nod. Waiting for the other shoe to drop.

"Like you said, this is wildly unprofessional..." *Here it comes.* "But I also have feelings for you."

Wait, what?

"You do?" I regain my voice.

"Yeah, I do. I'm surprised you're interested in me."

Am I on *Punk'd?* I look around the room for the hidden camera.

"You're serious?" I ask.

Niyi responds, "Deadly. You're serious?"

"As a heart attack."

Niyi closes the distance between our hands and grazes my palm with his fingers, setting my hand on fire.

"I'll be honest. I didn't think past this," I say, giggling. Everything that's happened with Niyi has been against my usual methodology. Despite the uncertainty about the rest of the night, and a possible future, I'm excited.

Niyi opens his mouth, but a waiter—accompanied with a draft of cold air—comes in.

"Food first, and then we can figure this out."

We order some calamari, a whiskey for Niyi, and a margarita for me. Once the waiter leaves, it's back to business.

"We're technically still working together," I say, still holding on to his hand.

Part of me expects him to let go; instead, his grip tightens. "We are, but only for three more hours." Niyi smiles.

"Touché."

"There is something I'd like to tell you...to be fully transparent."

Rebelling against my nature, I stop him. "Unless it has to do with you actually *not* having feelings for me, let's table it and have a good night."

A myriad of emotions flash across his face. "We'll talk about logistics and other things later?"

"I could even send you a calendar invite," I reassure him.

A different waiter delivers our appetizers and drinks.

"To us, three hours from now." Niyi raises his glass.

Still holding hands, we clink glasses.

The night continues with even more drinks and fabulous food on the *Cupid's Bow* tab.

I don't know what's changed for him, but his typical tension is nonexistent. For the first time, Niyi looks completely at peace. "Only two hours now," he says, giving me a sip of his drink.

Two hours, then he's all mine.

Moyo

WITH AN HOUR LEFT ON THE CLOCK, WE DECIDE TO SHARE a ride from the restaurant. It's the economical and environmentally conscious option. Not at all fueled by a desire to be near one another. At my house, I expect to walk to my front door alone and pick up whatever this relationship might be tomorrow, but I hear Niyi's footsteps behind me. I turn around and raise an eyebrow. He gives me one of his looks, but I don't budge, not this time.

"It's the right thing to do to walk a lady to her door." He stops his stride, hands in his pockets.

"You want to walk me"—I look at my door and then back at him—"four steps to my door?" I chuckle.

"The dat—*practice* date," Niyi corrects himself, "is still currently happening. Let me walk you to your door, please."

The coolness in his voice forces me to nod. I can't with this man. He catches up to me and we walk in step. Our hands hover next to each other but don't touch. Heat is radiating off him.

I reach my door. "This is me." My voice shakes as I dig out my key.

"It is you," he says, looking anywhere but at me.

I place the key in the lock and open the door. We speak at the same time.

"You—"

"I—"

We laugh at the same time.

"You go," he says.

"Wanna come in for a drink?" I ask, and his eyes widen slightly. "Or you can go home, and we'll talk tomorrow."

"A drink would be lovely. Thank you."

He walks in behind me. I take off my coat and hang it behind the door. He does the same.

I lean on my heels and point my thumb toward the kitchen. "Let me go get you that drink. Any requests?" I walk backwards, not wanting to take my eyes off him. The back of my calf bumps against the couch, and I stumble a bit. God, this is embarrassing. He moves to help, but I wave him off. "I'm good." I find my footing and heat rushes to my ears.

"I'll take anything that won't kill you."

"Comedian." The air feels lighter now that my calf is in pain. One burden for another. I look at the lone bottle of red and raise it so he can see. "Red?"

He responds, "I'll have what you're having."

I crisscross the stems of two glasses in one hand and grab the bottle with the other. I make an obvious effort to sidestep the couch on the way back, and it earns me a slight chuckle. He takes the glasses from me and sets them on the coffee table before us. I take a seat beside him on the couch.

"Glad to see you made it in one piece." He examines the bottle of 2019 Tignanello that I purchased years ago on a whim. It was an expensive wine, but what is life without leaning into the finer things it offers? I hurry back into the kitchen to grab the bottle opener.

"This is the wine you've been saving," he says. I'm hyper-aware of the distance between us as I sit beside him, our knees a hair's breadth away.

"Yeah...I've always wanted to be one of those people who has a fancy bottle they could show off," I say. Because of my student visa, I couldn't work as many hours during college as other people who needed money. And despite my dad, bless his heart, doing everything he could to ensure my upkeep was decent, I never had enough for extras. After I got my green card and started earning the big hospital dollars, I started making little frivolous purchases like this one as a token to the younger me, who went to bed many nights on Indomie instant noodles.

"And you want to share it with me?" Niyi shifts his weight and pivots to face me. The earnest look on his face is piercing. I struggle to pinpoint whether it's happiness or sadness.

"Good things must be experienced sometimes." I reach for the bottle. Let's get this show on the road.

"Thank you," he says while I twist the corkscrew in. Our silence amplifies the pop as I uncork the bottle.

"I mean it." He slows my hand. "Thank you for sharing a part of you with me."

He takes the bottle from me and pours us two perfect glasses. He swirls the glass at the base with his thick, steady fingers, making the almost purple liquid slosh in the bowl. He brings it to his nose. I already know the scents that are attacking him. It might've been a spontaneous spend, but I did my research afterward. The top notes of blackberries, dark cherries, and plums seem to please because he smiles. He takes a sip and smacks his plump lips as he deciphers the flavors before taking another sip. He makes drinking look so good.

"Thoughts?" The hoarseness in my voice surprises me.

"Taste it yourself," he responds, raising his glass. I reach for mine, but he gently holds my shoulder, moving me away from the coffee table and toward his face. He tips his glass towards me, like he did at the restaurant, but this time, it feels more intimate.

"That's your glass." My voice comes out low.

"And I want to share mine with you." The bass in his voice is more prominent.

He scoots towards me, and our legs touch. I lean forward, and his fingers brush the side of my face as he places the glass on my lips. When the dark liquid touches my tongue, colors burst before my eyes. Blacks, dark reds, and purples come to light. As it settles, hints of vanilla, oak, and cinnamon linger. I close my eyes and take in the flavors. I go back for another sip and moan lightly as each taste finds its place on my tongue.

"Thoughts?" He tries to mimic my earlier tone, but it comes out more rugged.

"It's delicious," is all I can say while I look at him and attempt to keep my composure. It might be the drinks I had at the restaurant or this gorgeous wine, but I'm feeling frisky.

I take the glass from him and place it on the table. He shoots me a look. "So, are we at the 'kiss-and-goodnight' part of the date?" I ask. "Or are we gonna wait and do a countdown like on New Year's Eve?"

Instead of my desired reaction, I'm met with silence. Did I ruin the vibe?

"Ignore that. Too many drinks. I know you're still on the job. Ignore me," I blurt out and jump off the couch, turning my back to him. I am so stupid. How could I be so stupid? Jumping the gun when all I had to do was wait out the hour. He's definitely going to leave, and it will be awkward, and I'll never see him again. Great job, girl, you killed it (the mood, that is).

I hear him rise from the couch. Soon, his body heat mingles with mine.

"Moyo." His voice is low, serious. "Ignoring you is not an option."

"No, you don't have to make me feel better." My mouth is running like a broken tap. "I know we said three hours—and there's still time left—but if tonight's not the night, we can circle back later. It's fine." He pulls my hair to the side, his breath kissing my earlobe.

"You're insufferable, do you know that?" he asks. "I said, ignoring you is *not* an option." His body pushes up against mine. He's so firm and hard, all the air rushes out of my lungs.

I feel dizzy.

"I am..." he pauses, "your coach for another thirty minutes." The strain in his voice is undeniable. "I shouldn't want to do this, not before I—not this soon after we decided to wait."

I tremble at the weight of his words, the tension in his voice, his fingers lightly caressing my neck. I attempt to face him, but his other hand holds my waist in place. I gasp at the contact. I didn't know he was this strong.

"Moyo," he moans, and my name sounds like a desperate prayer on his lips. "If you turn around, I will kiss you. If you don't, I will leave here, and we can pretend this never happened. You can call me tomorrow if you'd still like my company. It's entirely up to you." His warm breath fans my ear, and I clench my thighs. Who cares about thirty extra minutes? It's midnight somewhere.

I turn around, and his eyes are on mine. He keeps one hand at my waist and moves the other from my neck, lightly trailing down the space between my breasts. I can't look away as his fingers tease me. I want to yell at him to move them lower already.

"We shouldn't do this," he breathes, moving a hand to my face. He holds me sternly—his thumb is in the center of my lower jaw, and his fingers relaxed on my cheek.

"And why not?" I flick my eyes up to hold his gaze, keeping still to savor his steady hold on me.

I pull my lower lip between my teeth. "You know you want to," I tease. Niyi's head tips back, a breathy exhale falling from his parted lips. He returns his heavy gaze to mine, and my mouth becomes increasingly wet.

Every second increases the cravings...my desire to be touched by him.

"Moyo." He leans in and whispers directly in my ear, "Know what you are to me?"

I can barely register his words, the pool between my thighs is so distracting. He pulls me close and takes my helix between his front teeth, nipping my ear hard.

"Mhmm," I whimper, completely forgetting the question.

He presses his head against my cheek. The friction from his facial hair rubs against my smooth skin, further lighting my body on fire. I can't see him, but his groan reverberates against my throat. "You're my favorite," he breathes, then puts his lips to mine.

I thought the wine was good, but it's nothing compared to this. How did I ever think I'd kissed anyone before this? Our lips move in unison to choreography my consciousness isn't privy to, but somehow my mouth knows all the steps. Niyi's like a never-ending wine glass overflowing with lust, and I'm drunk on him.

In the past, I've always led, and my partners followed. No one chal-lenged or compared to my passion until Niyi. We are perfectly in sync—a finely tuned orchestra moving towards our crescendo. My head tilts left, and he follows suit. My tongue rises, and his falls. A whimper falls from my lips, and he answers with a moan. There's no clashing of teeth or awk-ward panting. We are pure, unfiltered fervor. Bliss.

We fall into the comfort of the couch. Taking a second to breathe.

"Moyo," he rasps, "come here." He lifts me from my spot and pulls me onto him, so I straddle his lap. I'm a big girl, always have been, and my weight has never been a problem during sex, but it's never been this easy. Where boys have hesitantly squeezed and prodded, Niyi—the epitome of a man—grabs confidently and firmly. There is no second-guessing or reluc-tance in his movements as he gently pushes me backwards. My back hits the soft cushions of my couch. He pulls my sweater off and unfastens the buttons of my white shirt from the bottom up, exposing me in increments, then tortuously leaves a trail of wet kisses from my navel to my sternum on his way. He chuckles at my shaky breaths and uncontrollable whines.

He unclasps my bra as his lips find mine again, slower and longer this time, like we have all the time in the world and he plans to savor each second.

Everything within me is moving at record speed. The pounding of my heartbeat, the rush of blood in my ears, the ever-growing puddle between my legs. We're so deeply entangled, physically and emotionally, I can't fig-ure out where I stop and he begins; can't distinguish his moans from mine. He pulls away and rests his forehead against mine, and his eyes flutter shut. His fingers lightly trace across my collarbones, then move to my breasts, pinching my nipples till they're taut before taking them into his mouth. Niyi sucks and bites them till ecstasy flows through me like nectar.

Niyi gives me one sharp tug before letting go and focusing his attention on my lower half. Without any fanfare, he takes off my pants. I instinctive-ly try to shut my legs, but his wide palms keep me open. He doesn't say a word as his hands travel to my black lace-covered center.

"Niyi," I moan. His eyebrows lift, and his glossy gaze lands on mine. "Fuck me."

I'm ready, but not because I haven't had sex in almost two months. I'm ready because I've never had sex like this before. Everything about Niyi pushes me toward the edge. The shifts between delicate exploration and commanding touches are setting me aflame. His muffled moans spur me on. His weighted looks will forever be burned into the fabric of my soul.

"You sure?" he asks innocently before giving me a smirk. I want to smack him so hard because I know that he knows I'm sure.

I push up against the armrest. "If you don't get to it, I'll handle things myself."

He chuckles, and it's a dangerous sound. The rumble in his voice sends tremors all over my body. He lowers himself onto the couch and slides to the other end. He keeps his eyes on me, and I know he's checking to see if I'm serious. I raise my chin.

He nods silently and rests his weight on the armrest. "Handle it then."

I clench my jaw.

"Go on," he purrs. "Show me what you like."

I'm not gonna make this easy for him. I take it slow, toying with my lace thong. I pull it forward and spread my thighs, giving him the perfect view. His Adam's apple bobs.

I can't focus on my body and its needs when I'm staring into the eyes of a man I want to jump, especially when he looks like he could devour me at any second.

I close my eyes, and I'm back in the room at Cole's house. I remember my excitement and then the shock of being discovered so vulnerable. His words scream in my ears.

"Moyo." Niyi's voice brings me out of the memory. I open my eyes, and I'm staring, not into pale blue orbs devoid of joy but warm, chocolate eyes full of concern. "Are you okay?" The huskiness in his voice is gone, and all that remains is care.

I choke back the unease. "I'm good. Zoned out a bit," I say with a tentative smile. It's not real, but I hope he accepts it.

Fuck Cole. It's some bullshit that the first time I try to get back to myself sexually, I'm reminded of that horrible night.

"We don't—" he begins.

"No!" I yell a little too loudly. "Didn't peg you for the running-away type," I say, trying to brush off the awkwardness and reignite the passion my trauma pushed aside.

One thing I adore about Niyi is he always follows my segues.

"Oh, I don't run away. If you ever want to share, I'm here," he whispers, settling back into his seat. He watches me for another second, searching for a crack, making sure I'm okay. I am okay. I have to be okay.

Suddenly, he stands up.

"Thought you said you don't run," I comment.

He whips his shirt off and throws it to the side. "Does this look like running off?"

I'm too mesmerized to pay attention to his words. He is perfectly sculpted, with thick muscles, a densely packed torso, and exquisite, rich dark skin. He's stunning. His pants soon join his shirt in the pile. Standing in black boxer briefs, with shimmers of moonlight and his gold chain illuminating his skin, Niyi looks like a god. I can't help but stare in awe. After that holy demonstration, he plops onto the couch like nothing happened. He spreads his legs wide and palms a prominent bulge that I somehow failed to notice.

My mouth runs dry. I reach for the long-forgotten wine and take a gulp. He doesn't comment, just closes his eyes and gets busy. Groans fill the silence.

"What are you doing?" I ask.

He takes his time opening his eyes. "Giving you a show. What does it look like?"

I blink rapidly. "Why?"

"I asked you to show me what you like, and now I'm showing you what I like. I can stop. We can stop. It's up to you."

I can't believe he's doing this to make me comfortable. "No, no, carry on." I beam. "But first, let me get you some things."

I hurry into my pristine bedroom and reach for the lube and wipes in my bedside drawer. I also grab my bullet vibrator, just in case. He's staring aimlessly at the ceiling when I return, but his eyes brighten when they land on me. "Now you can begin."

He squeezes lube into his hand. "Your wish is my command." His hand goes inside his briefs and he turns the heat up with a moan.

I've always enjoyed it when my partner watches me. There's something powerful about controlling my pleasure and starring in a spectacle that makes someone salivate. However, being on the other side of the equation is something I can get into. His eye contact alone makes me squirm in my seat, and we're not even a minute in. His tortured, heavy, lust-filled stare is irresistible, and I find myself itching to join in. So I do, closing my eyes as my fingers get to work.

"Don't look away," he commands. "Keep your focus on me while I keep mine on you. I'm here for you. You're safe."

He slows down to marvel at me. "You're perfect. I can't wait to taste you. You deserve this," he coos. My body unwinds with every affirmation. "I wish you could see how you look right now. You're perfect, Moyo, absolutely perfect." My legs tremble, and I struggle to keep eye contact. He looks so golden despite being utterly disheveled.

"Breathe with me. Breathe," he repeats, taking a dramatic inhale, and I follow suit. "You almost there?"

"Mmhmm," I whimper, my walls contracting with each passing second.

"I'm right here with you. Keep breathing." Sweat forms on his forehead. "Let go for me," he directs, and I reach my crescendo.

I hit the wall hard. My limbs shake, my toes curl, and stars pop up in my vision. I am completely and utterly wrecked. He's still going, watching me with a pained smile. He's smiling because I'm satisfied. He only cares about me, no regard for his release.

I don't know what it feels like to be filled by him yet, but I know what it feels like to be desired and supported by him.

I raise my eyebrows, offering something in return. He fervently nods. I take my time moving towards him.

"Moyo, please," Niyi moans, his chest rising and falling. I'm turned on by the sweat forming on his hairline and the pleading in his deep-brown eyes as he opens his mouth.

My cum-covered fingers are barely in Niyi's mouth when he starts sucking on them.

"Fuck," he moans. The expletive sparks a smile from me. "Sunshine," he adds.

"Sunshine?" I question, resting my back on the armrest.

"Don't get too cocky."

"No, from 'your favorite' to 'Sunshine.' What's next?" I laugh.

"I'll take care of you," he says. I already know what he's thinking.

"Go ahe—" Before I can get out the words, my legs are on his shoulders, and he's lying prone with half his body hanging off the couch.

"Moyo," he moans, and the sound echoes through me. I'm at the edge, ready to chant his name like a chorus—when the doorbell screams instead of me.

"Moyo! Open up!" Anjie's voice booms from outside. "I left my key at home, so you actually have to open the door." Another onslaught of bells.

Shit.

Niyi lifts his head, and I tighten my legs to retrieve some lost pleasure. We glance at each other. There's so much more to say, so much more to do, but all we can do is get dressed because of the incessant doorbell ringing. I throw on my sweater and hurry to get on my cargo pants. Niyi returns to his green-and-black ensemble, his bulge unmistakable from any angle.

The doorbell rings again.

I can't keep Anjie waiting any longer without looking even more suspicious.

"Hide," I shoo. Niyi shoots me an incredulous look, and I give him an equally exasperated *What do you want me to do?* look in return. He stalks off into a dark corner of the kitchen. With the lights off, you can barely see anything in there.

Anjie doesn't let me get a word out before she storms in.

"How did you know I was home?" I ask, trying to distract her and keep her away from the kitchen—and off the soiled couch.

"We have each other's location?" Her inflection makes it a question. "Anyways, that's not why I'm here. I need to talk to you," she huffs. I want to kick her out, but her face is flushed, and her tone is more hurried than usual.

"Wait." Anjie pauses, ignoring my attempts to move her away from the living room. "It smells a little weird in here." Then she notices the half-drunk wine glasses, the lube, and the wipes on the table.

"You have someone over. Where is he?" she demands, raising her voice. I hope Niyi knows what's good for him and doesn't come out.

"*Had*," I lie.

"Hmm, interesting," she says and then sprints to the kitchen and turns on the lights. Niyi flinches in the corner. "I knew it!" she yelps and claps her hands, laughing like a kid who's just won at hide-and-seek.

"I really needed that tonight." She sighs and turns back to me, forgetting Niyi. I mouth sorry to him, and he smiles and shakes his head.

"I'll head out," Niyi finally speaks up. Not that it matters now that she's found him anyway.

"You're not gonna introduce us, Moyo?" Anjie asks, feigning innocence.

After I help this girl with whatever it is, I'm banning her from my residence.

"Anjie, this is um—" The words run out. How do I introduce him? I'm not ready to tell them he's the *Cupid's Bow* guy because what do I say? I know I said that nothing will ever happen with us because he's not part of the plan, but I changed my mind, and he just ate me out like a starving man. I could mention his name and pretend he's a friend they don't know, but I have explicitly named him on multiple occasions, so I'm not about to say it now.

"Just a friend," Niyi provides, and relief floods through me. "A friend who is leaving. Thank you for the drink, Moyo. Have a great night," he adds respectfully, like he didn't just talk me through an orgasm and nearly cause another one.

"I'll walk you out," I say.

He grabs his shoes from behind the couch, and I hand him his jacket as I open the door. I shut it gently behind me and check that the curtains are closed. I don't want anyone else to see this. What this is going to be, I don't know. Are we going to kiss? Are we pretending this didn't happen? Are we finishing up tomorrow?

We stand awkwardly, and I'm transported back to earlier tonight, before everything changed. The fog of uncertainty is thick considering we've just seen each other naked.

"Uh," I say to fill the silence.

"I hope your friend is okay," he says.

"I'm sure she's fine."

He pulls me closer with his free hand and places a kiss on my forehead.

"Now go back in there and be a good friend." He releases me and points his head toward my front door.

"You'll text?" My lower lip finds its way between my teeth. Completely giddy, drunk on him. I can't believe how routine this all sounds.

"Of course." He places another kiss on my cheek. Part of me wants to stand there and kiss him all night, but going to help Anjie is the more responsible option.

I give him a final wave as he heads to his end of the street. He walks slowly backward, waiting for me to open the door. As I step inside, Niyi winks, making my legs go weak.

Anjie better have something serious to talk about because I'm about to murder her for ruining my second orgasm of the night.

25

Moyo

THE DOOR CLOSES BEHIND ME WITH A THUD THAT SOUNDS eerily like the pounding in my chest. My hand flies to my cheek, remembering Niyi's warm breath over my flushed skin.

Anjie coughs obnoxiously, her eyelashes batting overtime like a plane about to take off.

"So…" She draws out the final syllable and cups her face as she looks at me all starry-eyed. What this babe does for gist.

"So, what?" I roll my eyes as I retrieve the emergency ice cream pints from the freezer.

Late-night visits like these are rare and thus extremely important. The vulnerability of showing up at someone's house late at night—even when you're basically sisters—isn't lost on me. So, to increase our comfort and reduce tension, in all our freezers, we girls each always have three pints of ice cream on hand: cookies and cream for me, butter pecan for Sewa, and chocolate fudge brownie for Anjie.

Anjie takes her googly-eyes off me when I place the mini bowls and spoons in front of her. She heads towards the couch when I latch onto her gray hoodie.

"What?" She looks at my arm, and I quickly let go.

"Let's talk in my room."

Anjie narrows those piercing brown eyes at me and kisses her teeth in the dramatic way my mother does. "You were fornicating on the couch, abi?"

I bow my head and angle my body towards my door. "Anjola, nitori Ol- orun, let's sit on my rug."

"You're a nasty, nasty girl." She snickers behind me. I don't let her see because that would be admitting defeat and affirming the accusation, but I smile a little as we step into my room.

The ivory shag rug in front of my bed is one of the softest things I own and truly one of the best purchases I've made since moving in. We usu- ally don't eat on it, but since the couch is out of commission, it's the sec- ond-best place. Anjie sits crisscross on the rug while I lie back against my footboard and spread my legs out. She expertly scoops some chocolate into her bowl, and I do the same with my cookies and cream.

"What's up?" I ask. The spoon hangs in my mouth.

She takes another spoonful before she answers. "Can we talk about you first?" Her eyes are gooey, her version of puppy-dog eyes, which she hard- ly ever uses. I give in.

"It was..." I pause, and Anjie leans in expectantly. "Amazing!" I yell, and she squeals. In seconds it's as though we're back in our college dorms, sharing hookup stories and giggling the night away.

"I will need the couch cleaned immediately!" she exclaims, but it's all punctuated by smiles and shrieks of laughter. "Who is he? Will you see him again? Will *we* see him again?"

"Okay, promise not to scream or to call Sewa right now," I demand.

Anjie's eyes question me, but she crosses her fingers, kisses them, and places them across her heart. The little gesture signifying promises we've made since the days of sharing bunk beds and public showers.

"It's the app guy."

She screeches like a freaking owl. "I knew it!" She shoves her spoon in the bowl so she can properly dance using her arms. She looks like a baby learning motor function. I bust out laughing. "Sewa owes me fifty dol- lars," she mutters as she kicks her feet.

I almost scoff, but at this point, *we're* the suckers for getting roped into one of Sewa's bets. "Normally, I'd feign upset, but I'm happy she lost. What did y'all bet on?"

"Oh, she said y'all would fuck in a month."

I blink rapidly. "And you said?"

"Six weeks. I knew you needed more time to warm up to him." She licks her spoon, realizes it's empty, and refills her bowl.

"I hope you guys know I hate you."

"Love you too!" Anjie reaches over to squeeze my neck, and I allow myself to be drawn into her embrace.

"How did y'all know it would happen?" I suddenly feel self-conscious. Knowing and accepting my attraction to Niyi is one thing, but it's another thing for my friends to cosign it. I don't need their blessing, but their approval means something.

Anjie recognizes the change in my tone. "The fire behind your eyes and voice whenever you talked about him was enough to heat several rooms."

"I—"

"Abeg, don't even start. You'd brush us off whenever we mentioned him, but there was always some underlying heat. You were attracted to him. It was a no-brainer." She shrugs and returns to eating her ice cream.

Her words force me back to my initial interactions with Niyi. How he looked at me on the first day. The way he's looked at me since, when he thinks I can't see. Apparently, when you're the one involved, it can be tough to see past the fog.

"I need half of the cut, by the way," I chime in once I'm done going down memory lane.

"You didn't even tell me anything apart from 'amazing,'" Anjie says. She mimics my voice horribly with some high-pitched mess.

"I don't sound like that," I bite back.

"Sure, love-struck."

Anjola is the most insufferable person on this planet.

"All I'll say is that you did indeed interrupt something," I divulge, and her mouth goes wide. "Now, tell me why you interrupted my night before I kick you out."

Anjie puts one last scoop in her bowl.

"Heard about *The Cook-Off*?" Her eyes grow clear and serious.

The name doesn't ring a bell, so I shake my head.

"New TV show. A culinary contest for small restaurants owned by BI-POC in the Greater Boston area. The winner gets a hundred thousand to invest in their business."

I smile, and the tension between my shoulder blades relaxes. A cooking contest? I am not worried one bit.

"No, don't look excited," she says. "I didn't apply."

The confession blows me out of the water. Anjie loves her restaurant. She's constantly recipe testing and ensuring the best customer service and working conditions for her handful of chefs. She does everything herself and frequently laments about not having enough money to grow the restaurant. There's no logical reason she wouldn't want to apply for a contest with a hundred thousand big ones on the line.

"Don't look at me like that." She crosses her arms.

"Like you've lost your mind? I will keep doing that because a hundred-fucking-thousand isn't chicken change."

"I know!" she whines.

"So, you're regretting not signing up?"

"Not at all. You know regrets aren't my thing," she hurriedly corrects.

Now I'm utterly confused because if she didn't sign up and isn't regretting it, then why is she here? I cock my head and wait for her explanation.

"Someone signed me up. And I don't want to do it," she reveals.

"Why?"

"Moyo, how am I supposed to know why the mystery person signed me up? If I knew who they were, I'd ask," she snaps, voice dripping with enough sarcasm to flood a small country. She reaches to pick up the pint of semi-melted ice cream. "Sorry, that was snippy. I'm a little overwhelmed and stressed."

After knowing someone for all your adult life *and* all of your teenage years, it's hard to be surprised by their moods. Despite being the most serious of us all, Anjie's mood has always been all over the place. Once, during our first year of secondary school, we went three weeks without talking. It was miserable, but over time we learned to communicate through grunts and glares.

"It's okay," I say, and rub circles on her palm, tracing the age spots from our many years braving the Lagos sun without sunscreen. "But I meant, why don't you want to do it?" Her silence lingers for a few beats. "Talk to me. What's really going on? 'Cause it can't simply be food."

Anjie pushes the pint away with her other hand and sighs deeply. "It's reality TV."

"Oh."

"See?" She jumps up. "You hate the idea of me on reality TV. You know I can't control my tongue."

"I never said any of that," I interject, but the whole idea does stun me. Anjie doesn't have the bubbly personality needed for those kinds of shows. She finds them abhorrent. This explains why she didn't sign up.

"I'm gonna be so screwed," she moans.

"You're the best chef. You'll be fine," I say in my most soothing voice and reach for her hand once more. We sit there a second, and I wait for her breathing to regulate before I speak again.

"Do you have to go alone?" I ask quietly.

"We get to bring one person along from our restaurants."

"Mike?"

"Who else would it be?" she deadpans. Mike, the man I'm almost certain is in love with Anjie, has been her pastry chef since the beginning.

"Asked him yet?"

"He doesn't know. I'm still trying to get out of it."

"Because it's reality TV?" I ask, and she nods. "A hundred-freaking-thousand dollars would do so much for you," I whisper.

"I know..." She trails off wistfully, looking at the ceiling.

"It does seem fortuitous that you were signed up," I say, and she shoots daggers at me. "In fact, someone would call that fate." I wink, and she hisses.

"Stop stealing my lines. Fake spiritualist." She eyes me but then mouths a solemn "thank you." She rises from the rug and moves to shake out the worries—a thing we usually do to end our heart-to-hearts—but I stop her 'cause I'm not done.

I lift myself from the ground and look her in the eyes. "Anjola, darling. I have been your friend since we were prepubescent kids. I have seen you at your worst—"

"Are you talking about the three-week fiasco? It's been decades."

"Like I said, at your worst, and I've seen you at your best. Which was yesterday, today, and will continue tomorrow. You're hilarious, brave, and talented. You'd be amazing on TV. And I hate to think I'll have to share you with the rest of America, but I'll manage. Don't let your insecurities stop you." I give her my most reassuring smile and squeeze her palm.

"Thank you," she says, audibly this time. "I needed that." She pulls me in for a hug, and we embrace like we always have. She gives me one last squeeze before we pull apart, her eyes glistening with unshed tears.

"Awww," I coo. "Are you crying?"

"Allergies," she sniffs. "You know I might not even be on the show."

"What do you mean?"

"There's an initial mini-cookoff where we make one appetizer and one main for the producers before they decide which final ten teams go on the show."

I can't believe my ears. "You got all pissy over some TV show you're not even on yet?" She nods quickly. I pinch the bridge of my nose. "So, technically, you might not even be chosen? And this whole convo would've been for naught?"

Anjie rubs the back of her neck. "Well, when you put it like that, it does sound a tad bit overdramatic."

"A tad?"

"Okay, it sounds very overdramatic. Is that what you want to hear?" She playfully shoves my arm. I've got to laugh at the ridiculousness of it all. Here I was, getting some for the first time in months, only to lose out because my best friend was feeling too many things about maybe, possibly, potentially being on TV. It's hilarious, but I wouldn't change a thing.

Okay, that's a lie.

"When you think about it, this is me being confident that I'll nail this informal round and get to the reality TV portion," she says.

"You know what? You're right, and I'm very proud of you." I pull her into another hug, and when we let go, we shake out our worries. As always, we start with our arms, flinging wrists every which way until we feel satisfied, and then we move on to our feet.

When we're done, Anjie's face is relaxed.

"Know what you're making for the initial mini-thing?" I ask.

She gives me her smug, all-knowing, Anjie smile. "The mini-cookoff? Why do you think you've been taste-testing a lot more dishes these days?"

"Wait, how long have you known about this?"

"Right after Thanksgiving."

That was weeks ago.

"I initially thought it was a joke but then decided the menu needed a revamp anyway. But last week, I got another email asking for co-chef registration and everything felt a little too real," Anjie explains.

"You submitted it, right? When's it due?"

"It's due tomorrow at noon."

"Anjola Kuti, you call Mike first thing in the morning and get this sorted!" I yell.

She jumps back. "Okay, okay. I hear you. Don't eat me like he was—"

"Don't."

The annoying mischief in her eyes doesn't die and neither does my stern look. Luckily for the both of us—because we would've stood at a deadlock till someone broke, our record is eleven minutes—my phone rings. The caller ID makes me smile, and before I know it, Anjie looks over my shoulder and nudges me.

"Answer," she whispers.

I do, and somehow my smile gets wider.

"Goodnight," she calls out, exiting my bedroom, and I hope my entire house.

"Who was that?" His voice comes through, and heat shoots to my core. It's barely been an hour and my body already misses his touch.

"Anjie. She's leaving." I flop into my bed, getting comfortable.

"Everything good?"

"Impostor syndrome reared its ugly head, but yeah. She's good."

"Lovely. Is your Saturday free?" he asks.

It takes everything in me not to immediately say *yes*. "Can I check my schedule and get back to you?"

"Take all the time you need. Just know, I *need* to see you again." There's no mistaking the bass in his voice.

"Why do you *need* to see me again?" I ask playfully. My stomach tightens, and my inner thighs get wet. I hope he follows my lead.

"Because we have unfinished business," he says with some strain.

"What kind of business?"

"Moyo." His voice is harsh.

"Niyi." Mine is smooth.

"This woman," he chuckles, and I wish I could see him laughing. He looks stunning when joy outlines his features. "Are you free tomorrow? Well, technically today?"

"For what?" I question. Regardless of his response, I know my answer, but if I don't make him sweat a little, then who will?

"Wine tasting...and maybe some other tastings."

I smile. What better way to follow up tonight than with more wine and, hopefully, a room where we won't get interrupted this time? The infinite possibilities run through my mind: Niyi's mouth on mine. And after that, all over me.

I smile, not bothering to keep the rasp from my voice.

"It's a date."

Niyi

BEFORE I REALIZED MY FATHER AIN'T SHIT, I SPENT MOST OF my childhood studying astrology. Post-realization, I spent the rest of it working towards a financially sensible career, so I could leave my ain't-shit father. As a result, young Niyi didn't get a lot of time outside. Especially not doing things like jumping rope or skipping.

Therefore, I'm shocked to find myself skipping all the way home. I didn't even know I could do that, but I can't help it after being with Moyo.

I held her in my arms, looked into her smoldering, brown eyes, and tasted her. It was everything I didn't know I needed.

Each step is like walking on a cloud. Almost as if *I* am Mercury, winged feet and all. The cold is inconsequential with Moyo's captivating scent lingering on my skin. Every gust of wind brings the intoxicating smell up to my nose. I make a mental note to send a thank-you letter to Elder Teda, Uranus, wherever they are...possibly the Amazon, for the blustery winds.

Still giddy on Moyo, once I get home, I pull out my sketchbook, turn on my classical music playlist, and get lost exploring abstract shapes and unconventional designs to try out in the studio.

Vivaldi's "Spring Largo" permeates the room as my designs go from malleable structures to pieces I'll need Aaron's help with taking from 2D to 3D. Most are a mess, uncoordinated, raw, but they flow effortlessly. The sketches begin to lose form, my pace decreasing and inspiration lacking until I think, *What would Moyo like?*

Her smile pops into my mind, and this time, her image fuels my concentration. The music fades and all that's left is her. The full cheeks, wide smile, and hair that rivals the clouds. She comes into view, and I move faster.

I think of her love for her work, her organizational prowess, her dedication to her friendships, and her movies.

Her movies! The idea strikes like lightning. The idea doesn't take shape in my head, but my fingers interpret it expertly, putting form to paper. Recalling the green all over Moyo's home, the perfect complimentary color comes to mind—ochre. Earthy, to mesh with her aesthetic, but dynamic enough to contrast with the space.

When I'm done, the adrenaline lessens, and I feel a hand violently shaking my shoulder.

"Yo, Merc, what the fuck?" I move away from my cousin's grip. A wave of nausea hits.

Merc's face is transfixed in a face-splitting grin. "When did this happen? Why didn't you tell me?"

"What?"

"You did it."

Still lost, I reply, "Yeah, I did some sketches..."

"You didn't feel it?" Merc asks, and my confusion magnifies. "You activated The Sight, right? I think you were just using it. Why didn't you say anything? Change your mind?"

My head snaps back and I shake it wildly. The Sight? I'd know if I unlocked that. Wouldn't I? I should've felt a buzz in my veins, or my blood should be charged like Sprite.

"There's no way," I reply. I was only drawing and thinking about Moyo. "It's morning."

As soon as the words leave Merc's mouth, I open my blinds to sunlight. It's been hours and I didn't even notice the time passing.

"I did it," I mutter, stunned. Time flew by and I rode the wave.

"I came over to apologize for the other day..." Merc says softly, sitting beside me. "I shouldn't have gotten heated like that. Your experience with this family thing is yours, and I should've listened. I should've stayed and heard you out."

"'Preciate it. I shouldn't have raised my voice first."

"I know the job's been hard for you, but I've enjoyed our time together. Yeah, we work together, but we're also like…" Merc pauses, seemingly searching for the right word.

"Like family?"

"It's been different, with you as Saturn. Your dad made Vee and I efficient—*Cupid's Bow* at its prime. But with you, we've learned how to not only focus on the work."

They learned something from *me*?

"Y'all taught me parts of this family are worth having," I say, honestly.

"So…we good?" Merc asks.

"Yeah, we good."

We hug it out.

When they pull back, they say, "I also came over to ask if you *really* wanted me to find the Jakandes, but you were locked in." I roll my eyes. "Plus, I've never seen a Saturn work before. What was it like?" they ask.

Is this just a Saturn thing? Is this how my father felt? Is this why he quit? Is this why he was never around? Is that why he never noticed what was going on with Mom? Questions bang around in my skull. My stomach bubbles, the contents threatening to rise in my throat.

"Ah, the nausea," Merc says, their voice drifting like it's a fond memory. "It'll pass."

"Is there a way to…" I struggle to find the words, "*not* get that sucked in?" I never want to experience this unsettling feeling again. The zone was easy to slip into, and I'm not gonna lie, it was addicting. If Merc hadn't stopped me, I'm not sure I would've stopped.

"I'm not sure how it works for you, but for Mercuries, the trick is working through an anchor because unfortunately, we have to be all-in for it to work. It's why we love our gadgets."

"I was just sucked into a zone." My stomach flips over.

"It's called The Sight because it gives us insight into another plane. For the most part, we're humans cosplaying gods but when we're in that zone, our consciousness no longer exists in this realm." Merc shrugs and carries on like they didn't just provide life-changing news. "Didn't Uncle B mention it?"

My head shakes on its own accord. "No," I say, remembering all the moments I'd ask about how work was, or I'd tell him how weak Mom was, and he wouldn't reply. When I was older, I'd ask if I could help him, and he'd respond that he needed to focus. All the times between elementary school and going to college, I wondered how exactly being Saturn and playing matchmaker took up so much time.

Everything feels like it's turned on its head. I thought The Sight would be something I could control, not something that would control me.

"You should ask him. Maybe he has advice," Merc says. "Now that you have The Sight, do you still want to relinquish the role?" they ask slowly. "Really think about it. If it is what you want, I'll help, but consider everything before deciding."

I have The Sight. I finally unlocked it. I could do the job...be Saturn and become someone who loses hours at a time. I thought my dad was special, getting together with my mom and having me, but after seeing the full extent of the power, I know he was selfish.

My mom passed when I was about ten and she seemed happy, despite everything, but there's no way that Dad could have been a healthy partner when his very being didn't allow him to be present. I will not be making that mistake. Maybe that's why Dad gave me the power when I was single. Maybe he thought I'd fall in love with being Saturn, the way he did after Mom passed, and I wouldn't find the time to fall in love with anything else.

Unfortunately, that wasn't the case. One thing is clear, I can't bring Moyo into this complicated situation.

"Niyi," Merc says, redirecting me back to our conversation, "do you still want me to find the Jakandes and see if there's anyone willing to take the mantle?"

With the freedom to live a normal life on my mind, I answer, "Abso-fucking-lutely."

Date #3

THE DOORBELL RINGS, AND FOR ONCE, I WELCOME THE
sound.

I look in the mirror, fluffing my curls and applying one last coat of gloss
before opening the door. Niyi's there, smile wider than ever. The black
sweater he has on contrasts with my white sweater dress.

"Hi," he says.

"Hey."

I lock my door, then step closer to him. His fingers immediately find
mine, and we fit like a glove. The spark from all the earlier times we've
touched is present, and this time, I get to appreciate the current.

"So, where are we going?" I ask, noticing his car isn't here.

"Wine tasting, except it's my personal collection." He pauses to assess
my reaction. "Thought going to my place would give us privacy, and the
space to talk after."

"You're inviting me over?"

"If you'd do me the honor."

"Let's see how you live," I say.

He laughs. "Why do I feel like I'm about to get judged?"

"Lean into it, you'll survive. Maybe."

"I'm at your mercy, Sunshine." He squeezes my hand. I squeeze back,
fighting the urge to kiss him on our walk. And from the gleam in his eyes,
I imagine he's thinking the same thing.

I pause when my favorite house in the neighborhood catches my eye.
The light green roof and complementary mint walls with stone veneer
siding at the bottom look as stunning as usual.

"You like that house?" Niyi asks.

"Gorgeous roof, well-kept lawn, what's not to love?" I respond and then notice the amusement on his face.

"What?" I ask.

He reaches into his pocket and pulls out a set of keys. "Ready to see the inside?"

My jaw drops. The longer I'm in his presence, the more things I discover, but this takes the cake. There's no way Niyi owns my dream house.

If all his surprises are this good, I might have to deviate from my plans more often. If I'd stuck with my perfectionist ways, I never would have met Niyi. Funny how life works.

"You're joking?"

"I'd never." He leads us up the steps. "Welcome to my humble abode."

The black leather couch catches my eye first. Then I'm drawn to all the ceramic details littered around the living room. A white-and-green striped jewelry bowl sits on the coffee table, along with a thin, dark-green cylinder vase and a few white-and-gray marbled coasters.

"How'd I do?" Niyi asks, recapturing my attention.

I take my eyes from the beautiful details to his stunning face. "Better than I expected. Not perfect," I tease, and he rolls his eyes, "but decent."

"I'll take it. Let me show you where we'll have our date."

The exterior of the house is gorgeous. The details in his living room are comforting. But this scene he created in the garden is spectacular. When did he do all this? It's barely been twenty-four hours since he was at my place.

A table with multiple wine bottles and different glasses sits on one side of the garden. The table beside it has different dishes wrapped in foil. The most shocking details are the giant white tent and the inflatable movie screen.

"Niyi, this is..." My words trail off as he guides me around, and I take everything in.

Like our practice dinner date, strings of lights beautify the environment. Up close, I see five different wine bottles and containers of small chops. When we get to the tent, the heat welcomes me, and I happily take off my jacket.

"You didn't have to do all of this," I say, settling into the cozy pillows and blankets.

"I didn't have to, but I wanted to. I always want to do things for you," Niyi says, and like all the previous times he's told me, my heart flutters. Is this the kind of care my dad talks about? Is this what I've been missing out on?

"Where do you want to start? Food, drinks, movie—all of the above?"

"One of everything," I say, feeling cared for.

"I'll be right back."

"Wait," I call after him, and Niyi pauses. "What's the movie?"

"You'll see."

Soon, he's back with a bottle, two glasses, and a plate of snacks. The plate rests on his forearm, and his eyes are focused on the puff-puff, spring rolls, and samosas. I almost laugh at his concentration, but I help him by taking the plate and setting it on the blanket. Niyi puts the wine in an ice bucket on a stool and the glasses beside them.

He wipes his hands on his dark pants and joins me on the soft cream blanket. "I didn't think through the transportation part of this."

"Maybe not quite," I laugh.

"Must you agree with me?"

"When I disagree, it's an issue. And now, when I agree, it's a problem. How do I win?"

"You win all the time," Niyi says, cozying up to me. His face rests in the crook of my neck, allowing me to smell the lavender and sandalwood of his cologne.

"That is true," I whisper, shutting my eyes as I breathe him in. The scent takes me back to the night before, and I squeeze my thighs.

Niyi pulls back. "Sorry, I got a little carried away."

"No, it's fine."

"I'm not being a great date." Niyi clears his throat. "I have some drinks to introduce and a movie to show you."

"Or we can continue where we left off yesterday," I say suggestively, listening to my hormones.

"Moyo," he says, and my name, usually a prayer on his tongue, comes out like a growl. "One drink and let me show you the movie. Then you can devour me. Is that okay?"

My thighs clench. I nod.

Niyi exhales.

"Here's a Cava. It's from outside Barcelona." Niyi pours us two glasses.

The bubbles dance on my tongue. It's different from what I'm used to, but there's a familiarity I struggle to name...because of how intently Niyi's looking at me.

"Not drinking yours?" I ask.

"I'm thirsty for something else." He winks, and I practically choke on the wine. "Enjoy the drink. I'll be right back, just turning on the projector."

I don't care what the movie is. When Niyi returns, I'm kissing him, and that's that.

This time, Niyi returns with a remote control and a different type of wine.

"Pinot Noir," he says, placing it in the ice bucket. "And our movie. I think you might know this one."

The screen is dark, but I know exactly what it is even before the title card plays. Still, I wait an additional second for confirmation before freaking out.

Scream pops up on the screen, followed by the iconic telephone ringing.

"How did you know?" I ask, ignoring Drew Barrymore as she unknowingly talks to Ghostface.

Niyi studies the mixed look of shock and delight on my face. His smile widens as he watches me, and I beam back in response.

"I wish you could see the look on your face. You look so happy, and I love that I'm able to do that for you." He caresses my cheek. I lean into his touch.

"I love it, but how did you know *Scream* was my favorite movie?"

"I arranged your Blu-rays—"

"You didn't say DVDs, I'm so proud," I interject.

Niyi laughs. "And *Scream* was the most worn-out."

Again, I'm left speechless.

"You always do this."

"Do what?"

"Shock me with your kindness and thoughtfulness." I throw my arms over his shoulders, pulling him closer. This time, I don't hold back. The kiss starts soft as our lips get reacquainted, slow and delicate.

Niyi pulls away. "But...your...movie..." he stutters as my nails graze his nape.

"Niyi, darling, who gives a fuck about movies?"

I pull him into another kiss. I can rewatch *Scream* another time; I need Niyi now.

Niyi

MY SWEATER IS OFF, AND THE SPACE HEATER ISN'T DOING enough to fight the cool air, but it doesn't matter because Moyo's pressed against me.

"We should go inside," she says, and my brain springs back into action. I grab her coat, pause the movie, and take her hand.

"Your sweater?" Moyo asks.

"It'll be there," I say, which makes her laugh, and it's the prettiest sound.

The walk to my room feels never-ending, but in reality, it only takes us a minute. Once the door swings shut, we pick up where we left off. Moyo takes off her white thigh-high boots. I lift her dress to see more of her skin. With restless fingers, my shirt is next to go.

My muscles tense slightly as my hands go underneath her voluminous ass to lift her, forcing her thick thighs to wrap around my waist. The yelp that falls from her perfect lips is the reaction I desired.

"Niyi," she breathes. Melting into her brown eyes is an experience I'll never get used to.

"Sunshine," I say, equally as breathless. My chest heaves in rhythm with hers.

"Don't drop me," she says, her voice small. I lift her again in response, bouncing her around to show her she's safe. When she's ready to share all her fears, she will, but in the meantime, I'll show her I'm not planning to go anywhere.

"I'll never drop you," I whisper. I want to say more, but not until I'm rid of the mantle of Saturn.

Little droplets form in the corners of her eyes, and I'm about to provide additional reassurance when she leans in for the most romantic kiss I ever had. Our tongues move slowly and cautiously in unison as I maneuver us to my bed. I lower her onto the white cotton sheets, but she doesn't disentangle herself.

She smiles between the kisses and my tongue licks her teeth. "Thought you'd never put me down," she jokes.

"I said I'd never drop you," I correct, laughing with her. "I'm setting you down gently, the only way you should be. On a soft surface, with a man between your knees."

"Oh, is that man coming soon?" She breaks apart and looks behind me in a mock search.

I shake my head in disbelief with a chuckle. "He canceled, so I'm filling in. Hope that's okay?"

Her head cocks for a beat before she moves back into my personal space and tugs on my lower lip. "I can manage."

Our moment goes from romantic to lustful. I nip at her top lip, pull back, and watch as she discards her dress. Moyo is gorgeous, no question about that, but watching her dark skin against the white sheets with her eyes on me is the most breathtaking sight. I'm never having sex with her in the dark. Every curve, roll, and bit of skin must be illuminated so I can worship at her altar.

"You're beautiful," I breathe, and lean in to kiss between her breasts. Her hands fly to her bra straps, but I stop her. I need to take my time with her. Slowly, I pull each strap down.

I make my way down her body, kissing every inch of skin before kneeling. My tongue swipes at my lower lip in anticipation, preparing to enter the promised land again. With shaking hands, I slide her thighs apart. And like anyone before a deity, I lay offerings in the form of kisses.

"Niyi," she whimpers.

My hands slide under her thighs to pull her closer to the edge of the bed. She lifts her head, and I see the top of her forehead and her beautiful wavy hair. She moans my name into the air—the most gorgeous sound in the universe.

"Niyi," she cries out, clawing at the little curls on my past-overdue hair-cut. She tugs harder when my only response is a moan against her center, so I look up. She's sweaty, her eyes glossy, and absolutely gorgeous.

I can't help but smile. This woman is everything, and it validates my entire existence that I give her some happiness.

"Mr. Looku Looku," she pants. "Are you just gonna stay there?"

I'm hooked. "Just admiring."

Moyo's heavy breathing fills the room as she watches me take off my pants. Her rosy lips part and her gorgeous nipples harden as I slowly put on a condom.

The bed dips as I join her. And like unleashed animals, it's a frenzy of kisses from the both of us, mine across her décolletage and hers across my neck. She grazes me several times, nicking and sucking. Her hot, wicked mouth leaves marks, but I don't care. Anyone can know I am hers; it's already written in my heart. There's no hiding it.

She grabs my sheathed, throbbing dick and places it at her entrance, slathering it with her wetness, making me draw in a sharp breath. The feel of her sends me into a form of primal madness. Sex has never felt this urgent or essential. Have I ever genuinely felt for someone before?

"What are you thinking about?" she asks, breathless.

I answer without thinking, "About how I've never felt like this."

She pauses several seconds. I'm about to take back everything when she pulls me closer and kisses me with an intensity that takes the breath from my lungs.

"Neither have I, if I'm being honest," she whispers. My forehead drops to hers, and we stay there, eye to eye, as Moyo guides me in. It takes all the restraint I can muster to keep from cursing once I'm fully inside. Her eyes shut and her nails suffocate my bicep. We pause for a second, taking in the new sensations of being physically joined.

"Shit," we say simultaneously, and then both laugh.

I start with slow, steady movements. Taking my time with each stroke as I adjust to the intoxicating sensation. As I stare into her hooded eyes, tension builds and I shut mine. After craving this for so long, letting it end so quickly would be criminal.

"Hey." Moyo caresses my face, and my eyes open in response. "Look at me," she commands. "Are you getting close?" She bites her bottom lip, and it almost sets me off.

"Yes." The word comes out jagged. It's becoming harder to worship her without finishing too fast.

Her hips raise and buck, spurring me on. To keep pace, my strokes gain speed and power.

"Sunshine, you feel so fucking good," I moan as I thrust into her, the bed moving to our rhythm. She responds, but the words get lost in the motions. Desperate for more, I place one of her legs over my shoulder, letting me sink deeper.

"Harder, baby," she mewls, and the term of endearment makes me snap. I thrust in and out of her with quick, hurried movements like a starved man finally getting a meal, sweat and expletives dropping with every stroke. Her big, beautiful brown eyes haven't once strayed from mine. The intimacy unravels me.

"I'm coming," I announce and let go, collapsing on top of her. Moyo squeezes everything out of me, and a spasm ripples through my body. It takes me a moment to remember how to breathe, but when I do, she's staring at me, wide-eyed and giggling.

"That was—"

"Amazing," she finishes. I lift onto my forearms to get my weight off her, but she pulls me back in. "I like your weight on me," she says as she nuzzles into my chest.

For a moment, we lie there, her head against my chest. Nothing is happening, nothing other than breathing, but it feels more fated than the stars, the planets, and the rest of the cosmos. Breathing with Moyo is larger than life, and I am content.

"Your heartbeat is so soothing," she whispers.

I raise my head to look at her. "I could say the same."

Moyo

"DO YOU NEED ANYTHING?" NIYI ASKS AS HE PLAYS WITH A strand of my hair, the curl wrapping around his fingers in a practiced rhythm.

I raise my head from his chest, pulling my attention away from his soothing heartbeat and devoting it to his handsome face.

"Any more wine?" I ask.

"Of course. Coming right up, Gorgeous."

I do a double take. "Now, who's Gorgeous?"

He barely chuckles; instead, a gust of wind erupts from his nose. "So sorry, *Sunshine*," he corrects, and I smile at him. "It's barely been twenty-four hours, and you'll only answer to that now?"

"Don't introduce me to things you can't maintain," I say.

"Duly noted. Now let me go get you that wine. Red or white? Or rosé?"

"Red, please."

As soon as he leaves, the cold sets in, and I put on a black sweater I find strewn across a chair.

"Keep it." Niyi's voice startles me, and I jump.

"Sorry for scaring you." He laughs. "It's just—wow!" He drops the open bottle of Pinot Noir and two wine glasses on his bedside table, then grabs my hips. "Please, keep the sweater. It looks better on you." He wets his lips, and I lean in for another kiss.

This time, the kiss is sweet. Our hands roam, but it's not a frenzy. We're no longer filled with insatiable hunger. We're full, but still indulging because who doesn't like a sweet treat?

We land back on his bed, and I pull back from the kiss. We switch to a comfortable resting position with him seated, resting against the backboard, and me in between his legs.

After Cole, I honestly didn't expect to find someone else. I thought that after finding The One and promptly losing him, I'd never experience the love I always craved. But now, as I rest my head on Niyi's broad chest and he plays with my hair, I know that Cole couldn't have been my soulmate. I've met someone who makes me feel seen and cared for in ways I never knew existed.

With an overwhelmingly full heart, I reach across Niyi for the wine bottle. I pour two glasses and hand him one.

"To us?" I raise my glass cautiously, because is there even an us? We haven't spoken about it in specific terms, but it feels natural to say.

Niyi raises his. "To us." The steadiness in his voice reassures me that we'll figure it out.

There's no set plan, but I'm leaning into this because perfection has led me nowhere. One thing is certain—how happy Niyi makes me. It's a little terrifying, abandoning my dating plan, but an *us* feels inevitable. Written in the stars.

Grounding myself back in the moment, I clink my glass with his and take a sip. After two more glasses and a greedy amount of kisses, my stomach growls.

"Small chops? Or I still have leftovers from the Nigerian restaurant a few days ago?" Niyi offers.

In the past whirlwind of a day, I forgot I'd bumped into him at Anjie's. "What's left?"

"Mercury couldn't finish their food, so I brought home their leftover jollof," he says.

"They were at Anjie's restaurant? Was this a *Cupid's Bow* meeting?" I ask. Anjie's gonna freak out when I tell her Mercury was in her private dining room while we were chatting in the kitchen.

"Your friend I met last night? She owns that place?" Niyi asks, bewildered.

"Small world, huh?"

"First, we live close to each other, now my cousin's favorite restaurant is owned by your friend. Extremely small."

I do a double take. "Mercury is your cousin?"

"That's part of what I wanted to talk about," Niyi says.

Remembering our first meeting with Mercury and the tidbits Niyi has mentioned about his relationship with his father, I say, "Is that why you were awkward in that first meeting? You don't get along with family in general?"

"How about we get you something to eat first? This might be a long conversation."

My interest in the *Cupid's Bow* familial organization negates my hunger.

"No, I'd love to hear this," I say excitedly, but Niyi's sullen expression tempers my buzz.

"Aside from Merc, my family owns the company," Niyi begins.

I nod, listening intently.

"My dad used to work as one of the matchmakers till he retired about two years ago, and I took over his position."

"You're a nepo baby? Got it." I say, wrapping my head around things.

Niyi lets out a soft chuckle. "Yes. The other thing is...I don't know how to explain this without sounding downright ridiculous."

I take his hand, my concern brewing. "Explain it however. I'm listening."

"Okay," Niyi huffs, "Mercury is not their actual name or simply a moniker. It's their title."

"Title?"

"Stay with me here. This is where things sound like something out of a book."

"Niyi, please go on." I'm trying to remain calm, but my anxiety is starting to spike.

"Every planet has an essence, and some people here on earth embody the planets," Niyi says.

"Elaborate."

"My family is one of these vessels for the planets. Merc is Mercury...and I'm Saturn."

Am I drunk? Is this all a weird dream? When I thought Niyi looked godly when naked, I didn't mean it literally.

"Let me get this straight...you're saying you and Mercury are the planets that orbit the sun in the sky."

"In many ways, yes. Not literally of course, we're not billions of years old. We're conduits with the ability to harness the planets' qualities."

"So, how are you the planets then?" I ask, trying to make sense of the unimaginable. I hope he's joking.

"The mantles have been passed down our bloodlines for generations," he explains, deadly serious.

He believes every ridiculous word...great! Instead of falling for a cheater, I fell for one of the "we wuz kangz" hoteps. But instead of believing his family descended from Egyptian pharaohs, he thinks he's from the cosmos.

My eyes narrow. "Prove it."

Niyi chugs the wine left in his glass and then reaches for the half-empty bottle of Pinot.

"Okay, what do you know about Saturn?" His serious tone reminds me of the cold Niyi I first met, and not the man who'd ask "how high" if I said "jump."

It reminds me of the change in Cole's demeanor the night he walked in with his wife.

This can't be happening again.

"Lessons, maturity, longevity." The list comes out automatic, devoid of my usual brightness.

"Amazing," Niyi says, offering a wide smile that feels more like him, but garners no reaction from me. "So, we have powers. Everyone has different capabilities, and one of mine is time." He pauses and rests his palms on the bottle. I'm unsure what he's doing, but he has the same hardened concentration of kids who visit the hospital for constipation.

His breathing slows until I no longer see the soft lift of his chest. My medical training kicks in. His grip on the bottle is strong and unrelenting, despite my efforts to separate the two. I check his neck for a pulse and I feel it thudding, but it fades with each beat.

"Niyi, wake up!" I yell, rubbing his sternum. Nothing.

I lift his eyelids and examine his pupils with my phone's flashlight. Unresponsive.

What the fuck is going on?

"Niyi!" I put my hand to his lips and feel soft exhalations. Good, he's still breathing. He's alive but unresponsive.

"I don't have my car, but everything will be all right. I'm here, and I'll be taking you to a hospital. I don't know if you can hear me, but I'm taking you to a hospital," I repeat. Instead of calling 911—insurance rarely ever covers it—I order an Uber.

Right before I confirm the destination, Niyi gasps.

I scream, "Thank God! What the fuck, Niyi? You scared the living daylights outta me. I thought you were—"

"I'm sorry for scaring you," he says. "But I've aged up the wine."

"What?" I say and swiftly cancel the Uber request.

"I can manipulate time in objects. Wine has been my favorite test subject. Try it and see if it tastes the same." His voice comes out strained, and not in a good way.

Niyi hands me his glass after pouring a hearty amount. Part of me doesn't want to taste it because what he's saying is impossible, but another part is intrigued.

I take a sip, and instead of the basic red wine from earlier, it has an even richer flavor than my Tignanello. For extra measure, I take another sip of my almost empty glass and return to Niyi's new pour. I repeat this series of motions like a wind-up doll with one setting. And just like the automaton, I return to the same conclusion, back to my starting point.

"It's true," I whisper in utter disbelief.

"Yeah, it's true," Niyi confirms.

"You're gods?"

"Technically, yes."

The truth only creates further questions. "So, *Cupid's Bow* not using an algorithm is true?"

"For the matches Merc, and our other cousin Vee—Venus—set up, yes."

Here I thought it was a marketing gimmick.

I play back Niyi's words. He mentioned Mercury and Venus, but what about him? "Do you make matches too?" I ask, and he rubs his nape, as he does in awkward situations.

"As Saturn, I used an algorithm because up until literally yesterday, I didn't have full control of my powers."

"You just said…" I peter off, confused. First, he has powers, now he's saying he doesn't have powers.

"I was given the role, but unlike Merc and the rest of my family, I couldn't get a handle on it. Probably because I hated it. I never wanted to be Saturn, except when I was a kid."

"So, what changed? Why do you now have full control to go comatose aging wine?"

"You."

That knocks the wind out of me. "Me?"

"My cousins have always said our powers are connected to our emotional state. I thought conceding to my father's wishes and trying my hardest at the job would suffice, but I've struggled for months. Until last night, when I stopped pushing aside my feelings for you," Niyi explains.

I'm speechless.

"You reminded me that I needed to do me and choose my path, even if it's contrary to what I've been brought up to do. Using my full powers has been the scariest experience of my life, as you saw," he says. "I never want to experience it again."

"So what? You're quitting *Cupid's Bow*?"

"Quitting the job won't be enough. I've been figuring out a way to get rid of everything."

"Everything, meaning your powers?"

"Yes."

"What does that mean for us?" I ask, my voice shaking. "What if you can't get rid of them?" The image of his unresponsive body fills my head.

"I will," Niyi says, determined.

That's not enough. "But what happens if you don't?"

Niyi takes a deep breath. "I wouldn't feel right doing that to you. I can't expect you to be with someone who won't be around due to his job. I know what it's like to be raised by such a man, and I refuse to repeat the cycle."

"That means..." Realization hits. I went against my better judgement only for things to end.

"I'll find a way. Moyo, I promise you." Niyi takes my hands. Where I'm unsure, he's unwavering. The determination emanating from his every pore should bestow me with faith, but unfortunately, I can't muster it. Once bitten, twice shy.

I pull my hands away.

"I need a moment. Or several," I say, getting out of bed. I retrieve my dress from the floor.

"I understand," Niyi says sadly.

Niyi follows me to the living room as I don my coat. He even opens the door for me.

"I'm not giving up on us, Moyo. Take all the time you need, but please don't give up on me."

With a stony face, I say, "Okay," unsure if that's even the truth.

What the hell am I supposed to do with a god who goes into unconscious states?

Moyo

I TEXTED THE GIRLS SOS AS SOON AS I GOT HOME. IT'S EX-hausting and slightly embarrassing to keep having relationship problems. It's even more embarrassing to have relationship problems with a guy I wasn't dating.

Anjie comes in holding two plastic bowls of goat meat pepper soup. She beelines for the kitchen, no trace of fatigue even as it nears midnight, while Sewa takes in my fallen face.

"What's wrong?" Sewa asks. When I don't say anything, she pulls me in for a tight hug. "Moyosore, talk to me."

"Let's sit," I say.

I guide the girls to my room, and they look at me as I gather the words.

Anjie speaks up. "Ready to tell us what happened?"

I relay the new information I learned, and their jaws drop. A pregnant silence fills the air as they process what I'm still trying to wrap my head around.

"I know, right?" I ask bitterly.

Sewa waves her hands in a circular motion. "Wait, so you mean to tell me you've been messing with the shadow man?" she deadpans.

"Can you be serious?" Anjie attempts to chide her, but she cackles. I burst out laughing as well. The laughter soothes my aching heart.

"She's laughing," Sewa whispers, obviously pleased with herself. I give her another hug. You can only laugh at the ridiculousness of this entire situation.

"He was very charismatic," I croak, recalling the line from *The Princess and the Frog*. Sewa made us watch it one night in college when we'd been reminiscing about Disney movies and Anjie and I confessed we'd never seen it.

Anjie gets our ice cream from the freezer, and I nuzzle into Sewa's embrace.

"I feel like a fool," I confess when Anjie comes back.

"Why?" Anjie lowers herself back onto the rug.

"I fell for another liar."

"Babes." Sewa shakes me gently, and it clears Niyi from my mind.

"Hmm?"

"You're not a fool. Especially not for getting to know someone for almost two months before sleeping with him." Sewa strokes the edges of my hairline.

I can't help but blame myself. Two months of interacting with this guy, and I didn't see it. I even mentioned his downright godly looks, and I didn't see it.

I tell them as much, and Anjie hisses a long, winding hiss that transports me back to Lagos.

"Anjola," Sewa warns.

"I need to say this," Anjie says with an edge, and I grunt my approval, preparing myself because I know whatever is about to come out of her mouth won't be pretty.

"You aren't a fool. You didn't see it because you didn't know. How were you supposed to know? No one would've guessed regular-ass people have the spirits of celestial bodies."

"But—"

"Let me finish," Anjie says. "He told you the truth the moment it looked like things would become serious, right?"

I nod begrudgingly. "I don't get how you're so chill about this."

Anjie exhales, "Because you were happy, Moyo—aside from this, you were happy. I don't care if you end up with the fucking Loch Ness monster, if it makes you happy. Unlike previous times, you haven't been performing joy and ticking boxes. You've been living! And for that, I would say this burgeoning relationship may be good for you."

"*Great* for you!" Sewa adds. "Plus, he said he's finding a way to end the whole thing."

"Also, when I found him here last night, he seemed way more polite and respectful than Cole ever was," Anjie mentions, and I wince because Sewa's eyes bulge. I have so much to update her on.

My head tilts back to rest on my bed frame. I'm not ready to listen to them, so I stare at the ceiling and tune them out. I understand where she's coming from. Realistically, there's no way I could've known if he hadn't told me, minus the comatose state. And if he hadn't, I would've kept falling for him. Part of me feels like I should've known, the same way I should've known about Cole. I'm tired of being blindsided and not being in control when it's my life.

"I want some control over my life." I sigh.

"And you have that. You left and you called us. That's what you can control," Anjie says.

"I need more than that. The men I choose constantly disappoint me, and I'm tired of it."

"Niyi isn't like the others," Sewa says.

"Not one bit. You didn't find out the truth. He told you. He trusted you with a secret that could change his life and the entire app," Anjie says. "For the first time, you aren't the only vulnerable one."

"And that's what a relationship is, sharing vulnerabilities. Even the scary parts," Sewa says.

They're right. I chuckle. The first time a man has disclosed something serious, it's that he's part-god. I start laughing wildly, and my friends exchange a look.

"Everything all right?" Anjie asks cautiously.

I try to stop laughing, but each time I think about the situation, a new wave of laughter hits. I fell for a god. A god who hates being a god. A god who, if he can't stop being a god, I'll lose. The first guy I've been truly excited to date.

"My life is like a bad CW show," I say through fits of laughter. That makes the girls go from concerned to laughing as well.

When I finally calm down, Sewa asks, "Are you sure you're good? What if he can't *not* be a god?"

"Then...I'll try again," I say, and Anjie all but hollers. "I know what I want in a partner. I'm sure I can figure things out."

The past few months have been a rollercoaster, but I can confidently say I'm not who I was at the beginning—I'm better for it.

"Thank god we've stopped the 'I no longer believe in love' thing," Anjie says, and I roll my eyes.

"Since I've stopped, you have to stop pretending you and Mike aren't a thing," I fire back.

"Here we go." Anjie sighs.

"Did you know she's going on a reality TV show with Mike?" I say to Sewa.

"Wait, what?"

"Moyo!" Anjie yells, trying to push me over, but Sewa blocks her.

"Well, Moyo should tell you how she and Niyi were fornicating on the couch yesterday," Anjie counters.

"Anjola, one matter at a time," I shush.

Sewa laughs at our bickering. "Guess now is the perfect time to tell y'all I dropped out of grad school."

Anjie and I freeze like it's a game of Simon Says.

"Yep. Decided right after Thanksgiving break."

"Spill," Anjie demands.

I ask, "Why didn't you say anything?"

"I wanted to sort things out for myself..." Sewa begins.

For the rest of the night, we take turns sharing the eventful, dramatic moments of our lives over ice cream.

30

Moyo

EVERYTHING REMINDS ME OF HIM. AND I HATE IT.

Well, that is not entirely true because I've spent the day sprawled on the couch, reminiscing about our time together. If I truly hated Niyi, I would've gotten the couch replaced, or at least cleaned to rid my comfort zone of his scent. But I can't because it's been only two days, and I'm trying Anjie's whole "feel your feelings" thing, so I miss him.

I miss Niyi. And I'm learning that's okay. It's not a moral failing. I'm not weak. I just miss the man I was falling for, who has somehow fallen off the face of the earth. Not that I expected him to show up at my house boom box-style, but the silence has been unpredictable.

I wonder what he's up to? Is he truly going to relinquish his powers? Or is this his way of ghosting me?

The questions crowd my mind, and unlike most situations in life, I don't have any answers. But like I told the girls, I'll be fine. Niyi or no Niyi.

The doorbell blares, launching me out of my moping. I pause the afternoon's background movie, *Saw*, and slowly get off the couch. It isn't until the second ring that my curiosity piques.

Could it be Niyi? I know the girls aren't coming over, and I didn't order anything. A spark of hope begins to crackle.

I open the door and the spark fails to thrive. I come face-to-face with Cole. And he's carrying another bouquet of fuck-ass roses.

He stops my attempt to slam the door with his foot. "Moyo, please hear me out."

"Leave." I push the door harder, crushing his foot. He winces. Unlike the Cole I knew, this man has facial hair now. A bushy mix of dark and light strands. His eyes look even more sunken than before. If I didn't recognize his voice, and his propensity for roses, I might've wondered who it was.

"I made a mistake. It's taken me months to admit it, but I fucked up. You were kind, sweet. You took care of me, and I took you for granted," Cole pleads, his voice wavering on each word. The same tone he used to have when he'd be apologetic about a last-minute cancellation.

I'm not sold. In fact, the spark is back and it's burning quick and hot in anger. I should stop his meaningless ramblings, but I'm curious about how he intends to spin this in his favor, so I let him continue.

"I broke up with Clarisse," he says, and I raise a brow. "My life has been colorless without you. I should have told her the truth that night. I should've stood by you, but I was scared. I made a mistake. But I'm not scared anymore. I know what I need in life, and that's you, Moyo. Please, what can I do to show you I've changed? I promise, if you give me this chance, I'll never take you for granted again."

His blue eyes shine with hope. He gives me a crooked smile and pushes the roses closer to me.

"Cole," I say, and his name no longer sounds like a prayer. It's a curse, and he notices. His brows scrunch and he frowns.

"First, I hate roses."

"But—"

"Second, she left you, didn't she?"

He looks away, confirming my suspicions. "I'm here now, Moyo. I'm here for you."

"Leave." Done with the conversation, I push the door, and he stops it again. This time with his hand. It takes everything in me not to slam the door and break his fingers.

"Moyo, we're made for each other. I'm single, you're single. Like *Cupid's Bow* said, we're soulmates."

I can't help but laugh in his face. "Maybe if this was hell. You're single because you're a cheating dick." My anger is on full display now. He has so much fucking nerve coming here and spouting this shit. "You're not my soulmate, and even if you were, I'd rather die than be with you. Leave. I swear to God, if I have to tell you one more time..."

"You have a boy—?"

"As if that matters," I sneer.

Cole's eyes brighten, a smile tugs at the corner of his lips. "See Moyo, we're meant for each other. You say you'd rather die, but I know that's not true. You're a romantic. You love the company. The comfort. The sex," he smirks, and I wrinkle my nose. "We were good together...easy. I know you, Moyo."

He's right. I did love the comfort, the company, the sex. And our relationship *was* easy, but that's because there was nothing there. It was more akin to an empty dollhouse on display. Looks like the real deal but is truly made of cardboard.

Cole beams in anticipation. His chest is puffed out and shoulders rolled back. The little bitch still thinks he's got it. He still believes I'm the woman he knew, who cared more about the label of love than the action.

"Cole..." He leans in, his smile taking root. "You must be out of your goddamn mind." His smile slacks. "Like I said, I would rather be single for the rest of my life—a hundred cats and all—than be with you."

"You don't mean—"

"Oh, I do. You think I'm still like you, searching for someone to give life meaning because being alone is too suffocating. Your inability to face your pathetic self has brought you to my doorstep, and I know you've spent the last few months praying that I remained the same. Well, sorry to burst your bubble, but I know what a real partnership looks like now."

Cole takes a step back, blinking rapidly, like a computer going into overdrive, before settling on one emotion.

He clears his throat in a last-ditch effort to change my mind. "You'll regret this," he says with an air of superiority.

"Like you regret your existence? Hmm, I'll pass." I shrug. "Now get the fuck out my neighborhood."

"Moyo—"

"Say my name one more time and I promise you'll regret it."

The useless guy holds my impenetrable gaze, once again searching for an in. But seconds pass with the only change being the increased tension in my jaw.

Cole looks away, stumbling backwards towards his parked car.

Still by my door, I watch him to make sure he leaves. He tosses the bouquet into the backseat before moving to the driver's door.

"Cole," I call out and his head juts up. "Fuck you."

Niyi

"Did you find them yet?" I burst into the *Cupid's Bow* conference room, expecting to find Merc and Vee, but there's a third person. The last person I expected to see—my dad.

"Why is he here?" I ask. Merc was supposed to find someone willing to take over the Saturn mantle, not bring my father to headquarters.

"Saturn," my dad says with his gruff voice. It's the first time I've heard it since the transfer ceremony.

The formality I grew up with threatens to come back, but I discard it. This isn't the time. Especially not for the man who might've ruined my life with this role.

"It's Niyi," I correct.

Dad raises his brows and erupts in a slow clap. I look behind him at Merc and Vee, who are also confused. "You're Saturn. I'm proud, my son."

Proud? He's proud.

I've wanted his pride and validation my entire life, especially after Mom passed. Even when I disliked him. Even when we didn't talk. Even as I moped about joining *Cupid's Bow*. Deep down, I wanted his praise. Aside from being the only one for the job, it's part of why I stayed. But to hear it now feels hollow.

"I'm not." I clench my jaw. Here goes nothing. "I am the worst Saturn there will ever be. It took me almost two years to unlock The Sight."

"It takes everyone different amounts of time," Dad scoffs. "Like Saturn, low and slow. You're a natural. Don't throw it away because things have been a little hard."

"I've been faking it the whole time. It wasn't that reading the charts was taking me time. I developed an algorithm," I reveal, but no one looks shocked.

Vee speaks up. "We knew from the beginning. Sorry, Niyi."

"What?"

"We knew you were out of practice, living away from the family and all, so we double-checked your work," Merc explains.

"And your pairings were basic," Vee deadpans.

All this time...they knew. They saw I was anxious and trying my hardest to keep up and they didn't cut me any slack.

"You were trying so hard. We didn't want to embarrass you," Vee says.

Wow.

"So why show me the complaint?"

"You were wasting away. The Sight is activated by action, so to give you someth—" Vee begins.

My dad cuts her off. "They informed me about your progress and asked for my advice." I shoot Vee and Merc death glares. "You are my son. I knew you needed motivation, so I asked them to find something in the complaints. We always get highly emotional complaints."

My head throbs.

I look to Vee and Merc. "So, your argument that day...the thing about the board?"

"Not entirely true." Vee winces. "The Board has been stricter since Uncle left, but we negotiated other things. All our new charity and community endeavors. One complaint wasn't going to make or break things, but we thought we were doing what was best for you and the family. Again, sorry, Niyi."

I can't believe what I'm hearing. All this work was to make sure I wouldn't let them down. I didn't want to be the shit Saturn for the perfect Mercury and Venus, but it didn't even matter.

My dad clears his throat. "And it was the best thing. We have a Saturn again. You unlocked The Sight, and that's what matters. You're doing well, my son. Don't give it up because of a woman."

The venom with which he speaks pisses me off.

"She's not just any woman," I say, and he wrinkles his nose and waves his arm in the air like he's swatting away flies.

"And you can have both. You don't have to discard your birthright. I know in the past Saturns have ended up alone or divorced, but I had both. You are my son. So, it will happen to you too."

His words don't make any sense to me.

"You were barely there."

That shuts him up.

I continue. "You were obsessed with your work. With having The Sight and floating through time. You barely committed to human reality. I tried to get your attention, to alert you that something was wrong with Mom, but it was impossible. You never cared about us, but somehow when Mom passed, it became worse. You stopped living."

"Watch your tongue! I was always there when your mother was alive, and after she died, I did my best. I put myself to work and provided for you. You went to the best schools and lived a good life. Now it's your turn to give back." My father's gesticulation is wild, and his volume increases.

Luckily, the conference room is soundproof.

Vee and Merc watch, hearing snippets of the ugly truth I wasn't ready to share days ago.

"A child needs more than an ATM. And I don't care about The Sight. I don't feel the buzz—"

"It'll come," he interrupts. "You'll come to appreciate it." He ignores my childhood pain, but I'm not even upset. I don't expect him to acknowledge it.

"I won't because I hate the feeling. The Sight allegedly elicits euphoria, but I feel worse off." My volume has also increased. It's greater than his, and he's forced to listen. Dad watches me with intense eyes that mirror my own.

"Merc," I call, and they perk up. "Remember when you told me I had used The Sight?" They nod. "That happened because I was thinking about doing something I love. Making art and thinking about the woman I care for. I'm not very good at this Saturn thing, but I'm good at those two things."

Vee nods, and I continue. "I'm grateful I got the role because it forced me to move here, meet Moyo, create more art, and build an actual relationship with my cousins." Vee and Merc look bashful. "But I think that's my extent of being Saturn."

My dad kisses his teeth. "I understand," he says softly, and my eyes almost pop out of my skull. "You love her, you like making your bowls or whatever, and you like your cousins. But why give up working with the cousins you now adore? You can do your job, love her, and make bowls in your spare time—as you're currently doing. Regardless of what you think, your mother and I understood each other. I showed love in my way, and she loved me in hers."

He's right. It's confused me most of my adult life, but he's right. My mother did love him till her last breath. She was fine with him living in the stars, but I wasn't. I've tried to be him, tried to be Saturn while at *Cupid's Bow*, but knowing how the power manifests, I know it'll cost me my life.

"It worked for you, but it's not good enough for me. I don't want to be a slave to time. I want to move with it. I want to live. Ever since I joined *Cupid's Bow*, I haven't lived. I abandoned most things I love in an effort to keep up. That isn't life."

"You plan to give up your birthright?" He's horrified.

"I stopped wanting it after I saw what you became. You gave it up for a reason—"

"But you accepted it. Like me after your mother, your heart was broken. Working helped me, and clearly, it's helped you too."

"I thought I had no other choice. I even thought maybe I'd like it. But neither of those things happened. Instead, I discovered new things to care about—a woman I'd love to be with, a possible job that won't involve living in front of a screen, and a section of this family that truly is family. Isn't that ultimately what Saturn does? Teaches you lessons that force changes?"

Vee and Merc nod their agreement, but my dad isn't amused.

"And what if this girl doesn't accept you for you, since you don't accept yourself? What if your artwork doesn't sell?" The words have some sting, but it doesn't hurt.

"Then I'll keep living. Each day I'm alive and not enslaved to time is another chance at my happiness. So even if Moyo and I don't work out, or I learn my work isn't up to par, I'd at least have the strength to carry on. And trust me, it's easier to work and forge new relationships without waiting to drop the 'I'm a god' bomb."

"I can't watch you throw away your life." He shakes his head.

"You don't have to watch. I've already made up my mind." I give him a solemn smile, but anger lingers in his eyes.

"Don't call me when you regret this," he huffs, brushing past me.

"I won't call you. Period."

I watch him walk away. I expect to feel conflicted, but I only feel peace.

Vee walks up to me. "Are you all right?" she asks cautiously, probably wondering if I'm upset with her and Merc. I want to be mad at them for manipulating me, but I wouldn't have met Moyo without their interference. Maybe that's the natural *Cupid's Bow* effect.

"I'm better than expected. But I'd love to be rid of this thing. Merc, tell me you found someone willing to work with you and Vee?"

"First of all, anyone would be grateful to work with us," Merc says. "To answer your question, yes, I did. Finding the specific Jakande family was near impossible, till I called Moon. Turns out she inherited a master list of the celestial families. And in case you're wondering, it's a tome."

I hug them. "Thank you." Vee joins in, making it a three-way hug.

"You're suffocating me," Merc wheezes.

Vee and I pull back, and Merc bends at the waist.

"Inhaler?" I ask Vee.

"It's in their office. I'll be right back."

Merc stands upright before Vee gets the chance to leave the room. "Just fucking with y'all."

"Not funny," Vee says, straight-faced.

"C'mon, it was funny. Right, Niyi?" Merc asks.

I fold my arms, mirroring Vee's stance.

"Tough crowd," Merc murmurs. "Well, let's get going to find our new Saturn. Hopefully the next one appreciates my sense of humor."

I roll my eyes. Merc is ridiculous, but I would be lying if I said I wouldn't miss working with Vee and them.

We step out of the pink-and-purple *Cupid's Bow* building. Taking in the sight the final time as Saturn, I say to my family, "A part of me will miss us working together."

"Awwww," Vee coos. "Don't worry, we're at your house most of the time anyways."

Wait.

"Speaking of, I need to borrow some wine bottles for a Restauranter event I'm hosting," Merc says.

"I should probably get you your own key," I say to Merc. I made Vee a copy after the third time she called asking for my whereabouts.

"Made a copy of Vee's, no worries," Merc says, and Vee laughs at my perplexed reaction.

"You're never getting rid of us, cuz," Vee says as we get to Merc's parking spot.

Two years ago, I would've protested. But now, post-Saturn, I wouldn't have it any other way.

32

Moyo

IT'S BEEN THREE WEEKS SINCE I HEARD FROM NIYI. AND I'M okay. The girls no longer mention him. I've been spending every waking hour at the hospital or working on getting more pro bono work approved.

I cashed in the *Cupid's Bow* check, bought a new couch ('cause the girls adamantly refused to use the other one, even after I got it cleaned), deleted the app from my phone, and started seeing a therapist for my relationship trauma. Dr. Whitney and Yaz have been appalled at how much I've been working, but they think I'll get the Clinical Excellence award at the gala tonight. All in all, I'm okay.

I'm staring at my gala dress when the door opens. Anjie's still in her apron, and Sewa looks stunning in a simple, black, sweetheart-neckline, floor-length gown.

"Why aren't you dressed?" I ask, taking the wine bottle from Anjie.

"I don't think I can make it," she says, and my face falls. "At least not at the beginning. I'm almost done with the final recipe test. I need to nail it before tomorrow evening."

Of all days for Anjola to have a kitchen-related emergency, it had to be this one. We squealed when we found out the date for her big event was the day after mine. But as the weeks neared, it became more and more evident that Anjie, the perfectionist, would need every last second to get ready for her shot on the reality TV show.

I shoo her away. "Run back to the kitchen. I'll see you when I see you." I kiss one cheek, and Sewa does the same on the other.

She hurries back into the driveway, Mike's keys jingling in her hand.

"By the way, I got you a date," she calls out before entering the vehicle. "Sewa will give you all the details after you get ready. Mwah. Love you!" The door slams shut, and she reverses before I can cuss her out.

Despite their thoughts and well-wishes, I don't need a date for this event or any event. Niyi is a thing of the past, and I'm taking a well-deserved dating break for peace of mind. I should've done this after Cole, but that hiatus would've been out of fear and resignation.

Like my dad said on our Christmas Day phone call: "Take your time. It's never too late for love." Right before attempting to set me up with some new co-worker's nephew.

"I promise, the guy is cute, and we vetted his suit." Sewa drags me back inside to get started on my makeup.

My white dress has a semi-sweetheart neckline and gorgeous, crystal-encrusted piping along the bodice. The cinched waist lines up perfectly with my natural waistline, and to add to the glamour, I've paired it with a white, faux-fur stole. The best way to attract money from donors is to look like money. I already have the silver shoes and accessories picked out, so Sewa helps with my hair and makeup. After an intense wash day, I placed my thick hair in heatless rollers last night. With Sewa's help, taking off the rollers is easy, and styling them into a wavy, old-Hollywood-esque style takes us less time than anticipated.

"All done!" Sewa exclaims, and I open my eyes to take in her handiwork. My makeup is flawless, the eyebags from sleepless nights poring over paperwork and intake forms are gone, and I look bright. Most importantly, I look like myself.

"You're a miracle worker," I say, hugging her. "Have you thought of doing this professionally?"

"Makeup or styling?"

"Both."

"It's on the table. Everything's on the table till after I rest up and recover from decades of academia-induced burnout."

"You'll let me know if I can help in any way?" I ask.

"I will," Sewa says. "Now, let me show you the guy." She pulls out her phone, and at another time, I might've been moved. In the photo, he's in front of a body of water, hair trimmed nicely but still sporting some length. His honey-brown skin glistens in the sunlight, and his face is all right—robust features, a sharp jaw. All regular things from a Black man; he's not special.

"He's cool," I say, applying another layer of gloss.

"Cool?" Sewa asks. When I nod, she says nothing more.

"Where's he meeting us? Here or there?"

Sewa looks me over, taking in her hard work. "Moyo, you are too fine! Again, I can be your date. Since you're not keen on this guy."

"As I told you, I'm not keen on any guy, and I said he's okay."

"Yeah, yeah. He's meeting us there." She checks her watch. "Oh, shit. Where is time running to?"

· ⁺ ＊ ♄ ＊ ⁺ ·

The Boston Hospital Foundation Gala is hosted in a large conference space next to the hospital in case someone needs to be called for an emergency. The alcohol at the event is mainly for donors and guests. The medical staff must always be alert, so instead we sip on sparkling cider and make the donors think we're indulging like them. No one cashes out like drunk people.

We meet the guy, Alex, at the door. He's a perfect gentleman, who I can admit looks better in person in his handsome black tuxedo. He's now sporting a buzz cut with a mustache and a little goatee.

Once we find our table, I leave Sewa and Alex to make my laps around the room. After spending countless minutes discussing the importance of early intervention across the different domains I work in—language delays, learning disorders, and neurodevelopmental differences like ADHD and autism—numerous donors bring out their checkbooks.

I'm making another lap around the room, watching for breaks in conversation or, better yet, a swarm of donors with too much drink and not enough conversation, when a voice draws my attention.

"You're even more magnetic in your element," a cool voice says from behind me, and I come face-to-face with someone I never expected to see. They extend a hand. I, and the countless people around me who stop and stare, recognize their face—it's Mercury.

"Vinny Carr." I plaster a smile and shake their hand.

Their smile is wide, every single tooth on display. They smell divine, a woody yet floral scent. If I wasn't so shocked, I would ask what it was. They have on all black and a jacket with abundant gold detailing. Their locs are in an intricate bun on the top of their head. They look regal and important.

"Moyo, darling. We're already well-acquainted. No need for formalities. Call me Mercury or Merc, whatever you prefer."

Their presence is a surprise, but not an entirely unwelcome one. I scan the room for another face, to no avail. Mercury watches me, their bright smile unwavering.

"Mercury, can I interest you in donating to the early intervention fund for Black children?" This is the first time this evening I have mentioned the specifics of the fund. White donors can be finicky when they learn their money isn't going to their demographic.

Before they can answer, the hospital's CEO taps into the microphone.

"Unfortunately, that's my cue. Please excuse me, Moyo." Mercury walks off before I register their words.

"Good evening, everyone, and thank you for joining us in raising money for children's healthcare at this year's Boston Hospital Foundation Gala," the CEO says, and applause fills the room. He drones on about the importance of research and development in advancing medical practices and technology. He also goes off-script and announces the staff recognition award super early. Typically, it's done towards the end of the night.

"This year, we've decided to bestow the Clinical Excellence award earlier because a special guest has graciously offered to present a grant to this year's recipient," he announces, and the crowd livens up. The buzz among the staff is incredible. Yaz's words come to mind, and for a second, I imagine winning it. But I'd never win because of who I am and, most importantly, how much pushback I give the administration.

"To present the award, I call on our sponsor, Vincent Carr."

I can't believe my ears. As if we're connected, my eyes find Sewa's.

"No way," she mouths, and I gesture, "*I know, right?*"

Accompanying Mercury is a gorgeous woman, who I'm guessing is Venus. She holds the massive check, looking radiant in her mustard dress.

"The name's Vinny, not Vincent, by the way," Mercury says, and the CEO turns redder than rodo. "My family and I"—Mercury begins and gestures to Venus, who grins—"are very interested in improving people's lives, especially those of children. Changing lives requires a lot of money, expertise, and most importantly, time."

I look around for the Master of Time himself, but I only see Sewa, my blind date, and surprisingly, Anjie coming towards me. The girls put their hands on my shoulders, and I kiss the backs of their hands. I'm no longer checking for Niyi. These two are my pillars. Come rain, come sun, they're always here. The guy they set me up with, whose name I've already forgotten, gives me a curt smile.

"We cannot give these deserving children more time or expertise; you're the professionals in the room," Mercury jokes, and everyone—except us—laughs on cue. "But we can donate money." Another round of laughter. "Along with my lovely cousin, I'm happy to present this year's Clinical Excellence award recipient with a check for one hundred thousand dollars to invest in their practice."

The "wows" in the room are hushed, but they echo. Mercury pauses to give people time to collect themselves.

"Hopefully that is enough to impact some change in this world," Mercury says.

After my first year at the hospital, I knew not to get my hopes up about winning the award because they would never give it to a person like me—headstrong, always pushing back against admin, and focused more on patient satisfaction than productivity. This year is no different, but getting money towards my work sounds like a dream. There's so much I could do. Too much research on pediatric developmental issues is focused on white children, and there's barely anything on the Black children of the world. But with access to funds like this? I could do surveys and adequately compensate people.

I could open a clinic.

Once the idea enters my mind, it's a done deal. A clinic to better serve minority populations in Dorchester and Roxbury, where most of my pro bono clients have been from. Fuck the need for insurance or for patients and their families paying out of pocket. Or even worse, fighting red tape. A free clinic is what I'll build if I get the money. It's decided.

"Without further ado, since I can see you're all vibrating in your seats"— Mercury pauses for the wave of laughter, nervous this time—"the grant recipient, for her stellar work, as recommended by her peers and bosses, is Dr. Moyo Adegbite."

It doesn't register as my name till Sewa nudges me and Anjie says, "Girl, get on stage."

Anjie and Sewa practically carry me to the stage, where I hug Mercury and Venus.

"Thank you," I say, addressing the crowd. The spotlight makes it hard to see anyone below the stage. "This is an honor. I'm so grateful to *Cupid's Bow* for this incredible donation. This money isn't only for me but for the nurses, psychologists, OTs, PTs, SLPs, neurologists, psychiatrists, and everyone else I am most likely forgetting because of my nerves and this bright spotlight," I say, and the crowd chuckles. "I can't wait to brainstorm ideas and use this money to serve our wonderful clients and offer our services to those who currently can't afford them. Again, thank you." This time, my gratitude is directed towards the two celestials.

Once I'm out of the spotlight, I am greeted by my girls and the guy.

"You were amazing up there, and now you have a shit-ton of money!" Anjie squeals.

"It's work money, it's not mine. But yes, it is a lot!"

"Knew you were going to win." Sewa beams. "Pay up." She gestures at the new guy, who reaches into his wallet and pulls out ten dollars.

"You can't help yourself, can you?" I laugh.

"I like easy money," Sewa says with a shrug.

The four of us make our way back to our table. The girls walk ahead while the guy, the one Sewa called Alex, lingers behind with me. He spends most of the time watching me accept congratulations and cheers from people as we walk to the back of the room.

"Congratulations! Your friend Sewa talked you up," he says, rubbing the back of his neck sheepishly. *Like Niyi used to do.*

"Thank you. But you should know that if you let her, she'll take you for everything you own."

Alex moves closer, allowing me to hear him better above the mingling room. "How about you? Will you let me take you out sometime?"

He's smiling at me with his nice suit and his nice manners, and he's sufficiently mingled with the overwhelming women I call family. But something is missing.

"I'm still getting over someone," I say. This is the first time I've admitted it to someone other than my friends.

"Sewa also mentioned you might say that."

Why is that girl telling everyone my business? Might have to murder her after this.

"But, when you're ready, I'd love to take you out sometime," he persists, and I can't even be mad. I hand him my phone, and let him put his number in.

Good old-fashioned dating might've been the way all along. I don't know when I'll be ready, but I like knowing all hope isn't lost.

33

Moyo

"MOYO, YOU CAN'T EXPECT ME TO BELIEVE YOU DON'T AL-
ready have a plan for the money," Anjie says, raising her volume over the
chatter of the guests. The gala is still in full swing.

"I'm sure she knows what outreach centers she wants to partner with
already," Sewa says.

"It's only been ten minutes," I laugh, and take a mental note. Outreach
centers would be good. Why didn't I think of that?

Anjie rolls her eyes. "You always have a plan for everything—" She suddenly goes quiet, and Sewa's eyes widen.

"Moyo." The voice from behind me is strong yet soft. I don't need to
turn around to know who it is, but I do anyway.

"Niyi." I keep my face neutral. I won't react before I hear what he has
to say after disappearing for weeks. Niyi, in a snowy white tux, fights
back a smile as he takes in my appearance, and I tell my muscles to do
the same.

"Hello, all." Niyi nods to Anjie and Sewa, then he scowls at Alex, who is
still on my arm. "Moyo, may I talk to you outside?" he asks politely, and
before I can answer, Alex does.

"She's here with me tonight," Alex says, unwisely entering a conversation that isn't his. I want to smack him upside the head, but the girls beat me to it. When I let go of Alex's arm, Anjie holds him by his elbow, and Sewa creates even more division between us.

Anjie, now tightening her grip on this poor man, raises a brow, giving me one of our looks. I know she's asking if I'm comfortable talking to Niyi after everything. I'd like to say I no longer care about him or what he has to say, but that'd be lying.

I nod, letting her know I'm okay.

"Please, go talk," Anjie commands. She flashes a happy smile at Niyi and me, and scowls at Alex. The duality of Yoruba women.

Niyi and I walk side by side as we exit the brightly lit event space.

"So…" I draw the word out, waiting for Niyi to explain himself. Silently hoping he says something that allows us to return to our budding relationship. The past few weeks made me realize I don't *need* him, that I'm fine without him, but I do miss him.

"I'm sorry. Let me start there," Niyi says, his voice raised as the wind howls around us.

We're the only ones in the empty back lot, and I like it that way. It might be cold, but if I have to say goodbye to Niyi, I'd rather it be where our only audience is the Dunkin' Donuts sign across the street.

"I am so sorry it's taken me this long to get back to you. To decide what I wanted to say to you. I am sorry for not telling you who I was earlier. We built our relationship on mutual understanding, and finding out I had this secret that meant we couldn't be together must've hurt."

I take a moment to digest his words because it did hurt. I won't lie. "I appreciate the apology," I say.

"I'd also like to say thank you."

"For what?"

"For giving me the space to realize what *I* wanted for my life. When I was given the Saturn role, I took it because I thought I had no choice, and I thought maybe it'd change a few things in my family dynamics. Which it did, but in unexpected ways. My dad still didn't come around, but Vee, Merc, and I are closer than ever. It also led me to meet you. You planted the seed that allowed me to step out of my father's shadow. So again, thank you, Moyo, for inspiring my new lease on life."

"Did you give it up?" I ask.

"The *Cupid's Bow* job, Saturn, all of it."

I'm stunned. "How?"

"It's a long story, but the abridged version is Merc and I traveled, pretty much across the diaspora, to find a distant relative open to taking the role. Unlike my dad and the other Saturns before him, I explained the downsides, which lengthened our search, but we found someone. She starts at *Cupid's Bow* next week."

"It took three weeks to find someone?" I ask, slightly skeptical. I have no idea where he went or how big his family is. All I know is I need more info before accepting him back with open arms.

"A week, but—and don't freak out—I slipped into a coma after transferring the powers. Woke up a few days ago. That's why I didn't reach out till now," Niyi says breezily with a sheepish smile, as if it's no big deal.

Unsure of where to begin, I ask, "Are you okay now?"

"Moon, another cousin, healed me. We weren't sure of the consequences of breaking the commitment, but luckily, since I wasn't in tune with my powers for very long, it was easier to detach."

"You're gonna have to re-explain all of this with charts and diagrams," I say, not bothering to hide my confusion.

"Absolutely."

A final question pops to mind. "Prove it. How do I know any of this is true?"

"Thought you'd never ask. Come with me? Please? I'll show you."

We walk back inside, and Niyi heads straight for my table with the girls.

"Everything good?" Sewa asks.

"TBD," I respond as Niyi grabs the open wine bottle, along with some empty glasses.

"Hey!" Anjie protests.

"I'll bring it right back, Chef," Niyi says.

We find a quiet spot in an adjacent room away from the rest of the event. Niyi pours one glass, and I take my first sip of the night.

It's a very basic wine. Despite the caliber of the event, it's cheap. It's always cheap.

Niyi laces his hand around the body of the second glass, and I wait with bated breath.

Niyi takes about the same amount of time as he did in his room, except this time his eyes don't gloss over, his breathing doesn't slow, and he doesn't slip into a frightening comatose state. Once done, he hands me the glass and watches as I tip it, waiting for the wine to reach my tongue.

Do me this solid, please, I beg whatever forces are out there. In the moment it takes for the wine to run out of the glass and reach my tongue, I realize I want Niyi to be true. I want *us* to be true.

The wine touches my tongue, and a smile takes over my face.

"It's shit?" he asks.

"It's shit!" I respond, absolutely overcome with emotion.

"Any more questions? You can also ask Vee and Merc to confirm. I know they're related to me, but you can ask. I wouldn't be offended. I don't want any more secrets between us." He looks at me breathlessly. I wonder what he's thinking.

I force down my smile. I want to scare him a little. "Two more questions."

He looks petrified but accepts.

The first question is a thought I've had ruminating that might change things, but I need to know.

"We met when you were Saturn, ruler of my seventh house. How are you sure you're the one for me? And question two: how are you sure that once this attraction, lust, infatuation, or whatever you want to call it, is all out of your system, you won't be done with me?"

Niyi doesn't even take a beat. "Because like every other bit of astrology, the stars have to align perfectly. People have to align. I'm sure I made hundreds of mistakes—trust me, I was a horrible Saturn—but the stars brought me to you."

He edges closer, hesitating, before he grabs my hand. I'm ready for him to touch me again. "Everyone has a birth chart, but when I was Saturn, you were my life chart. I was living on autopilot, trying to be someone

I was not, until we met. The first time I unlocked my full powers, I was thinking about you. You helped me realize I didn't have to be Saturn, I could just be me. You are my Sunshine. You helped brighten up the darkest time of my life. And I wouldn't have it any other way."

His forehead touches mine.

"To answer your second question, I could never be done with you even if I tried, Moyo. It's like asking if we'll ever be done with oxygen. Until my dying breath, I will be yours if you'll have me. And lastly, only you can say if I'm the one for you. But I know that you are the one for me, and I'll work every day to make sure I'm worthy of you."

The tears in my eyes threaten to fall as I process his words. For the first time in my life, someone can't stand to lose me. I'm not the only person fighting for this relationship. The foreign sensation leaves me stuck.

"Moyo. Are you okay?" Niyi asks. His tender voice brings me back into our bubble.

"Yes, one more question."

"Please."

"Did you just give up immortality for me?" It's cheesy, and he might correct me on the technicalities, but it's worth asking.

Relief washes over his features. His shoulders droop, his neck relaxes, and, most importantly, his smile returns.

"I always said I'd do anything for you. Who cares about controlling time with you at my side?" He grabs my other hand and pulls me close.

I don't hesitate as I sink into the warm body I've missed so much over the past couple of weeks. My arms go around his neck, the white of my bodice blending with his white tux. Niyi's arms find my waist, taking their rightful place. I look into his eyes, and he stares into mine.

"Can I ask *you* a question?" he asks with a goofy grin on his face.

"Sure," I giggle.

"It's almost New Year's, so I must ask, are we at the kiss-and-goodnight part of the evening? Or are we gonna wait and do a countdown on New Year's Eve?"

It takes me a moment to place the words I said to him weeks ago. "Do you remember everything I say?" I ask between fits of laughter.

"I'd be a fool not to." His arms tighten around my waist, and he pulls me even closer. "You're the light of my life, Sunshine. I'd be a fool not to place you at the center of it," he says, his voice dropping to a low bass and his eyes filling with adoration.

He leans in, and I can't contain my smile when his lips meet mine. The taste of shitty wine gives way to sweeping tongues and roaming hands.

I pull back. "Still your favorite?"

He wiggles his nose against mine. "Always and forever."

Epilogue

Date #4

Niyi

I'M NOT BUILT FOR THIS LIFE. THE CREDITS OF OUR THIRD two-hour movie roll and so does my back. I know I was insistent on the movie marathon, but I grossly underestimated the mental fortitude and resilience needed to watch four straight movies.

Moyo has been easing me into it with her twelve-week, specially-curated "Make-Niyi-Fall-in-Love-with-Horror" course. The initial plan was to have the marathon at the end of the twelve weeks, but my unwavering desire to spend every moment with Moyo persuaded her to up the timeline, given I'm now a pro at a double feature.

Turns out I should've stuck to Moyo's plan.

Moyo places our handmade popcorn bowls on the coffee table and heads to the kitchen to grab another pack of Boom Chicka Pop's Sweet and Salty Kettle Corn. In her absence, I stretch even more because, regardless of how unfit I am for the movie-binge-watching life, I am built for the cuddling-with-Moyo-for-hours-on-end life.

My stunning girlfriend saunters in and, as if seeing her for the first time, she takes my breath away.

Girlfriend.

Every day since the Gala has been the best day of my life. I spend my days working on Ceramics Central items with Aaron; hanging with Merc and Vee if they catch me at home or rather, if I catch them using my living room as a third place; and after work, catching up with my Sunshine.

"You ready?"

I stifle a yawn. "Absolutely. Bring it on."

As we've done throughout my horror-movie training, I turn away while Moyo selects a new movie from the floating shelves I built for her. When she's done loading it up, she pulls me back onto the couch before taking her rightful place between my legs.

I kiss her hair as our limbs intertwine.

We're barely through the opening credits of *Bones* when Moyo says, "You're tired, aren't you?"

I huff. "What? No. Why would you say that? And miss Snoop Dogg in a silk press?"

Moyo pauses the movie and twists to face me. She's stone-cold silent, assessing me. I've never been a talkative person, but when Moyo gives me the look, I know it's time to come clean.

"Only a little."

"I knew it!" she exclaims. "This is why we had to stick to the plan. Do marathon runners just up and do the entire thing?"

I chuckle. "Are you comparing running twenty-six miles to watching four movies?"

"I'm so serious." Moyo joins in with her adorable giggle. "Runners start small with a 5k, then work their way up. But no, Mr. Niyi had to go from 5k to the big leagues."

"Ah," I gasp dramatically. "You and your sharp tongue."

Moyo rolls her eyes. "You love it."

"Do I?" I lean over her and whisper. My index finger trails her neck in languid movements that stop time.

Moyo's chest rises and falls with increased exaggeration. Her eyes track my movements as I get closer to her parted lips. I'm a hair's breadth away when I say, "Movie time."

My girlfriend sits up, and if looks could kill, I'd be decaying. But I can't help but laugh.

"You think you're sooo funny."

My palms go up in mock surrender. "Just following your rules, Sunshine." One of my first lessons was "cuddling is acceptable, but other distractions are strictly prohibited."

"The movie was off," Moyo whines.

"That's not what you said two weeks ago when I wanted to kiss you during a bathroom break when we watched *Final Destination*."

"It was a bathroom break. Not a break break."

"A break is a break is a break."

"What if I break you?" Moyo gets up in my face. Her eyes are hooded.

"As if you could." I hold on to her hips and maneuver our positioning till Moyo's straddling me.

She grinds against my groin, and I know I should've worn something underneath my sweats.

"You sure about that?" Moyo taunts as she feels my growing arousal.

My hands begin aching "You're wicked."

"Next time you'll be sure not to tease me like that," Moyo whispers before nibbling on my earlobe. Shivers rip through me, dwindling my restraint, but I won't give in. After our first kiss, I've done well to maintain enough control till she's begging, much to Moyo's annoyance. And she's been attempting to break me ever since.

"You won't get me." It comes out strained.

Moyo picks up her pace. "You're confident?"

She's going to kill me. I'll die happy, but she's going to kill me.

"Yeah," I moan, unable to hold it in.

This is about the time where, after turning both me and herself on, Moyo kisses me and we either dry hump to our satisfaction, or we have sex. But instead of the usual, Moyo gets up and heads to the kitchen.

I shake my head. *What just happened?*

"Moyo?"

"Yeah, babe." She comes back with a glass of water. "Ready to continue the movie?"

"Uh, yeah...uh...of course."

Her unhurried movements give me pause.

"Is everything all right?" I ask tentatively.

Moyo faces me with a wide smile. "Of course. I'm about to watch one of my favorite movies with my boyfriend, whom I love."

I freeze.

"Um, can you say that again?"

"I'm about to watch one of my favorite movies."

Nodding rapidly, I say, "Yeah, yeah, yeah, but not that. The thing after it."

"I love you," Moyo repeats, softer this time. Her smile gets wider, her eyes crinkle at the corners. Staring at her makes me develop sunspots in my vision.

Unable to control myself, I pull her onto my lap.

"Say it again, please, Sunshine."

Moyo holds my face, locking me in with her gorgeous brown eyes as she says the words slowly.

"I love you, Niyi," she breathes, her lips inches from mine. "I'm in love with you," she says, louder, bolder this time. My heart is about to rip out my chest.

Closing the distance between us, I kiss her, and she smiles.

"Told you I'd break you," she giggles.

I kiss her nose. "No fair."

"All's fair in love and war." She squirms as I line her neck, face, every section of skin available to me in kisses before pulling her into a deep kiss.

It's undeniable how much I adore this woman. I pour everything into this rough, hungry kiss. My hands roam all over Moyo's body, unsure where to start from, overcome by love, desire, lust, every sensation in the book.

Moyo, in only an oversized shirt and panties, gets even wetter, making me even harder. I'll probably pass out if any more blood rushes to my groin.

"I love you, Moyo. Today, tomorrow, and however long you'll have me," I say, out of breath with bruised lips.

"And what if I say I want you forever?" She tilts her head.

"Then let me go ring shopping."

Her jaw drops slightly. "No pub—"

"Public proposals. I know," I say, moving in to kiss the corner of her lips.

"How?"

"I know you, Sunshine. You're the light of my life. I pay attention, I know."

She leans away from my kiss and raises a brow.

"I've, maybe, also asked Anjie and Sewa about it," I concede.

Her satisfied, megawatt smile returns. "You've been planning a proposal?"

"If you stay ready, you never have to get ready." I wink.

"You're ridiculous." Moyo laughs. "I never even said I love you," she says, shifting in place, suddenly self-conscious.

I rub circles into her thigh and kiss her forehead. "You didn't have to say those words for me to feel it. You've shown me love every day. Every single day, Sunshine. I was just waiting for you to feel comfortable and say it on your terms."

"I love you." We share a small kiss. Our lips touch, sealing the promise.

"I love you too, Sunshine. And trust me, it was worth the wait."

Moyo's hands go into my hair and my hands go under her ass. As we've done countless times now, without stopping, I carry us to her bedroom.

"You know we'll finish the movie later, right?" Moyo says in all seriousness, as I pull down my sweats and she takes off her shirt.

I pull her into another kiss as my hands trail her body.

"I wouldn't have it any other way."

Acknowledgments

Writing this is surreal, and I honestly didn't know where to start. But after weeks of heavy contemplation, I'd like to first say thank you to whoever's reading this. Writing and publishing a book has been a dream for me since I can remember. Therefore, you reading this means a dream came true. And for that, I am eternally grateful.

Next I want to thank my parents, especially my mom, for instilling the love of books in me; I guess all those trips to Iponri market really paid off. To my sisters, the extensions of my heart, thank you for being there and cheering me on.

And of course, to my extended family, if I were to name you all, that'd be another book in and of itself, but I love you always!

To my agent and the entire Keylight team, thank you for pushing me to be a better writer. This book would literally not exist without all of you.

To Alex Copeman, my illustrator, you brought these characters to life in the most gorgeous way. Thank you for your patience, your understanding, and for being in this with me, there's no one's work I'd rather have on the cover of this book.

There are so many people who helped shape this book, be it in the ideation stage, or when listening to me rambling about these characters, or through reading and providing feedback. Shonna, my astro sister! Thank you for helping me figure out the astrology for this book; Teniola Ladi-Williams, thank you for talking about books with me and your infectious enthusiasm; Karl Egbe, my Karlito, thank you for providing the French translation.

The Book'd Brunch girls: Tomiwa Sobande, I will never forget meeting up for the first time and asking what you thought of my idea for a romcom;

your edits initially traumatized me, but I wouldn't have it any other way. Jakeyvia White, the number one Cosmos fan (and she will fight you if you think otherwise); Jasmine Bell, chef extraordinaire and my querying buddy; Trinity Love, the lovely poet; Without y'all's friendship and our writing sprints, I don't know where I'd be.

Atianah Thomas, Mohini X Katyayani, Jessica Carmichael, Zakariya Gordon, Christine Cowan, Daniela Ricchezza, thank you so much for reading and accepting this book (and me) in all its different stages, and for letting me text you all the time.

To the best friends in the entire world, Ebun Adedeji, Fayokunmi Adenuga, Melanie Ligale, Flower Akaliza, Bella Ntete you have all contributed to this book in ways I don't think you even understand.

To my boys, Cedric Bansah, Mike Lawson and Max Addo, you're extremely annoying, but you keep me going on a daily.

I'd also like to thank my teachers throughout the years for shaping my love for literature. Particularly, Mrs. Awofisayo, the way you approached literature, quite literally changed my life, thank you! And Dr. Siphiwe Gloria Ndlovu, I will never forget our creative writing class. I will also never forget the look of horror on your face when I told you my college major was psychology and not writing; it stuck at the back of my mind till I wrote again. I don't think saying thank you suffices, but it's all I can say.

Being a lifelong reader means having a wide pool of inspirations but its authors like Bolu Babalola, Kennedy Ryan, Tracy Deonn, JL Seegars, Akwaeke Emezi, Charish Reid, Christina C. Jones, that helped me realize I can tell this story how I want to.

As a child of the internet, I can't stress the love and support I've received from the online writing and bookish communities. You have cheered me on and helped me grow, I am grateful for every single one of you. To name a few: Torri, Robin, Bee, Dee, Reni, Aubrei, Marisol, and many many more.

And lastly, to Kieran Ozor Agyare-Kumi, boistory, I miss you everyday. Rest well.

About the Author

MOWA BADMOS is a Lagos-born Nigerian writer of stories about Black women and all the people who love them. As an avid traveler, she moved to the U.S. six years ago after spending two years in Johannesburg, South Africa. Mowa is passionate about incorporating her travels and showcasing Black love across the diaspora. When she's not writing, she can be found talking about TV online, baking, or updating her Letterboxd.